ANIMAL LUST

Books by Lacy Danes

WHAT SHE CRAVES

ANIMAL LUST

SEXY BEAST IV
(with Kate Douglas and Morgan Hawke)

Published by Kensington Publishing Corporation

ANIMAL LUST

LACY DANES

APHRODISIA

KENSINGTON BOOKS

http://www.kensingtonbooks.com

APHRODISIA BOOKS are published by

Kensington Publishing Corp.
850 Third Avenue
New York, NY 10022

All Kensington Titles, Imprints, and Distributed Lines are available at special quantity discounts for bulk purchases for sales promotions, premiums, fund-raising, and educational or institutional use.

Special book excerpts or customized printings can also be created to fit specific needs. For details, write or phone the office of the Kensington special sales manager: Kensington Publishing Corp., 850 Third Avenue, New York, NY 10022, attn: Special Sales Department, Phone: 1-800-221-2647.

Aphrodisia and the A logo Reg. U.S. Pat. & TM Off.

ISBN-13: 978-0-7582-2058-5
ISBN-10: 0-7582-2058-8

First Kensington Trade Paperback Printing: March 2008

10 9 8 7 6 5 4 3 2 1

Printed in the United States of America

To all you beastly bear men out there . . . We ladies love you!

To Crystal Jordan, for being my writing mistress and cracking the cyber whip so I made my goals each day. I don't know what I would do without you.

To Shelli Stevens, for being a good friend even though you don't always agree with my decisions.

To Lillian Feisty, thanks for always being available to give me your opinion when I am pulling my hair out.

To Robert, Jim, and Eric, for being available for male POV questions and brainstorms. You guys ROCK!

To Cathy and my mom, thanks for all your help. You are the best and I love you.

This book is for all of you!

Hugs and kisses,

Lacy.

CONTENTS

Long ago, the clan of Ursus was cursed with the blood of a bear. To all outward appearance they remained human. However, each one possessed powerful mystic abilities and hearty sexual appetites. Only one thing brings out the beast within: a male threatening one's mate. When this happens, only the strongest can control the animal that lives inside.

MARTIN

1

Cumberland, England, 1800

Sweet mother! What a blunder she'd made! Jane's hand shot to her mouth, and she bit the skin of her palm.

Jonathan had never loved her. He lied.

Tears blurred her vision and streamed down her cheeks. She tripped and stumbled, barely seeing the wooded trail before her. The flesh of her sex burned, and her legs ached. How she needed a nice long soak in a tub and time to sort this out. Dash it!

When had she misunderstood his intentions? They had been secretly touching and kissing behind his tavern for months. The whole town thought they would marry. Then, today at the fair, they'd snuck into the woods.

"Lovely, lovely Jane, ye give me a tickle, won't ye, love?" The smell of the ale from his breath wafted about her.

She shouldn't, but how she fancied him. What could it matter?

"You will marry me?" she breathed into his hair, her head spinning in aroused bliss.

He grunted as her touch ran down his muscled back.

He'd grunted! Her teeth ground together as she ran without seeing the trail before her. Sweet mother! He had never said he would wed her. She had craved his touch and the feelings he created in her so madly she'd mistook the grunt as an affirmation of his designs.

She'd given her innocence to a man who had no intentions of wedding her. Her fingers clutched her stomach. She could be with child, and she had no way to take care of a babe nor herself. Daft, truly daft.

Her head spun. She gasped for air as her legs tangled in her skirts, and she tripped, landing, limbs spread wide on the hard, damp earth. Oh. She lay, lungs burning, unable to breathe, and closed her eyes. Her entire life had changed in one act of wanton misdeed. She would pull herself together. She would find a way if she carried a child, but for now . . . she would grieve while no one could see her.

"Lovely Jane." He buttoned up his trousers as he inhaled a deep breath, the crisp air clouding as he exhaled. *"Not bad for a green tickle, and no worries about the clap."*

The clap. He'd rutted with her like she was no better than a tavern wench. He loved her. He said he loved her. Her eyes closed as tears welled.

" 'Twas a lovely, Jane. Ye have a sweet little honeypot. Take good care of it and we'll come out here again sometime." He *turned and headed off into the trees.*

By God. What had she done?

With her face down in the dirt, tears silently ran down her face. Her limbs trembled, and her head spun. She hadn't cried in an age. The act depleted and exhausted her. *Pull yourself together, Jane.* With a sob, she straightened and got to her feet on shaking legs. She was a wealthy merchant's daughter. He was friends with her pa. How dare he treat her ill?

Panic grabbed at her heart.

This act ruined her prospects of a normal life and brought shame on her family name. Her father's business would suffer. How could she be so selfish? Her family, she held dear.

Frantic, her gaze darted around the forest. Nothing but trees. *Think, think, you fool....*

Her fingers pinched the bridge of her nose. She would go to Jonathan and beg him not to say a word. Dash it all. Her eyes squeezed shut.

If she could only figure a way out of the woods. She held her breath, listening for any sounds from the fair. Nothing. What is the rule? Follow the sun and it will lead you to the north.... No.... Sweet mother, she should have listened to her father when he talked about directions.

She stepped toward the setting sun; pain spread through her ankle and up her leg, and her temples throbbed. Ouch! She put weight on her leg and swayed. She could limp but not far.

The forest grew darker. Where was she? She hobbled up the path. Dash it all. Lost, that's where. She picked up her pace. Frost eased up around her heart, and she pushed aching dreams down. Just ahead, a road loomed, and the sun dipped below the horizon. The lane, rutted and ill used, surely led somewhere....

Thunder cracked in the distance as she stared up at the large wooden door. Darkness brewed, and she passed not a soul on the road to this place. The house stood four stories tall, with huge spires that reached to the sky. She had resided in Cumberland for five years, and not once had she heard of an estate such as this. Lifting her hand, she knocked as rain plummeted to the earth in large wet thunks behind her.

She knocked again; shivers raced over her skin. The door creaked open.

"May I help you, ma'am?"

"Oh, indeed." She practically jumped at the man sticking his head out of the small crack. "I'm lost and injured." She pointed to her ankle. "And, well, you see, it is beginning to rain. Would it be possible for me to stay here this night? I could sleep in the kitchen or . . . or . . . the barn. I shan't be any trouble."

The man's eyes went wide behind his round spectacles, and his face twisted in what looked like horror.

"I . . . I . . . know this is highly irregular, but please?"

He schooled his features back to a serious line. "I'm sorry, ma'am. There is no safe way for you to stay here."

Safe? "Pardon?" *Oh, please just let me in.*

The wind whipped up and blew down the last of her pinned-up hair. A shiver racked her body, and her teeth chattered.

"Oh . . . Oh . . ." He glanced into the house. "Very well, ma'am. You will do as I say, do my bidding exclusively. Without fail. Women should not be in this house."

He was concerned about propriety? What a jest! She was ruined. Tears touched her eyes in shame, and she shook them away. What silliness! This man possessed no way of knowing that.

"I will do as you wish, sir." She had no choice. Either she stepped into this house and escaped drowning in one of Cumberland's deluges, or she would try to find her way back in the dark and probably die. She cringed. That was a bit too pessimistic, but she just couldn't go another step this night.

He hesitated and then opened the door just enough to admit her. She slid into the darkened hall and glanced around. A grand staircase stood twisting up to the roof. Dim light shone through a window above the door and illuminated the entry and the paintings that covered the walls. Where did the stair lead? An eerie chill raced up her spine, and she stepped forward, eager to see what lay at their end.

"This way, miss."

Startled, she spun around and followed the servant down a hall that went off to the left of the entry.

"I will put you in the east wing. You will lock your door.

Every bolt. I will bring you warm water to wash. After, admit no one to your room."

A bit protective for a servant, but then again, maybe his master was a real curmudgeon. The last thing she wanted was to end up back out in the rain now. "Very well, sir. I have no wish for you to lose your post. I can surely sleep in the kitchen."

"No!" His voice was a sharp shrill.

Her brows drew together as her eyes adjusted to the dim light in the hall they trod down. Why was he so nervous?

"Until I tell Lord Tremarctos you are staying with us, you will stay out of sight." The man swallowed hard. His hand moved upward as though to tweak his collar and then stopped midair as he glanced at her from the corner of his eye.

Odd! Surely she had nothing to fear. Besides, tiredness ruled her, and the events from the day shook her so terribly it would be no problem to stay locked behind a door in this house.

This house. . . . Her gaze darted around the hall, and she almost stopped and spun on the spot. What a beautiful house! The floors shone of a dark, polished marble. The doors stood floor to ceiling with massive iron hinges bigger than anything she had ever seen.

In the dim light she could tell that the house shone with delights she would never see again. Truly a pity. She wished she could see every detail. They turned a corner, and she followed the man up three flights of narrow servants' stairs. At the top of the hall another male servant approached, and the man who let her in waved his hand, calling him to them.

"Bring me hot water, a pitcher, and have Jack send up tea with cheese and biscuits."

"Sir." The man inclined his head and stared at her as she passed.

Her attire was a mess! Nevertheless, politeness dictated that he shouldn't stare. Her fingers picked at the mud that covered her dress, and her gaze settled on her dirt-splattered hands. She rolled her eyes. Just her luck! Finally she saw the inside of a fancy house, and she looked as if she'd spent the day gathering greens from the garden.

Halfway down the hall, they stopped and he pushed open a door. She stepped across the threshold and stopped. Her eyes widened, settling on the well-appointed room. "Oh, sir, a servant's room will suffice."

"No, ma'am. None of the servants' rooms have doors. And . . . well, you promised to lock yourself in."

She turned as he bent to light the fire in the grate. The sputtering flame cast more light into the dark room. Oh, how she wanted to get warm, wash the filth from her body, and curl up in that huge, heavenly bed. Her mouth dropped open. My goodness, the mattress was enormous; the posters were carved but with such dim light she couldn't see the design.

The linens looked a scrumptious deep shade, too dark to discern in the glow from the fire. The image of her lying on deep scarlet silk, naked, flashed before her. Her hair spread across the pillows as a lover caressed her thighs, his head between her legs, licking the entrance to her womb. Her knees wobbled as tingles scorched through her sex. Oh, my! Her hand shot to her mouth in shock, and she shook herself, trying to erase the image from her mind.

Never in her life had such thoughts entered her head. When she imagined the act with Jonathan, loving never involved a bed, and never with his mouth there. Her hand smoothed down the front of her dress to the apex of her thighs. Would kissing there be pleasurable? Her cheeks flushed warm, and she snatched her hand away. Thank goodness no one could see her thoughts!

She was tired; that was all. The man who had passed them brought up water and filled a tub for her to wash in; he was followed by a gentleman with a tea tray. She waited until they left, bolted the door as requested, and then sat down on the chair by the fire. Tears trickled down her face; they were the last she would allow because of Jonathan. Tomorrow would be a new day, and she would find a way out of this mess. But tonight . . . she let herself cry once more.

A noise pierced her slumber. What was that?

The sound increased as her eyes fluttered open to darkness. The fire in the fireplace burned no more, and the rain outside fell in a deafening pour.

Crack.

Lightning lit the edges of the curtain as a scratching from the other side of the door grew louder. Her heart increased to a fast beat. What was that? A dog?

She pushed back the covers, scrambled to her feet, and crossed the icy room to the door.

She shivered as she stood before the white painted wood. Her gaze scanned the line of eight locks the servant had requested she bolt. She had felt silly when she listened to him, but his nervousness about letting a woman stay here made her wonder what lay beyond that door. Leaning toward the door she placed her ear to the crack.

Sniff, sniff. A low rumble of a growl came from the opposite side. "I can smell you." *Sniff.* "The virgin's blood, the semen, dripping from you."

She jumped and scrambled back, an arm's reach from the door in outrage. How . . . how could anyone know what she did today? She had washed . . . thoroughly. There was no possible way anyone could smell her folly. Was this a dream?

"Who . . . who is there?" Her voice wavered as she reached out and touched the bolts she had thrown that night.

"Let me in." The growl, so low and throaty, made the hairs on her neck stand. "Let me taste what you have so freely given to another."

She continued to stare at the door; shame and panic boiled through her body until her body shook. The scratching increased. The sniffs echoed as if the person outside her door stood beside her. "Let me in.... Let me in...." the raspy growl rang, and sweat slid down her back.

It would not give up. Somehow she sensed it.

The sound of something dragging widened her eyes, and with a bang, the door shook on its hinges. "Let me in, damn you!" It howled in outrage. "I will have you. There will be no denying me."

"No.... Go. Leave me be!" She yelled into the blackness and stepped back from the door as the wood once again shook and creaked with the weight of the pounding.

This surely was a dream. Nothing like this could be real.

Her body shook, her gaze stuck on the door. *Please let the locks hold firm.*

A sharp cry of pain came from the other side of the door, and a breath tickled her neck. Her hand shot to that spot as she spun, expecting to see someone there. Nothing. The curtains blew, and the window snapped open with a crack.

Dash it all! She jumped and hurried for the window. The wind howled, blowing her hair back from her face in a gust. She grasped the sodden wood in her hands and tugged; she stared out at the night. Rain came down in sheets, and as the wood frame clicked shut, lightning lit up the gardens below.

A figure clung to the wall at the base of the building. Crimson eyes stared up at her. She gasped, bolted the window, and pushed away from the glass, the curtain falling back as—she swore—the eyes emerged above the edge of the sill.

The cry rang in her head once more. Her heart pounding, she spun and stared at the door.

Nothing. Not a sound except the pounding in her heart. Her body shook uncontrollably as every shadow in the room moved, alive and coming for her.

This is just a dream.
Close your eyes and things will all get better.

She jumped, nerves taut as she stumbled back to the bed and crawled up on the mattress. Her eyes darted back and forth between the window and the door, searching for anything she could make out in the black, but all stayed still.

Just close your eyes and things will be well. In the morning you can leave this place for home.

As she forced her lids shut, quiet met her.

2

The warmth of smooth silk surrounded her, and a pleasant aroma tickled her nose. Mmmm. She inhaled again.

Cinnamon.

Her mother's baking. She loved her pastries. Jane's stomach rumbled, and she lazily stretched, scooting her bum to roll on her side.

Firm pressure compressed her into the mattress, not allowing her further motions. What? She strained again as her eyes fluttered open to darkness. She was not home. This was not her bed.

She pulled, and her muscles strained as her gaze shot around the darkness. Her eyes gaped as she sighted the vague outline of the door. The white painted wood stood, unlatched and open into the room. Her heart rapidly sped. Jerking her body, she frantically strained. She couldn't move. Her muscles shook. Yet nothing restrained her. Another dream; this was just another dream. She squeezed her lids shut.

Sniff, sniff, sniff. Warm air tickled her stomach.

Sweet mother, that was real. Her eyes shot open. Still, she saw nothing. The bedclothes lay flat, but beneath the covers her shift slid up her torso to her breasts. What... "Stop! Don't touch me!"

She squirmed. Warm silk touched the peak of her nipple, and her lungs locked.

"Please!" Panic gripped her, and her body turned clammy. *This is what happens when you willingly participate in the act outside of marriage. You go mad with nightmares and dreams of carnal desire.* She squeezed her lids shut, and warm, moist air puffed up her neck to her ear.

"I said there would be no denying me."

The smell of cinnamon grew stronger, and her whole body trembled.

"What do you want from me?" She strained and pulled to move but couldn't.

Silence met her.

"Why can't I see you? Is this a dream?"

Still nothing. Chills raced her skin; she squirmed and strained her muscles. Warm smoothness dragged down her stomach, and her body trembled in the touch's wake. Heat flooded her core.

"I will not harm you," the male voice cooed softly, reassuring her. "To whom did you give your gift?" The warm cloth dragged up to her breasts and circled her nipples.

"Oh, God...." Her breasts grew heavy, and she groaned. Why... how... Oh, why did her body respond to this bizarre touch? "That is no concern of yours." This had to be a dream—a pleasant yet strange dream.

"Ah, but if this is a dream, what does it matter?"

"I—I guess that is true," she said tentatively. "But if this is a dream, why would you say such?"

A low rumble of a laugh shook her body as smooth wetness pressed to her neck, kissing her racing heartbeat. "You are beautiful. Your eyes... I have never seen such a shade."

Her body grew warm at the comment. "Thank you. They are my mother's."

He grunted as his lip reconnected with the skin at the base of her throat. Shivers of pleasure pulsed across her skin. What did it matter if she told him of her folly? This surely was a dream.

"I gave my innocence to the tavern owner in Sudhamly."

The pressure holding her tightened, and the air grew thick. A low gruntal growl pressed to her throat, and a tongue licked her neck from base to ear.

A burst of warm air caressed her earlobe. "You are very brave." His tongue swirled into the curve. "What did he give you in return?"

Her body shook, and she pulled her head away from the invasion. "I—I don't understand. The only thing he gave me was his seed and an aching heart."

A deep, angry hiss slid down her spine, and her body quaked.

"You love each other?" His voice sounded strangled.

"I—I thought so . . . but he did not." Her chest tightened as she said the words aloud. A true statement, and she needed to face that fact.

"He should have returned your gift. It is required to give something in return, especially when one gives her innocence."

"I'm sorry, I—I don't understand. What do you speak of? Who are you?"

The warm cloth circling her nipples vanished, and his mouth sealed upon her breast in a vise. Pain shot through the tissue into her breast, and her body arched off the mattress. He nibbled, and the ache swirled to intense pleasure, tingling down her belly to the flesh between her legs.

"Oh, God, what . . . what are you doing?" Her lips trembled as his tongue swirled the nipple.

He growled.

"I will give you the gift your mate stole from you."

"The gift?"

His warm breath slid down her belly, and a puff of steam touched the curls at that apex of her thighs.

Oh, my stars! This dream was exactly what she had envisioned would happen on this bed when she first glimpsed the monstrosity. The warmth of velvet brushed her thighs, and she bit the inside of her lip. After parting her legs farther, the spongy slickness of muscled tongue slid along the slit of her sex, and her womb clenched.

Virgin's blood, echoed in her mind. *Seed that does not belong.* The warmth pressed into her womb, and her body arched once more off the mattress.

Yes, enjoy the gift he denied you.

The tongue swirled the crevice, licking and sucking, as if he tried to remove every last ounce of the evidence from her folly. Oh, if she could only remove the memory from her mind!

Her heart pounded in her chest, and teeth grazed the flesh of the opening to her womb. Intense pleasure spiraled through the muscles of her legs, tightening them. Her toes curled, and her womb contracted, spending juice from her core. "Oh . . . oh!"

His tongue traveled across her scored flesh and lapped the honey that now flowed freely from her. Fierce sensation shot, arching her hips off the mattress. She rubbed her curls against the large head and wide shoulders she now felt pressed between her legs and bore down on his tongue. Oh, there truly resided a man between her legs!

Blissful tingling grasped every nerve of her body. Her fist clenched tight; blinding light flashed as every muscle in her body thrashed in wave upon wave. She screamed and then shook, her legs bucking to the touch of his tongue. He licked her clean from anus to curls as her muscles jumped and pulled away from the too intense caress.

"What . . . what was that?" Her gaze focused on the figure

of an extremely large man who, without a doubt, knelt between her legs. She squeezed her eyes shut. Oh, she'd gone daft!

"Your pleasure. For allowing a boar to mount you."

"Pardon? The gift," she whispered and squeezed her legs together about his thighs. Indeed, he was there.

"Yes." His large hands gripped her thighs and gently squeezed.

A howl pierced the air from down the hall. She started, and a swirl of air washed across her. The warmth of silk and body heat gradually faded, and the faint smell of cinnamon clung in the air.

She trembled and pulled the covers up close to her body. Was this a dream? She reached down and slid her finger into the slick flesh of her sex. It surely was.

Raising her hand to her nose, the smell of cinnamon clung stronger than her scent. How strange and too odd to think about. Her gaze shot to the closed door to the hall. In the faint light she counted eight thrown bolts. Exhaustion fluttered her eyelids shut, and she drifted into a strange and blissful sleep.

Tap, tap, tap, tap.

"Ma'am. Ma'am."

Jane woke with a start. Scrambling her body to the upright position, she stared at the door. She scrutinized the line of eight securely latched locks and then pinched the bridge of her nose. It had all been a dream.

"Ma'am, I have your laundered garments."

"One moment." She pushed off the bed and headed for the door. Sliding each latch open, she turned the knob. Surely a dream.

"Pardon, ma'am." A hand thrust through the opening; it was holding her dark gray wool dress, stockings, petticoat, and corset. She clutched them. "Thank you." Then she peeked her head through the crack in the door.

"Lord Tremarctos has been informed of your stay with us and wishes you to take breakfast with the family." He swallowed hard, his Adam's apple bobbing. "I will send Jerome up in a quarter of an hour to escort you to the hall."

"Very well." She shut the door and bolted the locks. All she wanted to do was depart and straighten out this whole day with Jonathan, but she would like to see the house in daylight. Leaving an hour later would not change the situation one whit. She frowned.

Turning back toward the bed, she gasped. Across the chair she had sat in the night before, a stunning pale green muslin dress lay. The color exactly matched her eyes. "Where did that come from?"

She raised her hand to touch the smooth, expensive fabric and noticed her hand wavering. She clenched her fingers into a fist. He had said he loved her eyes. It had been a dream, right? She turned away from the temptation and studied the room. No one could have gotten in. There was one door, and the window . . .

She rushed to the drapes and pulled them back. Rain came down steadily beyond the panes of clear glass, but the bolt remained latched. Certainly the dress had been there last night. How strange she had not noticed the garment. Then again, her mind had swum in other issues last night.

She glanced at the bed; the color of the linens shone a deep crimson in the daylight. The carvings entwining the posts depicted beautifully detailed bears.

Her fingers glided along the carved figure of one bear. Smooth and cool, the bear stood on its hind legs and fought with paws and mouth the next bear carved into the richly hued wood.

She bit her lip as her fingers stilled on the interlocking paws and mouth. Her stomach fluttered, and her other hand spread across the taut surface. How odd! Surely her stomach rumbled because of hunger. She needed to dress and feed her rumbling middle.

She gazed at the gray wool draped over her arm and then glanced longingly at the fine muslin stretched across the back of the chair. How silly to long for a piece of clothing. She had never owned such a fine-looking garment. Yet that dress pulled at her.

She wanted to put on the garment, to feel the slip of the fine fabric down her body. Would it be as smooth and as warm as the touch of her lover? She gasped and turned away from the dress. Nonsense, just nonsense.

"Bruno, are you sure she remained bolted in when you asked her to come to me this morning?" Lord Tremarctos shifted, agitated in his seat behind his desk.

"Yes, your grace. I heard the bolts slide. There is no way she could have faked it."

Very interesting. His brows lowered, and the corner of his lip curved up in concentration. His boars were all on edge this sunrise. The disquiet surely came from the smell of a woman inside the walls of Tremarctos.

"Still, none of this sits well. Does it, Bruno?"

"No, your grace."

With the torrential rain, she would not leave until the ill weather ceased. "Make sure all my boars are at breakfast. I don't want one of them coming across her without the knowledge that she is our guest. Or for her to be caught off guard by one of us." *If we are all in the same room, the situation will arise without much prodding.* Then he could decide what needed to be done.

"Yes, your grace. I will rouse them."

Lord Tremarctos stared after Bruno as he shut the door to his study. His fist clenched, breaking his quill in half. Please let the knife in his gut be for sane reasons, not for the dread that came to him in his sleep last night. Oscar. His teeth clenched. No . . . they all would surely want to fuck her. Even if she was not a mate, the smell of innocence shed pulled at even him. Let his unease be only that. His fist hit the desk with a loud thud.

Ursus . . . please stay dormant—he squeezed his eyes shut—and let his sons choose a mate without the turmoil that had stayed with him for a lifetime.

3

Beautiful. Jane stepped across the threshold into a magnificent dining room. Along one wall stood large windows partially covered by thick black drapes. In the center of the room, a large black-stained wooden table stood polished to a slick shine, surrounded by substantial black and gray upholstered chairs. She could see the dinner guests, in their fancy dresses, sitting in the large chairs. They laughed and sipped spiced wine. Sweet mother! The room glittered with the polish and sophistication of the moneyed.

With not a sound in the room, her slippers echoed throughout on the black polished floor. She glanced down at her gray wool once again and cringed. She looked frumpy and so out of place in such surroundings. Jerome, who escorted her, held out a seat for her halfway down the table. She smiled and sat. "Thank you," she whispered, afraid to break the tranquil atmosphere.

"What do you take for repast?"

"Tea and something sweet—no, cinnamon, if you have it." She could still smell the scent from her dream.

"Ma'am." He scurried to the sideboard and brought her a teapot and cup. She picked up the pot and poured the steaming liquid. Setting the pot back on the table, she glanced down at her lap. My stars! The chair made her dainty, and she was far from small.

"Now behave." A deep voice came from out in the hall, and her gaze shot to the door. An elegant, massive man paused at the doorway; then he entered the room with an air of control.

"Welcome to Tremarctos, ma'am." He held up a hand. "Stay seated. I am Lord Tremarctos, and these are my boars." The elegant, gray-haired man pointed to the door as man after large man entered the room behind him. All of them possessed something from the elder. Boars surely meant sons.

Boar? The word felt oddly familiar.

"What is Tremarctos?"

"Why, this place," the youngest-looking one replied as he slid out the chair beside her. "Devon Ursus at your service, ma'am."

His blond hair, pulled back from his face, displayed striking angles that lit up when he smiled. His icy blue eyes assessed her as if gazing straight through to her soul. Her blood heated with wicked sensations. He tore his gaze away, leaving a chill in her bones.

"And you are?"

Jane jumped and turned toward the voice that came from the other side of her. Another of the large men sat down, and awareness skittered through her body. "Oh, pardon . . . I am Miss Jane Milton."

The heat of the two enormous male bodies surrounding her tangled her emotions. How she wanted one of them to touch her—yet she feared that touch at the same time. Any one of them could crush her like a fly.

"Miss Milton. I am Mac, and that rogue there," he lifted his hand and pointed to his brother standing against the wall, "is Martin, my twin."

They did look remarkably alike yet different. Both possessed thick, dark brown, wavy hair—tucked back behind their ears—that brushed their shoulders. But their eyes . . . Mac's were a hard green, startling in intensity, and Martin's were a cottony pale brown, shining with the kind of gentleness she could get lost in.

Jerome leaned in and placed a plate, a sugary cinnamon roll perched atop, in front of her. She glanced up and smiled at him. The smell, so delicious, captured her senses as she stared at the cinnamon stickiness and licked her lips.

"Miss Milton, the last introduction is of my eldest son and heir." The father's tone sounded as if it scolded.

"Ma'am, I am Lord Orin Arctos." He stood formally at the side of the table, bowed to her, and then sat. Never once did he truly look at her.

Martin pushed from the wall, capturing her attention. With a small cup in his hand, he pulled the chair opposite her from the table and sat. Her gaze fixed on that cup. The same cup she held in her hand was dwarfed by his grasp. Hmph. Small cup indeed.

What kind of men were these? She had never seen such big, burly men. She glanced up, and Martin's gaze briefly touched hers. Lightning shot down her spine. Wh—what was that? Her teacup shuttered in her clutch.

"Orin is a bit formal, but nothing to fear," Devon whispered, mistaking the reason for her shaking hand.

"Oh, surely." She couldn't tear her gaze from Martin across the table; his brows stooped over his eyes as he assessed her, and her heart beat so hard in her chest she swore she visibly pulsed to the beat. What was wrong with her?

Her body had gone mad since yesterday. Each man's gaze created startling effects on her. Though the act of giving her innocence had been painful at best, her body now craved scandalous and wanton things. She shook herself. Maybe she had a fever, though she felt fine. Her fingers briefly brushed her cool forehead.

"Are you well, Miss Milton?" Mac's long, thick fingers pressed her forearm.

Martin stood up with alarming haste, his chair clattering to the floor. Everyone jumped; their gazes snapped to him.

"Sit now, boar, and behave," the father said from the head of the table as he studied his knife in indifference.

My stars! Was this kind of behavior common among these men? The air grew thick with tension, and Martin's cheek twitched as his gaze fixed on Mac's hands, which were still settled on her arm.

"Pardon, Father." Martin inclined his head. "I—I need to leave."

"Very well. Say your farewell." Lord Tremarctos's cool blue gaze slid over Martin and then shot to Jane and narrowed, only to settle on Mac.

Mac leaned back in his chair, and the corner of his lips crooked up. Good Lord! She had no experience with brothers. Maybe all male siblings regarded one another this way?

"Good day, miss." Martin bowed his head swiftly and headed for the door. What a strange and odd occurrence! Such hostility did not welcome her. She didn't feel safe at all. The time had arrived to leave.

"Your lordship, I—I am sorry to disrupt you . . ."

When the boars had all followed their father into the dining hall for the morning repast, Martin could just barely contain his rage as Mac had sat next to Jane at the table. Martin had schooled his features as her virgin blood heated in his veins. Last night had changed him.

Her openness about her feelings and the caring emotions that poured from her for the man in town shook him. She would make a good mother and excellent mate if he could only get her to accept him. He had wanted so much more from her last night, but he had barely escaped and bolted the door before Mac came raging up the hall, howling at her scent.

They always fought about women, and with the Ursus's healthy sexual appetite, squabbles happened frequently. Martin accepted the challenges, the wrestling. In most cases, he enjoyed the pleasure of the adrenaline of the fight . . . but Jane was not any woman to fight over. She was a possible mate for him, not a mere sexual release, and it remained unseen if Mac wanted more from her, too.

He had leaned against the wall in the dining hall and sipped his thick black coffee as he surveyed the situation. Her beautiful lower lip caught between her teeth. Her blond hair, down, pulled back from her slightly tanned skin, held him. She was utterly intoxicating.

What a sight they all made! Five men the size of oxen, sitting in substantial chairs dwarfed by their physical size. He'd wanted to show himself to her last night, but just couldn't bring himself to. His sure size would have sent her screaming in the night. So he'd used his mind to block her from seeing him.

As it was, she would notice his scent if he ventured too close. Damnit! No matter how he wanted to, he couldn't reveal his intentions in front of his brothers. She would surely leave if the claws came out, and he wanted nothing more than for her to stay . . . for a lifetime.

What did she think of him? Her gaze had scrutinized him as Mac introduced him. He had wanted to slip into her mind as he had last night, but his family would know the instant he did, and he couldn't hint at his desire. Not yet.

Repressing his intentions went against every lesson his father had instilled in him. Eventually his instincts would take him, and his family would know. But, for now, he needed knowledge, so he had sat back and watched . . . waited to see if one of his brothers desired more than mere sexual conquest.

Jerome had then leaned in and placed a cinnamon roll in front of her, and Martin smiled. She craved him. Devon caught his grin and winked. Yes, Martin did have a chance with her. Yet Devon had no idea Martin had already tasted her.

Orin finally sat, brooding in his usual silent way.

Martin had pushed from the wall and seated himself opposite Jane. Her gaze touched his, and the hairs on his neck lifted. She would be his . . . had to be. His instinct never raged this strong for a possible mate. He fucked several but never wished to start the mating ritual of Orsse. Jane. . . . Making her his was the one thought pulsing through his brain.

Mac had leaned toward her; his hand had risen bit by bit, heading in the direction of Jane's arm. Martin's blood had pounded through him; teeth clenched, his muscles had strained as he tried to control the will to defend her.

He would not permit his brother to touch her. She belonged to him. Damnit! He had tasted her. She infused each breath he took. Mac's hand landed on her forearm, and Martin's muscles had sprung him to action. His chair had clattered to the floor in alarming speed. He had barely suppressed a raging hiss as his vision hazed.

"Sit now, boar, and behave," his father had said from the head of the table as he feigned studying his knife.

Martin couldn't keep his rage controlled. Every thread that he held taut quaked. "Pardon, Father." His voice deepened and wavered in rage. "I–I need to leave."

"Very well. Say your farewell." *Gain your control, Martin, and say your farewell with grace.*

Of course, his father would test him.

His father's cool blue gaze had slid over Martin and assessed the situation in one glance. Then his father's eyes had shot to Jane and narrowed. What problems this caused! If either Martin or Mac were not sent from this house, another disaster like the one his father had initiated with Uncle Oscar would come full circle.

Mac had then leaned back, the corner of his lips inching up, mocking him. Damn him! Martin had wanted to jump over the table and tackle him to the floor. If he touched her again in any form, he would kill him. His fists clenched as the bone of his knuckles rose; his claws unsheathed. Damn him!

"Good day, miss." Martin had bowed his head, swiftly absorbing her beautiful pouting lips and deep honey-colored hair. His blood pounded through his ears. He tried to control this overwhelming desire for her and smashed his teeth together, snagging his tongue in the process. The salty taste of the virgin's blood that he had forced to flow anew last night flooded his mouth, and his semistiff erection hardened to full.

He had stepped forward. He needed her; she possessed him. His hands fisted, and his claws extended through his skin. *No! Get control of yourself! The green grass, the river . . .* He had inhaled a wavering breath in an attempt to gain control.

His muscles shook forcefully as he restrained himself from pouncing on his brother. He turned, leaving the room in haste. Striding down the hall, he picked out the tone of her voice. He stopped, anxious to know her thoughts, her feelings, and listened to her songlike tone.

"Your lordship, I—I am sorry to disrupt you and your family. I would like conveyance in your carriage. I wish to return home."

Damn it all. . . . She wanted to leave. Of course she did! What sane woman would stay in this madhouse? His hands shook with the need to possess her, lock her away, and make her accept him. His inner bear cried out in pain. Leaving was the only way to control this. . . . He would go for a ride. The rain, the smells of nature would calm him.

Jane sat at the table and waited for his lordship to answer. He stared after Martin, a deep, worried frown etching his face.

"My lord?"

His gaze slid to her and caressed her form. "I am sorry, Miss Milton, but our carriage needs repair, and with the rain so heavy, you will have to stay with us until the storm stops."

The same piercing cry from the night before rang out in her head. My stars! She did not think she could handle another night in this strange house.

Something of importance had happened between the twins in the moment when Martin had left the room. Her heart still sped when she thought of how fierce Martin had been; his soft eyes had changed intensity, and she'd half expected him to howl. The transformation had frightened her. All five of the men towered above her, their shoulders as wide as a door and arms as big as the trees by the river. She was so small, so helpless surrounded by them. She did not for one instant think herself safe, as the butler had said, "in this house."

4

Devon walked Jane from the dining hall. "My brothers are a bit rough, but they are all kind."

She tilted up her head to assess his eyes. A cavalier playfulness swirled about him. He appeared the calmest of the brothers. Her muscles relaxed. She didn't feel as skittish alone in his presence as she had surrounded by all the brothers.

"Did you sleep well? The storm—I mean, it was something, was it not?"

"Oh, quite. I awoke a few times but briefly." Under no circumstance would she tell him, or anyone, her dreams. He would take her first for a simpleton and then for a wanton. The first may be true, but the second. . . . The image of the dark figure kneeling between her legs last night returned. Her face flushed with heat, and she bit her lip. Wicked, wicked thoughts. She was a wanton. She turned her attention back to Devon.

He nodded. "We all are quite nocturnal. It is odd to have us all assembled for the morning repast."

"Oh, I'm sorry. I—I hope you were not stirred from your bed for me."

"I imagine we were. But we all sensed your presence any-way. I think Father wanted to see if any of us fancied you." He smiled, and playfulness lit up his face.

She couldn't help the giggle bubbling up her throat, and she raised her eyebrows. "A fancy would hold little consequence. I'm not of your station."

They turned a corner down the main hall. Sweet mother! She barely came to his chest. She glanced at the tight-fitting, ex-pensive coat, pulled taut with each breath he made. All of them were truly large. Large and handsome. She couldn't imagine any of them actually regarding her.

"Station matters little in this family. Instincts—that is what chooses us. Rules our lives. Father is firm on it. And none of us have selected a mate for our lifetime."

Her face flamed at such casual scandalous talk. "Sir, you shouldn't be so informal with me."

He gazed down at her and smiled broader. "Ah, well, that is true, but I won't tell if you won't." His long lashes closed over his eyes, and the lid shape turned round.

What? She tensed and blinked to clear her vision—oh, my stars—then she stared at his eyes as the lashes opened.

What was wrong with her? This man was just a man. Mad-ness. No one's eyes changed shape.

"Are you well, Miss Milton? You have gone positively pale."

"I—I . . ." *What do I say?* "I think I may have a touch of something. My vision keeps deceiving me."

He stopped and turned toward her, his blue eyes wide, an open, concerned expression on his features. "In what way? What did you see?" His lip curved into a grin, and his eyes changed from pale, crystal-blue ovals to round, solid blue.

She jumped and stepped back away from him. Sweet mother! Chills raced down her back. "What . . . what are you?" The hairs on her neck stood as her whole body trembled in shock and fear.

His smile turned devious. "What an odd question to ask your host. Why, I am Devon Ursus, youngest male boar of the Clan of Tremarctos." His eyes flashed and jumped, and the clear blue human eye returned.

"You . . . you . . ." her hand raised, and she pointed at his eyes, "are not human. What are you?" Her lips trembled, and she stepped back another step, unable to take her gaze from him in fear he would grasp her.

"Ah! That is where you are wrong, Miss Milton. I am human, only more."

She turned and ran. She needed to get out of this house. She had no wish to know what that "more" entailed. Ever since her arrival, strange things had occurred. This house possessed evil, a witch house, a house of the devil.

She would find her way home; she didn't care if she caught her death doing so. She didn't belong here. She hastened her steps as she ran down the hall, Devon's laughter echoing in the distance behind her.

"Miss Milton, I will not harm you. I only wanted you to know."

She pushed open the large front door. The rain continued to come down in sheets. She trembled as the damp air pierced the wool of her dress, chilling the sweat gathered on her skin. She glanced beside the door. There had to be a coat, a blanket, a hat, anything she could use to shield her from the rain. Nothing.

She glanced over her shoulder to see Devon mere yards away.

"Miss Milton, please don't be foolish. You will catch your death."

She bolted straight out into the rain. She needed to get home to see her mother, to know that what she had just witnessed resided only in her mind. Not that being daft in the attic appealed to her, just . . . well, craziness seemed better than believing such could exist. Was that wrong?

The rain seeped through her wool dress in a matter of moments as she ran down the slick road fronting the house. Her feet carried her as fast as she could manage as her slippers sank into the thick mud. Just what she needed, to lose a slipper in this sludge! She curled her toes, trying to ensure the shoes stayed put as she continued her fast pace away from Tremarctos.

Thick trees lined the road. She had no idea where she was headed. Her head spun, and her vision grew hazy. She stopped to steady herself. An agonizing cry sliced through her.

Don't leave. Where are you going? Stop!

The trees moved before her, inching in bit by bit. Her eyes widened. She'd gone mad! She swayed, the earth buckling beneath her feet as the forest closed off the road in front of her. She raised her fisted hands to her eyes and rubbed them. *The forest has closed off the road.* She squeezed her eyelids shut and shook her head; raindrops flew from her mane.

Pounding hooves shook the earth and vibrated through her. Sweet mother! They were after her. She darted into the thick grove of trees now covering the road. The branches were so thick she barely wiggled her way into the thicket. Her arm caught on a branch. She yanked, and the fabric of her dress tore; the bramble scraped her skin. Ouch! She wanted to cry out in pain but crushed her teeth together and whimpered instead. She needed to get farther in and hidden from the road. There was no room to turn. The branches snaked and twisted about in a thick mesh, holding her still.

She slumped beneath a large branch, unable to push against the bramble. She would never make it home! Her body shook, and she covered her face with her hands. The wet of her wool dress chilled her skin, and her teeth chattered.

Come back! Damn you! Do not fear me.

Leave, damn voice! Covering her ears with her hands, she tucked herself closer to the tree trunk and out of sight of the road. She would find shelter somewhere tonight! The pounding hooves stopped in a sloppy smash of mud. A loud whinny snort pierced the sound of the rain just beyond her shoulder, and she jumped.

"Damnation, woman!" came from the road behind her. That voice she had heard in her head; she remembered from her dream. It had been a dream . . . hadn't it? The man from her scandalous dream stood in the road! She needed to look, to know whose voice, hands, and tongue had caressed her so pleasurably. Her head turned without further thought, and she peeked through the branches at the gentleman in the road.

One of the twins sat astride a draft horse and stared into the thicket covering the road.

What a mesmerizing sight! Soaked through, the horse blew fog from its nose. Steam rose from its body as it stomped its foot, mud splattering. Rain poured off the rider's greatcoat and hat in streams. His broad shoulders and bunching muscles handled the large mount with ease. Her heart pounded, and her nipples pebbled hard. His beauty and confidence radiated power. She gasped. She'd gone daft. He was a beast. Her eyes widened as the rider's gaze locked with hers as he swung down.

You are not mad, Jane. Though at times I think things might be easier if we didn't exist, we do. Please don't run from me. Let me explain who we are.

She scrambled to her feet, but before she could take a step away from him, large arms wrapped about her and pulled her from the bramble.

She twisted and thrashed in his arms but to no avail. With the ease of someone holding a feather, he held her in his grasp. His body about her, the rub of his arm against her stomach and sides, set her skin awash in heated dew. Oh! Her body wanted this man! His breath deepened to the laborious sound she remembered from her dream. How could that be? It had been only a dream, yet her body knew and craved his silken touch on her bare skin.

"Hold still, damn you." The warmth of his breath heated her skin about her neck.

"Then release me." She inhaled and tried to calm the intense arousal pumping through her. The smell of cinnamon filled her senses, and moisture flooded her sex. He groaned.

"Jane. . . ." He pulled her tighter against his body. Through his greatcoat, his large erection pressed into her buttocks and back. She struggled, unable to control her body as her sex pulsed. Rubbing her bum back against the large ridge, she craved his phallus filling her. She was doomed to be a wanton.

"Let go of me!" Her voice held no fortitude. She cursed.

He backed up to his horse, muscles tremoring about her. "I will not permit you to drown nor catch your death out here."

He growled as he placed her in front of the saddle and mounted behind her in a movement so fast she had no time to slide to the ground.

You goose! Where would you go if you did leave? You have no idea in which direction Sudhamly lies. But where did he plan to take her? Not back to that house. If he could handle her like a piece of dust, all five together could squash her. What a terrifying thought! But this man alone. . . .

"What are you about, sir?"

"I'm taking you home."

"Home?"

"Indeed, back to Tremarctos."

"That is not my home, sir. If you are going to take me anywhere, please take me to Sudhamly."

Warm breath tickled her ear. "I have no intention of letting you go anywhere."

Her body responded traitorously to those words, trembling with longing so strong; the emotion frightened her. Her heart sped, and warmth peaked her nipples. He wanted her with such conviction. Desire and love with Jonathan paled in comparison. The passion of this man's voice, of his body when he touched her, spoke to her soul. She was too naive to know that such desire existed in the world.

The ridge of his arousal heated her bum through her dress, and she squirmed in his lap, eliciting a groan from deep in his chest.

Indeed, the passions were carnal. She could not befool herself otherwise. If she returned to Tremarctos, this man would do only one thing to her. The act. He would not stop until they joined completely. The flesh of her sex burned; the remembered sensations of this man's tongue sliding along her sex slammed into her anew.

His warmth radiated along her side, and she shivered, cozying her face into his coat to get away from the rain and closer to his heat, his intoxicating scent. His head rested on the top of hers. His arms circled her as she sat across his lap, rocking to the beat of horse hooves. He protected her from the rain.

His heart beat beneath her ear, the rhythm calmed her body and soothed her own rapidly beating heart. How could the embrace of this man feel so correct? Promise so much? He would surely do just as Jonathan did—bed her and then leave! No man would knowingly, willingly take a fallen woman. A woman who could be carrying another's child. And he knew of her folly.

Tilting her head up, she tried to see his eyes. Which of the twins carried her. Raw determination and concern etched his face. His cheekbones were all harsh angles, his dimpled chin set in harsh masculinity. He was ruggedly handsome, more so than any man of her acquaintance. Yet he remained not a man. Or he was "more," as Devon had said. More? He so desperately wanted to keep her. His intensity scared her yet peaked her hopes. She had never experienced desire this all-encompassing from a man. She needed to know his intentions.

"What . . . what will happen to me if I return with you?"

He didn't answer and spurred the horse into a gallop. Tremarctos loomed out of the mist, and she squeezed her eyes shut as her head spun. "Please don't take me back to that place. It frightens me."

There is no choice. Tremarctos is my home.

He pulled his mount to a halt in front of the great door. A groom came forth and gripped the reins. Grasping her firmly, the twin swung his leg over the withers and slid down, never letting her leave his hold. He strode up the steps and pushed open the door.

"Damned foolish woman." Devon strode up to them and then down the hall with them. "You will catch your death."

A violent hiss of warning came from deep within the chest of the twin who carried her, and his muscles clenched possessively about her.

"Back off, Martin. I'm not here to challenge you, and you know it. I was the one who spooked her off. I want to make sure she is well."

The muscles in Martin's body relaxed but did not release their possession of her. *Martin. . . .* The one with the velvet eyes.

"Pardon, Devon. I can't control it."

"I know, you never could. Just try to go easy. Father wants to see you. He said for you to come to his study at once. I think he is afraid of what you and Mac will do. We all felt you use your mind. It was strong. Like nothing we have experienced before."

Martin grunted.

He and Mac? What did that mean? Mac had touched her at the table this morning, and Martin had burst from his chair.

Would her presence in this house cause a family squabble? Would she come between two brothers? She couldn't allow that. Family was important, the most important thing. She rolled her eyes. Her own family! She should notify her parents of her whereabouts. But with the rain, how would they get any note she wrote?

"Martin?"

He grunted as he glided up the stairs, taking them three at a time.

"I wish my family to know I'm well and where they can find me. Is that possible?"

He shook his head but said not a word.

Blast! Ma and Pa would be worried sick at this point. Shame on her for not thinking of them before this!

With his shoulder, he pushed open the door and carried her into the same room she had stayed in the night before.

"Martin, I—I need to know more. . . . I—I can't stay here not knowing what is in this house. It frightens me."

His entire body tensed, and his breath blew out between his teeth.

"I will tell you. . . . You need to know—just not yet. What Devon showed you was enough for the moment. We are all different, us brothers. Devon has the best control of what he is, and he easily showed you by his command. The rest of us are not that way."

"But—but what of you, Martin? All this is rather odd, and not knowing what you are . . . unnerves me."

He nodded tersely. "As you should be." He deposited her on the large bed and stared at her with heat in his eyes. "Lock all the bolts. I will send up Jerome and Bruno with hot water for you to bathe in." His gaze assessed her dress, and he frowned. "Please put on the dress I left for you."

She gasped. "You left that dress for me? How did you obtain it?"

He stared at her with desire, and her knees jumped. Remembering the gift he'd given her the night before, she quivered. He was real. The man who gave her that bliss was real.

His lips were set in a serious line; she wanted nothing more than to kiss them. Her tongue slid out and wet hers in a blatant invitation. He didn't move. Her brows drew tighter. Why? She didn't know how to go about this or what she attempted to get herself into. But at this moment all she could think of was his firm lips traveling along hers as she tasted his warmth. Would he taste of cinnamon as well as smell of it? She assessed his face; warmth burned across her skin. His gaze locked on her lips. "Martin?"

"If I touch you at this moment, Jane . . ." He groaned and shifted his stance. "I had better not." He nodded his head, turned, and strode from the room, water trickling off his greatcoat, leaving a trail on the hardwood floor.

Sweet mother! She had practically thrown herself at him. What good did bolting the door do when he commanded that effect on her? Besides, even with them all thrown, he had entered last night.

She sat back on the pillows, staring at the shut door, and shivered. He said they all were endowed with different powers. Did that mean only he possessed the ability to unlock doors? Well, the locks surely did something. She scrambled to her feet and slid each one closed.

5

Arousal burned Martin's skin; he couldn't let her leave. If only she hadn't squirmed so much when he'd caught her up; every rub against his body had pushed the mating ritual of Orsse closer to beginning. Would she accept him? She'd arrived at Tremarctos because she'd loved and given herself to another. If Orsse started and she denied his body that magnitude of release . . . Pain ripped through his groin, and his eyes squeezed shut.

He would convince her. She was not indifferent to him. The smell of her arousal in his arms couldn't be faked. However, he wanted more than access to her body—he wanted her mind and soul.

He pulled off his thick leather gloves as he strode back down the hall toward his father's study. Where the hell was Mac? His hair rose in agitation on his neck.

Mac would know how Jane truly felt about him, about everything. His ability to read emotions surpassed all the family members. Unfortunately Mac never could read Martin. He wished in this one moment Mac could. If Mac knew his interest involved more than a conquest, he may back down. Or he would taunt him.

He turned into his father's study and closed the thick wood door. Many a shout had happened in this room, and that door, thick as the oak was, never stopped one whit of it. Everyone in the family always knew what happened in this room.

"Sit, Martin." His father gazed up at him from behind his large wooden desk, his sanctuary; his face was pale and twisted with worry.

"Father." He settled into the tiny wooden chair across from him.

"Is she well?" His father glanced up at him from beneath his lashes and scowled.

"Quite." He worried about her welfare? Something was not right. His gut twisted with unease.

"You did not touch her, did you?" His father's fist clenched, making his knuckles turn white.

"Pardon?" Why the hell did he care if he touched her? He had a mouse-sized amount of control over this, and his father damn well knew it.

"Your brother said she is a possible mate."

"Mac?" Where the hell was he? Martin shifted in the small wooden chair. He always felt like a child sitting here, but this was not a matter of childhood punishment. This was his future, his happiness.

His father stood and paced to the shelves behind the desk. The energy pouring off him darkened. Martin's blood shifted, eyes slowly sliding from pale brown to crimson. This wasn't good.

His father turned back toward him. "Devon."

Devon. . . . Martin's blood raged through his ears. Devon had lied to him. No . . . none of Devon's actions betrayed any effect that Jane inflicted on him. Yet Devon did have amazing control of his instincts, his nature.

Martin's teeth clenched. "Miss Milton is a possible mate for Devon?" His claws slowly unsheathed themselves from the backs of his hands.

"Control, Martin." His father paced back to the desk, and he placed his palms on the wood surface, leaning toward Martin. "Devon sensed Miss Milton was a mate for you . . . and Mac."

Where was this conversation headed? He knew. He needed to get back to Jane. He wished he could slide into his father's mind and speed this along. He had tried several times while young, only to be instantly blocked and checked.

"Why did you want to know if I touched her?" Opposition crackled the air between them. He wasn't going to like this answer. His muscles locked, and he held his breath in an attempt to calm himself. *The sound of rain, the smell of must and moss in the woods. Damnit.* The calming elements were failing him. He didn't want to switch. If he did, changing back may take hours, and he needed that time to convince Jane to accept him.

"You will not touch her," his father stated calmly, his gaze boring into him. "She will be removed from this house as soon as the rain lifts. I will not allow a woman to come between this family. I will not allow this family to relive my mistakes."

He wished Martin to turn and walk away from her? Martin's eyes widened in shock. He couldn't. He'd used all his strength, all the power of his mind to move the earth and stop her from leaving. No easy task. His father no doubt felt that energy pull. His father was not naive in this matter. Had his father learned nothing from his own mistake?

"If you had resisted . . . if you possessed the *ability* to resist, none of us would exist," Martin hissed as his fists clenched to the point of pain, claws extending fully through the bone of his knuckles.

"*Control, Martin!*"

He couldn't control this; none of them truly could. He

squeezed his eyes shut. *The rain, the water rushing down the stream, the smell of lavender in summer.* His eyes fluttered back open, hazy. He changed to the shape of the Ursus. Damn him! Rage burned though his every pore, like fire to the fall grass, the powers and emotions flaming through his veins. His height and breath expanded; his teeth developed sharp points for puncture.

His father sat back in his chair and sighed. "I see your instincts are as powerful as mine, my boar. Be wise with them, Martin, and lock yourself deep in this house. For if you come to blows with your brother, you may regret it."

"And what of Mac? Have you given him this speech? Or are you telling me to let him have her?" His voice was a roar to his ears. He surged up from his chair and loomed over his father in full Ursus height.

His father's eyes flashed, and his fist hit the desk. "Don't you bare your teeth at me, boar. I am not your competition for your mate. I am watching out for this family. She will not be one of us."

"No!" Martin reached across the desk and snagged his father by the cravat, lifting him out of his seat and up into the air. "You are trying to interfere with instincts I have no control over, desires older than time. Something you told us always to trust and obey."

His father tore from his claws. The linen about his neck was crushed and torn; he leered at Martin. "I will have you locked up, Martin. If you cannot stay away from her, I will make you."

"Try." His father had never been able to match his strength. He turned away from his father. *What happened to all you taught us?* He scoffed, disgusted by what came from his father's mouth. Thank goodness their mother no longer lived to see this. She would be heartbroken to know his father regretted his choice in her. They had seemed happy.

He glanced at his father, who stood undoing his shredded

cravat from his neck. "Were you not overjoyed with your choice in a mate?" Martin asked.

His father's blue eyes narrowed in anger. "Hold your tongue. Your mother centered my world. What I regret is that I fought and killed my brother to get her."

Martin flinched at the pain in his father's voice. He knew the tale; the entire family did, though his father never spoke of it. Why his father thought he had had any control over what happened to his brother or what would happen to his sons amazed Martin. Would he never learn? The more any of them fought the powers, the worse the outcome.

That outcome had happened to his father. He'd denied his feelings for their mother because of his brother's fancy. Then Orsse had started, and his instincts had overpowered his will. He'd thrashed his brother in order to mate with her. She'd had no choice but to take his father; that, or go through the incredible pain of shedding an unplanted Ursus–ready womb and end up ruined, a society outcast.

Her not having a choice was what bothered Martin. His father could have avoided that. If he had shown their mother his interest, she could have chosen.

He would not put Jane in that position. He would be damned if he locked away those strong emotions. He didn't know if he could. How his father had lasted to the point of Orsse without their mother knowing, he couldn't fathom.

"I will not allow you to lock me away in order to try to control actions you cannot. Where is Mac?"

"I don't know." His father's voice was a whisper.

He spun around to face his father. His father's face was pale, the wrinkles about his eyes deeper than the day before. Fear etched the frown on his lips. Terror of losing one of his sons made him act such.

Martin nodded. "If you find Mac, Father, leave him be. Let the powers work this out."

He strode to the door and opened it before his father could say more. Stepping into the hall, Martin strode directly into Devon.

Devon jumped back from him.

"Holy hell, Martin! Did you kill him?"

Martin pushed past him and continued down the hall. He needed to change back, and quickly. "No, killing your sire is considered ill-mannered. Not that the thought hadn't crossed my mind." He shook his head in an attempt to get his vision back to normal. Damnit! The heat and emotions hurt his eyes and made his body ache for release . . . for Jane.

He cast a quick glance at Devon, who hurried to walk beside him. "Devon, have you seen Mac?"

"Not since breakfast. He was quite shaken by your actions and I hate to say a bit intrigued." Devon ran to keep up with his brisk pace as he headed to the family wing of the house.

"Indeed. I won't be seen again until this is straightened out. Please check in on Miss Milton."

Devon stopped in his tracks, and Martin kept up his pace, wanting to get to his room and do all he could to change back with all haste.

"Martin, don't you mean to have her? To have her join us?" Devon shouted at his back.

"There is no doubt. She will be joining us," he growled.

But with who?

Jane couldn't sleep.

Her nerves held taut, her stomach in a knot. Terror of this night held her mind captive. But what did she fear? This house, for sure. But more so, the intense desire for this strange man, when only a day ago she would have married another. Was she that wicked of a woman? Jonathan had been in her thoughts in some form or another for the past year. Now Martin consumed her thoughts. Sweet mother! She was confused.

When Martin had held her and protected her from the rain today, she sensed something entirely different for her life. A lifetime full of being cherished and desired beyond any capability she imagined. But what was Martin? What was this family? He had said she shouldn't be afraid of him. She didn't believe they wanted to harm her; they would have done that already.

She rolled onto her side and watched as the embers sparked in the grate. The rain was a gentle pelting at the window; normally it would have put her to sleep in a moment. And this bed—any other moment in her life she would have drifted into a slumber in mere seconds in such comfort.

She wanted Martin to come to her. Show her what he was so she could put her mind at ease and either leave or . . . or what? Stay? What a shocking thought. Martin had talked to her with his mind. Could she do the same? If she called for him. . . .

Martin, come to me.

She giggled. How silly. . . .

The wind outside picked up, and growls and howling came from somewhere in the house. She counted the bolts on the door. All eight were locked. She closed her eyes, and images flashed of Martin spread over her. The smooth velvet of his touch caressed every inch of her body. His prick moved within her until she screamed, cinnamon filling her nose until she could smell nothing but him. Her body quivered, and she pulled the covers closer in an attempt to find the warmth his body had provided the night before.

I can smell your arousal from the other end of the house, filtered through her ears. *Would you shut me out if I came to you?*

Liquid coated her sex at his words. Her eyes squeezed tighter. She shouldn't want this. She should be rational. But Martin . . . She did want him.

Come to me, Martin.

Her body wanted this man beyond reason. She wanted this man. Her limbs shook.

A growl came from the direction of the door, and her body trembled.

Sniff, sniff. You desire me.

Her nipples hardened as warmth, hotter than any blanket or fire, slid over her, possessing her heart and soul. Wetness slid up her belly as smooth silk traced her nipples and then up her neck. How did he do that? She didn't dare open her eyes. She couldn't; she didn't want to see the red-eyed beast she had glimpsed last night.

Warm breath puffed at her ear. *I will make you feel like you have never felt.*

"Yes. . . ." Her sex clenched as she spoke the word, more moisture spilling to her curls, to her thighs. She was mad! She didn't know what he was, and she wanted this act with him. Wanted him in a way that defied all she knew. Her heart ached for him. Her body. She couldn't turn him away if she tried. He commanded her emotions, her thoughts.

He growled, and teeth grazed the flesh of her neck, dragging down the skin as his humid tongue slid.

Her hands reached out to touch him and stopped midair, unsure what she would find beneath her touch.

Touch me, he demanded, deep and gruff. Her hands connected with his head, and her fingers slid into his silky hair. Loose locks fanned out across her body, tickling her flesh.

His head wiggled beneath her hands as his mouth latched over her nipple, tongue swirling, teeth lightly biting and suckling. Her hips arched into his stomach, and her heat dampened her shift as cotton clung to the flesh between her thighs.

"Oh, Martin." Her hands slid to his back and discovered skin so smooth, so soft, like fine satin. His muscles rippled beneath her touch, and his hand tugged up her shift, so the garment pooled above her breast. Skin to skin, their bodies burned. Her legs slid apart to cradle him as his mouth descended back to her breast, sucking the now bare buds.

Sweet mother! This act exceeded last night. His hands slid to her hips, pinning her to the mattress with his weight, and her lungs locked. The velvet touch of his fingers cupped and scooped her bum, tilting her sex to ride against his abdomen. The friction, the tight downy curls brushing her flesh, tightened every muscle in her body. Her mind concentrated on that one spot where they pressed so intimately. She slid her hips back and forth against him. Each grind increased the delight of his touch.

Jane, Jane, your blood pumps through me. Jane. He shifted to the side and slid a finger into the slick flesh between her thighs. She cried out, and he captured her mouth. His tongue wrapped around hers, tugging and sucking. Oh! He tasted like cinnamon, but there was a hint of more . . . a darkness, an animal heat and possession, like drinking something naughty and so exquisite you just had to have more. She moaned and arched into his hand, craving more fingers to slide inside.

His hand continued to rub her silk lips as more and more moisture slid from her and coated his hand. He growled and pulled his lips from her.

"You are most ready for my mounting, sweet Jane." His breath warmed her cheek as he spoke aloud. "You are mine."

Indeed, she wanted this. She didn't care what people would think. She nodded her head and arched her hips into his hand probing her sex. He pressed three fingers into her opening and then fanned them out, stretching her flesh. The burn was so erotic it sent waves of pressure steaming up her limbs. He slid the fingers back and thrust in. Her hips arched, and she ground her drowning flesh into his palm with each thrust.

He shifted over her, his shoulder level with her lips. She kissed the salty yet sweet bare flesh hungrily. Biting the smooth curve, she pinched the muscles and flesh between her teeth. He hissed and grasped her thighs, wrenching them apart.

His sex branded the inside of her thigh, and she gasped. His prick felt thick, so thick, and oh, so long. She tried to relax, but every nerve jumped at the scalding, smooth head pressed against her slick lips. He leveraged himself upon his hands and leaned in to lick her neck.

Her heart hammered in her chest. She was about to join with a man, and she had no idea what he was. Should she do this? An overpowering wave of desire pushed through her veins. Her breath hitched. Yes. The need to have him fill her, to have this man who made her body feel so good thrust into her, dominated her soul.

She rotated her hips and pressed down against the head probing her entrance. He did not move but let her initiate this act. The taper pressed slowly in, stretching her wider and wider. He held back, muscles trembling, straining, as ever so slowly his large phallus squeezed in. Every slip of him, every stretch of her flesh to sheath him intensified her awareness of only him.

He snagged her earlobe between his teeth and hissed. Picking up the motion, he continued to press in with small thrusts of his hips. The head popped into her, and a wet sensation slid down her crack to her bum hole.

"Jane," he hissed through clenched teeth and lunged in one harsh movement, the head of his phallus nestled against the tip of her womb. She cried out, and her eyes fluttered open. His huge form covered her. The heat pouring from him dampened his body and hers. His hip arched, and he pulled the long phallus from her greedy sex. She whimpered at the overwhelming sensation of emptiness.

"Jane . . ." He thrust back in, harder than the last.

Her hips arched, and her knees clutched his hips, not wanting him to leave her body.

He growled. *I'm lost to you.*

Her hands dug into the muscles of his back. "More." Her voice sounded so harsh she didn't recognize it as hers.

Under her hands, his flesh grew taut. As he growled and hissed, his sex plundered in and out of her. Her body arched into each thrust, muscles tightening as she reached for the bliss he'd brought her last night.

"Martin! Martin!" Her sex clenched, pulsing, sending sucking noises from their join. He hissed again, encircled her legs with his hands, and leaned up away from her, tilting her bottom. His fingers burned the flesh of her bum, and pressure pushed at her bum hole; something was inserted into her. The sensation was so strange. Her sex spasmed, body bucking, as both penetrations continued with the push of his hips.

His fingers dug into the flesh of her legs. His lips came down hard on her nipple, sucking to the point of pain. Sweet mother! The craving, the desire in her, burst, spiraling her need for this pleasure. He suckled her nipple, and his body trembled. With a growl, he bit down. She screamed as pain-filled pleasure tore at her. His phallus pulsed, and he froze, muscles taut. He then heaved. A tingling prick hit her womb as warm wetness gushed into her. Pressure built, so delightful, and warmth radiated from her womb. He ground his hips into her mound, and her body erupted again, the walls of her womb massaging his hard staff.

"Jane." He rolled to the side, dragging her with him. She sprawled across his chest, her legs wrapped about his hips. The sounds of their matched heartbeats lulled her to sleep.

Jane awoke to wet warmth licking the length of her slit, her body arched on its own. "Martin?"

His head pushed up from under the covers, his eyes the same blood circles she'd sighted that first night. She jumped. He closed his eyes and shook his head. "Jane, you need to know more, now that you have accepted me."

She laughed. "I think it is a bit too late for that. I should have known more before you . . . we . . . I just couldn't refrain myself." Embarrassed heat washed her face.

"You are my mate. Your body knew even if your mind resisted." The backs of his fingers caressed her cheek, and she closed her eyelids, nuzzling into the caress. "I am sorry I made you bleed anew."

"Did you? Well, you are large." Her cheeks blazed further with warmth.

He smiled down at her and winked. "Indeed. Did you enjoy the last?" His eyes flashed with wickedness, and her body heated, the memory of the intense sensation of being penetrated twice assaulting her.

"Oh, yes."

"I will mount you twice more in the next two sunsets."

"You wish to keep me?"

His brows drew together, and he nodded. "Silly girl. The ritual for marking you began this night. This join will show others you are mine by marking you with my scent, my marks. Then the opening, readying your body to receive my seed. Finally Orsse, where I make you my mate forever." His entire body shook, and Jane tugged him and rolled. Her body nestled fully along his. "I would take you again tonight if I had not hurt you so." His body continued to shake.

"You are holding yourself back? That is why you shake?"

"Yes." His teeth clenched. "I have to leave you. I don't have the restraint I wish where you are concerned."

She nodded, and the flesh of his chest trembled with breath.

"Martin, tell me what you are?"

"We are all Ursus; we are human but more. And the more is what makes us all different. I have acute vision in the dark. I also have incredible strength. We all, in some form or another, can read thoughts or emotions." He pulled her tightly into an embrace. "And when threatened, we change."

Change? "How so?"

"Claws, height, teeth. It is our defense. How we protect what is ours."

She nodded and rubbed her face into the downy curls on his chest. "Is that why you feel like silk?"

"You think so? Well, not all of us do. Mac's hair is coarse, even if he is my twin." His heart beat wildly beneath her ear, and his erection grew firm against her belly.

Jane's cheeks grew warm. "We will do the act twice more, and then you go off into the woods and leave me here to bear more Ursus?" Or a human child of Jonathan's. How could he truly want her, knowing that?

He did not answer but pushed from her bed and kissed her. His firm lips nipped and sucked her breath from her. Her head swam in the presence of him.

"I cannot stay. I have grown stiff again. If I do, I will hurt you further."

She wanted him to stay, to do what he did with her again. She shifted and wrapped her hands about his shoulders, and the flesh between her thighs burned and ached. Ouch!

She nodded; he was correct. Joining again would not be as pleasant as the act could be. The weight of his body compressed the mattress. As he left, her eyes drifted shut.

6

"Miss Milton! Miss Milton!"

Jane stretched the muscles of her thighs and sex, aching. The sensations and images of what she and Martin had done the night before returned and heated her skin. A smile tugged her lips.

"Lord Tremarctos wishes you to join him in his study."

Oh! She was tired! Her eyes fluttered open to light pouring in around the curtain. The sun. She bolted up straight. She could go home. A smile touched her face, and she scrambled to her feet. The flesh between her legs protested the sudden movements.

Martin. . . . He would not be happy if she left. She gasped. Her heart ached at the thought of leaving him behind. How had her connection to this man fused so fast? She pinched the bridge of her nose. The decision to leave surely could wait until she saw Martin again. She could, however, send a letter to her parents with haste and inform them as to her whereabouts.

She glided to the washbasin and splashed icy water on her face. Gooseflesh covered her skin, but it didn't cool the heat raging in her. Wringing out a wet cloth, she dragged the damp cotton down her neck. Her gaze caught her reflection in the looking glass, and she gasped. Her lips were swollen—her tongue darted out and traced the plump surface—her hair a tangled mess, and a startling cranberry flush stained her chest.

Pulling out the edge of her shift, she gazed at her breasts. They, too, possessed the red hue as well as the skin around and beneath her curls. Her fingers skimmed lightly across the smooth-as-silk flesh. Martin. The skin felt just like him. How odd! A reminder of him? He had said he marked her. Was this what he meant?

She pulled her hair back and coiled the thick fair locks at the base of her neck the best she could; then she donned the light green dress Martin had given her. The fabric slipped down her body, and shivers pricked her skin. Martin. She ran her hands down her restrained curves, imagining his hands instead of hers. She turned back to the looking glass. Oh! How the color brought a snap to her eyes. The neckline, a modest square, covered the silk burgundy flesh. Besides her lips, no one would think anything different about her.

Opening her door, Jerome waited to take her to Lord Tremarctos. She followed him down the hall and the grand stairs to the main floor.

She stopped at the doorway to the study. The large wooden door stood open into the room. Lord Tremarctos sat behind a massive desk; on the wall behind him hung a full bearskin. Books and interesting artifacts filled the shelves that surrounded the room. She wished she could linger, to pull the books from the shelves and learn of the hidden secrets of this house.

"Miss Milton," Jerome announced her and bowed.

"Miss Milton, please come in and sit down." Lord Tremarctos didn't look up as he scribbled in an open ledger on his desk.

She stepped across the threshold and into the room on shaky legs. Lord Tremarctos was about to send her home. Her heart jumped into her throat.

Fisting her hands in front of her, she sat in the large wooden chair opposite his desk. He was truly elegant. His long gray hair was tied behind his back. His jacket shone the same dark silver as the threads of his hair.

An icy blue gaze slid down her, assessing, and he sighed. "The weather has lifted. I have a carriage prepared. It will be ready to take you home within the hour."

She bit her lip and pinched the folds of the soft green skirt. She didn't want to go. Did Martin know she was about to leave? She glanced up to see Lord Tremarctos staring out the window.

"Miss Milton, I won't play games. I wish you to leave this house. I can sense your indecision." He wouldn't look at her, and his hands fisted on the desk's surface. "I can see and smell Martin's mark." He closed his eyes, and his lips pursed; a crease pierced his brow. "I cannot, will not allow you to remain here."

"Pardon?" This was because of what Devon had said. His father feared what Mac and Martin would do. She had not seen Mac since morning repast the previous day. "What do you fear by me staying here?"

His gaze shot to hers, and anger flashed behind his eyes. "There is a history here, Miss Milton, something that you could not possibly fathom. I will not let my sons follow the same path. You *will* leave this house. I do not approve of you being here."

Her lower lip trembled, and tears pricked her eyes. He did not agree with Martin's choice? Tears welled further, and her throat tightened. Once again, she was undesired. She should have known that Devon's comment about station not mattering was a stretch of the truth. If she left, what would Martin do? Did he truly want her as his lifemate? Or had he said that so she would allow him to bed her?

She choked back a sob, her heart slowing to a painful thud in her chest. It didn't matter. Lord Tremarctos wouldn't allow her to stay. Without Martin here to defend her, she had no choice but to follow his request and leave. A tear slid down her cheek, cooling the humid flesh as chills of sadness raised the hair on her neck.

Maybe returning home would be for the best. She inhaled a shaky breath. She needed to reassure her family that she remained well and . . .

She swallowed the large lump stuck in her throat. Martin was different, and even though he felt so perfect, so many things were not right in this situation.

She was not of their station, and she truly still had no idea what the Ursus family was or of what greats and horrors they were capable.

But Martin.

Needles pricked the reddened skin beneath her clothing, and her hand raised and traced the neckline of her bodice. Her body and mind craved Martin. How long would the feel of his skin remain on her body? She may forget him in a day as she had Jonathan. Her finger traced the silk skin of his mark. She would hold on to this memory for as long as she could. Overwhelming emotion for Martin filled her heart to the brim. Tears stung her eyes, and she swallowed her heart.

She wouldn't leave without saying where she'd gone. If Martin decided he did indeed want her after his father's rejection, he would know where to find her. She would write a letter to him. She couldn't just leave.

"Very well, sir. Do you have pen and parchment? I would like to leave a letter for Martin." She had horrid handwriting, but she could leave a short note.

He nodded and then pulled out a few sheets, a quill, and an inkwell. "This is for the best. Thank you."

She pinched the quill in her shaking hand and scribbled across the parchment.

Martin
  I have returned home to Sudhamly to ease my family's worries.

                                          Jane

Jane stepped down from the Ursus carriage to the muddy street of Sudhamly. The streets bustled with noontime activity. People turned and stared at the black lacquered coach with the emblem barely recognizable on the side. If she had not lived in the Ursus house, she would have thought the symbol a mistake blurred by the mud.

To her, the red and green emblem of a bear print, claws extended, shone clear as day. Bear. . . . Chills raced her skin, and the marks on her skin burned. With each step she made farther away from Tremarctos and Martin, the marks stung. She walked away from the carriage with reluctance, her heart pounding with unease.

Did the townsfolk know of her fall from grace? She glanced at a few of the locals and smiled, but they stared at her in question of her conveyance.

Nerves shook her hands. Why did being here feel so wrong? She'd wanted the comfort of this place, of her family, but at the moment she wanted to scramble back into the Ursus carriage. She shook her head.

You ninny, you belong here, not there. You feel that way only because of your folly. Go put your parents at ease.

She straightened her shoulders and pushed open the door to her father's shop. The familiar smell of starch and crisp linen wafted to her nose, and she smiled.

"Be right with you!" her pa yelled from the back of the store. How odd. She had been gone only two nights, but she didn't know what to do. Should she go into the back? Should she wait here?

The front room of the shop, the largest in their home, felt incredibly small. The steam-thick air, from washing and dying, smothered her. She didn't belong here. . . . Yes, she did. She shook her head. She couldn't wait to see her parents and wipe the worry from their minds. She strode forward, her hands fisted, spine straight, determination pulsing through her. She paused. If they knew of her folly, would they tell her?

Her heart pounded in her throat; she walked behind the counter and pushed open the curtains that led to the back. Her mother stood behind a worktable, cutting cloth, and screeched as Jane caught her gaze.

"Jane! Jane!" She hustled over to her and wrapped her in a huge embrace. "Oh, dear girl, where have you been?"

"Mother." She squeezed her mother's fleshy shoulders tight, tears blurring her eyes. "I got caught out in the rain. And . . ." What should she tell them? She very well could not say she'd rutted with Jonathan and run off because he'd treated her ill. Or that she took shelter in a house filled with nothing but men.

Her mother pulled back and studied her face, a crease between her brows. "Are you well?"

"Quite." Her lips turned up into a smile.

"Thomas, Thomas, Jane is home. Jane is home!" her mother squealed.

Her father came from the kitchen, his hands blue with dye. "Ah! Jane, you scared us so." His gaze ran down her length. "But you look well enough. You surely found a place to stay out of the weather. Did you press on to old Mrs. Smithies'?"

"Ah, no . . . I got lost, but I did find shelter. I'm quite well."

"I just put on a pot of tea, and you can help your mother with some mending." He waved them back toward the kitchen.

Her shoulders relaxed, and she and her mother strolled through the door to the family side of the building. It was good to be home. Not once had they pressed her for any explanation. How odd! She'd never hid anything from them in the past. Maybe she should tell them.

No! They would be so ashamed of her, and at the moment she wanted to feel only comfort. Her heart constricted. They trusted her, and she'd done the unforgivable. What would they do if she carried a child? She could not keep from them what had happened. If the gossip leaked out to the township, her father's business would suffer. But how would she explain?

She sat down to enjoy the comforts she craved, family and home. Tonight she would tell her mother what happened. And tomorrow, everything would change.

The hair on Jane's neck lifted as Jonathan prowled into her parents' parlor. What was he doing here?

"Miss Milton, so glad you're well. Gave us all a scare, lovely."

Sweet mother! How was she going to get through this? She couldn't look at him. Heat flushed her face.

He is only here to see your father, you foolish girl. Your father is his friend.

She nodded her head and went back to her mending, not seeing a stitch.

He strode to the chair beside her and sat down with an ungraceful *thunk*. The needle pricked her finger. Ouch! She grimaced; she refused to let him see her nerves and forced herself to smile.

His dark blond hair was slicked back from his face, and he wore the same white shirt he always wore. She tensed, waiting for the flutter in her heart or the pain she'd felt running through the woods. Neither came. Only her cheeks burned of shame.

He was pale. Had he been ill of late? His blue eyes caught hers, and her stomach clenched. Oh! How odd! She had never experienced that reaction to him before. Her hand shot to her stomach and pressed against the unease.

"Mary, bring us some of those fine rolls you made and a pint," her father said to her mother. "I think we need to celebrate my baby coming home."

Her mother scurried to her feet and disappeared into the kitchen. Jane slid the needle back through the tablecloth she mended and held in a burp.

Jonathan leaned toward her. "Gave me a fright, you did, lovely. I'll be havin' no more of that." His eyes were hard as his gaze traveled to her breasts.

Thank goodness he wouldn't touch them again! She hoped he wouldn't try to lead her to indiscretion again, but she had given him her virginity, and wasn't that a good signal she would always be willing?

Now that she had Martin, she couldn't imagine allowing Jonathan to touch her again.

Did she have Martin? She had left his home. He could consider her gone, never to return. But she didn't think so.

She, oddly, could feel him. She sensed that he grew near and that he was determined to have her. The possessiveness probably came from his mark. A smile curved her lips as a warm contentedness filled her.

She would one day go back to the Ursuses, if only to stare at the house from afar and wonder. The raspberry marks on her skin pricked, and her heart constricted. She wanted to return to Tremarctos not one day but now.

Oh! What a bloody mess this was! She couldn't do that, and why did she want to so badly? They were not of her kind, and more than a little part of her feared Tremarctos. Her stomach gurgled, and she hiccupped.

Her mother reappeared with a tray in hand, her savory herb rolls and two pints of beer perched on top. The smell of rosemary and thyme eased her stomach's grumble.

Mary placed the tray on the sideboard and brought one pint to Jonathan and the other to her father.

" 'Tis a good thing Jane made it home safe." Jonathan raised his mug to her father and smiled.

Had his cheek twitched? Her eyes narrowed as she scrutinized him closely.

"Indeed it is. For if something had happened to her, I wouldn't have this joyous moment."

The way her father had phrased that was a bit odd. She quelled the shiver that ran down her spine. What was he about?

"I'm so happy to be home, Father, to relieve your worries. I did not intend to make you and Mother fret." Her gaze darted back and forth between the two men. Something was amiss.

"Indeed, child, as we are delighted of your return. And this day is all the more special. . . ." Her father's eyes filled with joy, and a radiant smile stretched across his face as he gazed from her to Jonathan.

Oh . . . Oh, no! Her lungs locked, and she gasped for air. He was about to say what she thought he was about to say. Her entire body tensed as bile burned a hasty trail up her throat. Her stomach twisted and heaved. Her hand shot to her mouth, and she swallowed hard, trying to fight back her crumpets, for she didn't want to embarrass her family by casting up her accounts.

"Yes, child, Jonathan has asked for your hand. . . ."

She choked as she attempted to swallow back the contents of her dinner. Jonathan reached out to grasp her hand, a conflicted smile on his face. The smell of him, hops and watered-down Scotch, collided with her nose. Her stomach would have none of it; vomit spewed from her mouth, splattering across the crotch of Jonathan's pants and his prized machine.

"Holy futter!" Jonathan screeched as he shot to his feet.

"I—I'm so sorry," Jane said, feeling a trifle better. "But—but I thought you had no interest in me for more than a tickle."

Her mother gasped. "Jane! H—have you . . . have you and Jonathan . . ."

Her father held up a hand, effectively cutting off her mother. "Jonathan came by after your disappearance. He was overwrought with guilt and said that when you came home he would marry you. We knew you had a fondness for him, so we accepted."

She should be overjoyed with glee. Oh, God. This was not happening! Two days ago, wedding Jonathan was all she had wanted. What she expected from her life. But now . . . she had experienced true affection, true desire, and this was not what she wanted.

Her mother brought two cloths from the kitchen and handed them to Jonathan. Jane's fingers pinched the bridge of her nose. Ugh. The stench of him! She shot to her feet and scurried to stand on the opposite side of the room. Her stomach clenched again as he stepped toward her. She'd always found the smell of hops so masculine, so Jonathan, but not now.

"Nuttin' to worry yourself over, lovely. I have been cast up on before."

Oh, God, Oh, God, Oh, God. What a mess she had gotten herself in. She spun around. "I—I can't marry—"

Rap, rap, rap .

She jumped, and everyone turned toward the door.

Her father strode to the back entrance and yanked the handle.

Martin barged past her father into the little parlor, dwarfing everything inside.

His wild eyes assessed her in a glance.

"Sir." He nodded at her father.

A wave of relief swept through her so strong she wanted to weep and throw herself into his arms. The smell of cinnamon wafted to her nose from across the room, and her stomach instantly stopped its revolt. His eyes twinkled. *All will be well, Jane,* filtered through her mind.

"Excuse me, sir. Who are you to barge into my home?" Her father's gaze slid down his massive form, studying the tailoring of his clothes.

He looked so finely dressed in expertly fitted blue coat and breeches. Something only a man of means could afford, and her father would never turn down business.

"I am your daughter's husband."

A loud thud sounded from the kitchen door. None of them turned to investigate.

"Pardon, sir?" Her father turned his gaze on her. "Jane?"

Oh, this . . . this . . . What a preposterous idea! They were married . . . how was that supposed to work?

"Haven't you told them, Jane?" Martin's firm, deep voice made her insides quiver. *Play along, Jane. I will not leave this house without you.*

Her fists clenched. She wanted to go with him. She had a real proposal of marriage and one that was fictitious. Her soul wanted the lie. What was wrong with her! No sane woman in her situation would turn down a real proposal.

Jane.

She stared at Martin, and her throat tightened. She couldn't refuse him.

"No. I—I couldn't think of a proper way to break the good news."

Relief shone in Martin's eyes.

"How about 'I ran off and got married'? My goodness, child." Her father studied Martin's shiny mud-splattered boots. "And, sir—it is 'sir'? Correct?" Her father tilted his head.

"Martin Ursus of the Duke of Tremarctos," he drawled.

Was that true? His father was a duke?

A thud and then a groan came from her mother as she fell to the floor again. Jane couldn't take her eyes off Martin, and no one else moved to help her mother either. They might miss something.

"Jane, child, why did you not tell us you were acquainted with a nobleman?"

Martin left her no room to answer.

"I met Jane on the road while in my carriage two days hence, and I was so captivated by her beauty my heart wouldn't allow me to live without her." He smiled and winked at Jane.

Lies . . . and more lies. Would she ever tell a truth again? She tried to smile.

"She refused to get into my carriage. My heart fancied it love, and I refused to leave her. After much persuasion, I finally convinced her to accept my plight and agree to wed me with haste. We left for Scotland straightaway."

Would he have done such if she had met him on the road? She closed her eyes. . . . By God! She wished that situation had been true. What a mooncalf!

She sat back and stared at him standing rigid in their parlor; his head was only mere inches from the ceiling. What did her father think? Jonathan had obviously told him of their folly.

She glanced at Jonathan; angry hurt shone in his eyes. Noticing her gaze, he strode toward her, his motions cutting off Martin midsentence as Martin watched Jonathan approach her. In one swift motion, Martin stepped between Jonathan and her. His eyes narrowed, and he stared down at Jonathan, daring him to step around him.

"But . . . but I . . . she . . ." Jonathan pointed back and forth between himself and her. "We."

"No!" Martin said in a firm voice that all but growled. "There is no 'we' where she and you are concerned."

Jonathan's eyes went wide, and he turned to search Jane's face. "Jane." He bowed his head. "I'm glad you are well."

Martin stepped aside to let him pass, and Jonathan hastily pulled open the door and went out into the night.

Jane swallowed hard. She'd just passed up her one chance at respectability. But Martin had come for her. Martin! Her entire body lit like a fire at his nearness.

"My dear girl." Her father grasped her hand and winked. "My lord. You will stay with us this night so we can get to know our new family member."

"I'm sorry, sir. I have estate business to be handled in the morning. We will head back to Tremarctos this night."

"Very well, very well."

"If you so choose, I will send a coach for you in one month's time, and you and Mrs. Milton can journey to Tremarctos for an extended visit."

Oh! That would be horrid! What would her family think of the strangeness that occurred in that house?

"So be it! That will do nicely, don't you think, Mary?" Her father turned toward the kitchen. "Oh, Mary!"

All three of them rushed to her mother, who groaned in her faint as her legs twitched on the floor.

Jane's father knelt down to help her mother to her feet, and Martin's warm fingers wrapped about Jane's arm, pulling her back firmly against his length. His hand traveled down her arm, eliciting small tremors in his touch's wake; then he laced his fingers in hers. His erection pressed into her bum.

Jane, Jane. I need you, Jane. I need you more than any of that romantic clad trap I spouted to your family. He spoke to her mind.

She closed her eyes as aroused awareness skittered about her skin. Did he mean it?

I should have warned you about the smell of other threatening men. . . . His chest rumbled in a suppressed chuckle against her back.

What? She turned and peered at him, and his lip quirked. "You mean to tell me I cast up my crumpets because Jonathan got too close to me?" she whispered.

"Something like that." He pressed his lips to her ear, and his frame shook.

Had he just barely suppressed changing when he saw Jonathan?

"Are you well?"

As soon as I am inside you, I will be.

7

Martin's muscles strained as he lifted Jane into the carriage. His horse was tied behind. He had met the carriage driver, who had dropped off Jane at home, as the driver was returning to Tremarctos. He'd had the driver follow him back to Sudhamly and it was a good thing—he needed to be inside Jane, and now, to begin opening and be one step closer to making her his. He sat on the black leather seat, wrapping an arm about her back and one under her knees, lifting her onto his lap.

"Jane." He nuzzled into her golden hair as the carriage began to move.

"Martin, I have to know. Will you make good on your words?"

He smiled against the soft fair strands. She had no idea how she possessed him. "Jane, you can have anything you wish from me. You desire our connection made legal? So be it."

"But what if I carry Jonathan's child?" Her cheeks reddened with color, and her breath hitched. "Will you shun me? Th— the child?" Pain and uncertainty poured from her and into his hands. "You know how I came to be at Tremarctos. Only time—"

"Shhh, dear Jane." He brushed a hair back from her face. "You are not with child . . . yet. I would smell it. However, the day after tomorrow you will be . . . with mine."

He grasped her chin with his hand and turned her face to his. Her blue eyes sparkled as he searched their depths, trying to read her emotions. "That is what you want, isn't it, Jane?" His thumb rubbed the soft surface of her cheek. "To be bound to me for life, to carry my children?"

Her eyes widened, and desire poured from her so hot the skin he touched burned. "Strange as it is, that is quite what I wish."

"Is it? Are you sure? Not that I would be able to stop at this point. You consume me, Jane. But I would try."

A tear leaked from the corner of her eye and caught his fingertip stroking her skin. "I want you, Martin." Her breath hitched.

The same kind of desperate physical desire sparked the air between them. It wasn't the emotion that was in his heart, but it would do for now.

She shifted in his lap, bunching up her skirts, her knees sliding to either side of his thighs, to face him. The smell of her cunt opening as her body straddled him pounded through him.

Egad. His cock swelled, and his eyes flickered red. "Jane?" His hands dropped to caress the curve of her waist.

"Indeed, here in the carriage." She nodded, a sensual grin lighting her face.

Indeed. . . . He growled, and his hand reached between them and into her buttered folds. The hot, drenching flesh slid about his fingers, pulling them deep as she arched her back into his palm and moaned.

Chills raced his skin as his cock pulsed. She soon would be his for always. She thrust her breasts toward him, and his tongue darted out and traced the edge of her neckline. Her skin spiced with arousal, and his scent slid down his tongue and pulsed straight to his cock.

She wanted him just as desperately. He pushed his fingers into her cunt, and her legs slid on the leather seat, parting farther, riding down on his invasion. The spongy flesh caressed his fingers in waves as she trembled in aroused bliss. She was exquisite! He had never felt so proud to have a woman want him. His gaze settled on his mark covering her breasts, and his head spun; the animal within him went wild with hunger for her.

His thumb wiggled back and forth in her slick folds, finding her nubbin and then gently scraping his nail over it.

"Martin!" She pushed against his hand, spending more of her sweet-smelling honey onto his fingers. Her fingers dug into the cloth of his coat. "I—I want you now, Martin." Her face flushed with heat, and she flinched slightly with shame.

"Don't be embarrassed by your desires, Jane." His voice came out a croak. "I want you with just as acute a desire. You must ask for whatever you wish carnally, and do not fret over it." He pulled his hand from her and fumbled with the buttons to the flap of his trousers, pulling his cock free. His flesh hardened, growing bigger without the confines of his pants. He groaned in relief.

Lifting her away from his body, he rubbed the swollen head of his cock into the balmy flesh of her cunt, sliding the head from clit to anus. The connection of their skin pulsed with lightning heat. He growled and placed the tip in her entrance.

"Push down on me, Jane. Slide my hard cock into you until your body is filled with me."

His mind focused on the spot of their join; his sac opened, and he pulled her tight to him. The seed from him this time would ready her for his seed within half a day; his next spend would make her full in the belly with his child.

She pushed down ever so slowly; her slickness caressed his

prick head as she descended. His lungs seized, and he tried to stay immobile to let her take the lead of her desires, but he needed to touch her. Damnit! He reached up and grasped her breasts; his thumbs rubbed her hard nipples, barely discernable beneath her corset; his head lolled back on a groan rippling through his chest.

The head of his cock pushed through her opening, and his gaze shot to her face.

She stared at him and bit her lip. "Martin." She pushed down in one motion and encased his entire staff in her steamy warmth.

His teeth clenched, and his heart beat madly. She arched against him, rubbing her mound against the curls of his sex, bonding their juices, their hairs, their bodies as one.

She pulled back to the tip of him and descended again with the same swift motion. His muscles jerked; again and again, she repeated her motion. Her velvet clasped his hardness and pulled his seed from the depths of his sac. It wasn't enough; he needed it faster, harder, deeper.

"Jane." He lunged forward, toppling her into the seat across from him. Kneeling on the floor of the carriage, his cock still lodged in her, he grasped her legs and hooked her knees over his shoulders. Her skirts pooled about her breasts; her face was lost in a sea of green muslin. His hands trailed down her stocking-clad legs to the bare skin of her thighs and caressed the aroused soft flesh.

She squirmed, and he possessed her hips, pulled his cock to the tip, and bucked into her slick body. She stretched, encasing him with her honey flowing freely from her, coating his stiffness as he probed her deep. He was wild with his actions; he was harsh, but he couldn't stop himself.

The entrance to her womb touched the head of his cock, and he stopped and pushed harder against hard flesh as his bags tingled, spending the opening fluid on her womb. He growled at the strange sensation like a mini spend that built and built his pleasure. Leaning down, he nipped the buds of her breasts. She cried out and arched into him. He pulled out again and pressed back in.

"Martin . . . oh . . . Martin!" The walls of her cunny clasped his hardness, and he kept the same rhythm, pumping in and out of her as his stomach muscles rippled and his chest tightened, his seed like a ball of fire coiled in his sac. The burning need to come inside her overpowered anything he knew.

His muscles strained, reaching for the euphoria. Her cunt glided along the skin of his cock; with a growl so loud it pierced his ears, he felt his seed erupt in bursts strong and hard, his entire sac emptying into her. His body burned, trembling with each blessed mind-numbing squirt.

He lowered her legs to his hips and pulled her body to him. He drank in the scent of her, him, and them. He had never experienced such an intense spend before. Exquisite!

He sat back on the opposite seat; she was straddling him, his cock still pulsing the opening fluid into her womb. His body trembled as it had the very first time he fucked, overwhelmed with pleasure and sensations. He felt as if he glowed, yet there was no light. He studied her passion-stained face, and his throat constricted on welling emotions threatening to take him.

Her nubbin rubbed against the flesh at the base of his staff, and she screamed; her womb and her body bucked, pulling the fluid deep within her. He grunted and hissed. How long would he stay hard?

The ritual texts taught him of this, but never had he thought the climax to be stronger and more pleasurable than a normal fuck.

"Jane." He nuzzled the skin at the base of her neck. "Are you well, Jane? Did I hurt you?"

"No, I'm quite well." Her breath hitched, and little tremors caressed his cock. "It feels different this time."

"How so?"

"It feels like you are still hard and blissfully filling me."

He growled as another burst pulsed from his cock. "Indeed."

"Sweet mother!" Her body rocked against him as his fluid oozed out onto his crotch. She put her forehead on his shoulder and wrapped her arms about him, clutching him to her. He, in turn, held her and cradled her in his arms. His breath caught, and his heart increased to a wild thumping.

He loved her.

He squeezed her tightly, placing his chin atop her head. He had never experienced this desire. If something happened to her, it would surely happen to him, too.

He knew she desired him; she was willing to spend her lifetime with him. That should be enough, right? The need to feel the emotion from her, that same desperation that poured from her on the night she came to Tremarctos over that twit Jonathan, maddened him. He wanted her to feel emotions, deep and strong, that wrapped about her and his heart. Would she? Or was it too soon after such an emotion belonged to another?

Jane rubbed her face into the soft lapel of Martin's coat. "Martin, Tremarctos still frightens me. I—I think if you told me more about the Ursus, it would ease my fret."

His arms about her tightened as the carriage hit a large rut, tossing them. His strong arms eased her mind and comforted her body. She was safe with him, but Tremarctos . . . Martin couldn't always be with her there. She needed to understand, to be able to stand alone in that house without fear. Her fingers toyed with the button on his silver waistcoat.

"Ursus." Martin's body tensed, and she rubbed her hand over his chest to sooth him. "We come from the north, across the seas, where the winters are bitter cold. Our clan was one of great warriors who believed in the Sacred Bear. It was part of who we were. Who we are. The men of the clan would adorn their skin with designs of the bear. Here," one of his hands dropped from about her, and he showed her the top of his thigh, "And here." He reached up and tapped the back of his shoulder.

"How so? Painted on?"

"Kind of, but with pricks of a tool into the skin so that it won't wash off. We all have them. You haven't seen me unclothed in daylight yet." His chest rumbled with a chuckle. "You will."

The carriage turned up the drive to Tremarctos, and Martin stared out at the structure. "I'll tell you more over dinner. Even show you my marks."

Jane gasped. "At the table, Martin? No!" she scolded.

"I will have a hearty meal sent up to your room, and we will dine in private and stay in bed. I'm not leaving your side again until you are thoroughly mine."

The carriage rolled to a stop, and a footman came forth and opened the door. Martin stepped out and stood, offering Jane his hand. She slid her small hand into his giant one. He was so impressive! The setting sun played warm hues of red and copper off his brown shoulder-length hair. The light brown of his eyes sparkled as he stared at her with possession in their depths.

Her knees weakened, and a smile tugged her lips. She would never get used to that look. With one swipe of his gaze down her body, every part of her trembled with lust and longing for more. She was adored. He cherished and desired her beyond reason. She almost stopped in her tracks. What a fretful thing! She desired him with no bounds. She wanted him no matter what he was. No matter what he wanted to do to her.

The door to Tremarctos opened, and Lord Tremarctos stood watching them ascend the steps. His brow stooped over his eyes, and a deep frown curved his lips. Her eyes widened, and the warmth that had been coursing through her muscles evaporated. He was not going to let her enter. He held up a hand, effectively halting them.

"Father."

"Martin, Miss Milton." Lord Tremarctos inclined his head.

"Let us pass, Father." Martin's fingers about Jane's hand tightened.

"By all means, Boar. But I need to speak with you. Now."

Martin glanced at Jane. "So be it. Speak."

Lord Tremarctos's gaze scrutinized her body and stopped at her hips. "I can smell the opening fluids on her; send her up to wash." He turned back to Martin. "You and I will speak after she is gone."

Jane lowered her eyes. Did the man have no manners? Her face flushed, burning hot. Why did he hate her so? Was he so threatened by her he had to humiliate her? He should let them pass and allow his son happiness.

Martin looked at her and inhaled, sniffing the air. "It is a delicious smell, is it not, Father?" The muscles in his cheek twitched, and the hand holding her flesh shifted.

She glanced down at their fingers and her eyes widened. On the back of his hands about his knuckles, slits appeared and pointed tips of bone poked through the flesh. Claws. Oh, no! Martin could not fight his family, not in front of her, not for her.

"Stop!" Jane stepped forward and turned, placing her free hand on Martin's chest. "I will go wash. Come to me when you are through, Martin."

Martin tensed; his grip on her hand tightened even more. "No, Jane. I will not permit you to be alone in this house."

His father nodded. "She is a good girl, Martin. She can handle letting go of your hand."

"No. She will not go about the house alone." Martin stared into the darkened entry. "Devon, will you stay with her?"

Jane gazed into the blackness beyond the door, and Devon stood in the hall shadows, glaring out at them. She smiled at him. Yes, Devon would keep her company. Martin could sooth his father.

Devon nodded slowly at Martin.

Jane dropped Martin's hand and pushed past Lord Tremarctos into the house. Martin followed on her heels.

She reached Devon, and he inclined his head to her. "Miss Milton." His eyes were sunken and his skin ashen. With his fair hair, he looked truly ill.

"Are you well, Mr. Ursus?"

He shook his head. "Quite. Just a slight sniffle, nothing to fret over."

Martin reached past her and grasped Devon's shoulder. "Devon, thank you. Father won't relent. I have no idea where Mac is, and I can't lose her. I don't want her to be alone, not with Orsse starting. If anything were to pull Mac from his hiding, it will be the scent of a fertile mate."

Devon swallowed. "Very well, Martin. She is safe with me." He turned to her and offered his arm. "Miss Milton."

"Wait, Jane." Martin grasped her hands and raised them to his lips. His tongue ran the line of her middle finger, halting at the apex of her hand. His wicked gaze trapped hers as he pushed his tongue through the web to tickle her palm. Oh! The sensation dragged along her sex, lapping the swollen folds. Yet his tongue was on her hand. Her body heated with desire so fast her breath hitched, and her sex grew tight. She didn't want him to leave!

"I will be swift, Jane." His eyes held concern, and he tensed; his gaze quickly darted around the entry. He shook his head and released her.

8

Jane paced her room, her eyes on the door. Devon stood in the corner by the windows, looking out onto the gardens below.

She wanted to change, to shed her clothes and lie naked on the bed in wait for Martin. Her skin grew balmy, and her shift stuck to her unbearably beneath her corset. Couldn't she shed her corset?

"Devon, would you mind stepping into the hall for a moment? I wish to refresh myself."

Devon's eyes grew round, and he shook his head, flipping them back to normal.

"Are you sure you are well, Devon?"

"Quite sure, Miss Milton. Do you require any assistance before I leave?"

Damn! She did. The tiny buttons on the back of her dress would have to be undone and then redone once she removed her corset.

She frowned. "No, that is all right. I will manage."

"Are you sure?" He stepped toward her, and her body sparked

like a flame on dry twigs. Her head grew light, and she wiped her brow with the back of her hand.

"Damn." His eyes flickered back to rounds, and in three strides he gazed down on her. "It has started."

"Pardon?"

His chest labored in and out, straining his silk waistcoat. He closed his eyes and inhaled, shaking his head. When he opened them, the human eyes returned.

"Let me help you get more comfortable, Miss Milton. I can feel your discomfort. You need to breathe." He shook his hands out as if he had been clenching them much too tightly.

"Devon, I don't think that is wise. What is wrong with you? You don't look well at all."

"I'm fine," he snapped and turned from her, but he didn't move from his close proximity. The heat from her body washed in waves through her muscles. A thick gush of moisture slid from her sex and down her legs. She shifted her stance and glanced at the door. Where was Martin?

A low groan came from Devon. It was the sound between pure delight and massive pain.

She didn't like how Devon was acting; she wanted him to leave. "If you will only step into the hall for a moment. Then you can come back."

"No! Martin has trusted me to watch you. You belong to him." He turned toward her, and his eyes had changed again. "Lord! The smell of you. I have to touch you." Devon's whole body shook, and her eyes widened. He was unwell.

"No!" He shouted as his eyes changed back again. "I—I thought I could control it, that I could stay away. He deserves you."

What was he talking about? "Control what, Devon?"

A painful howl passed his lips, and his eyes flipped back to round. He lunged toward her, and she jumped back, lodging herself between the large bed and a stand.

His gaze slid down her body, and he closed his eyes, tilting his head slightly up. *Sniff, sniff.* "You smell delicious. Sweet, like apples."

"D—Devon. You are not well. Martin will be here any moment."

"Not soon enough." His hand reached out toward her, and she placed her fingers on his arm. He stopped, and she gagged. What was left of her crumpets rose quickly in her throat.

"I have a choice, don't I? I choose Martin. I—I could never be happy without him."

A crash came from the door as it swung open. Her gaze darted to Martin, who strode into the room. "I heard a howl. Is Mac here? Devon?"

She swallowed convulsively. "Devon. Don't do this. You can turn and walk away. You are not who I choose." Her body began to shake. Martin would kill Devon. Fear shot down her spine, and her stomach dropped.

"Devon?" Martin's voice was a deep growl.

Jane stared at Martin. He stood a good head taller than his normal height; his shoulders were broader, and his eyes had changed to red as he stared at his brother; he was ready to kill him. His teeth clenched, and a low hiss came from deep within him.

Devon stared at Jane; in the depths of his eyes, she could see the struggle swirling like a vicious storm. His mind didn't want her, but his instincts did. His eyes flickered madly as he fought to gain control.

"Devon, step away from her. . . ."

Devon spun around and bolted straight at Martin, knocking him backward and into the fireplace mantel. The thud was so loud and forceful the mirror shook on the wall above.

Jane screeched. "No! Don't do this, Devon! Martin! No!" Her hands wrapped about her stomach, holding herself in place. What was she to do? She wanted to rush forward to pull them off each other, but she was so small in comparison! And they had claws!

She stepped forward, and they rolled, grunting and hissing, claws flashing over and over again. Please don't let them hurt each other! The sounds of tearing cloth, of tearing flesh, made her scream.

With a howl, Devon jumped back. His arm was slashed open, his eyes deepened, widening in shape and color. An agonizing whine ripped from him, and he bolted from the room.

Martin leaped up to follow, and Jane bolted at him. She threw herself into his heaving chest, grasping his torn coat as he struggled to get past her. "No, no, let him be! He did not want what happened. He tried to control it. But his desires won in the end. Martin!"

His arm locked about her, his hands fisted in her skirts at her bum. With an animalistic howl, he ripped up her dress and petticoats and pulled the material from the front of her body. "You are mine, Jane."

Oh! Her chest labored for breath. "Indeed, I am yours, Martin. There is nothing to worry about. I will not deny you."

He dropped to his knees; he pushed up the fabric of her shift and kissed the soft skin of her belly just below her corset. Her hands slid into his long, thick hair, and he slid his tongue into the crevice of her button and then lower to the curls of her mound.

His body shook. "You are in Orsse. That is why Devon could no longer conceal that you *were* a possible mate for him." His warm breath puffed against her drenched flesh, and she arched as she pushed her curls into his mouth.

"Martin. Make me yours, Martin."

He growled, and her hands reached down, pushing his torn coat and waistcoat from him. She wanted to see him naked before the last bits of sun faded from the room. He lifted her, and in two strides he placed her on the bed.

As he unbuttoned the flaps to his trousers, his cock popped out from the opening, and she gasped. When she said he was large before, she had no experience really to compare.

His prick stood straight up from his belly; the head was the size of a small apple, the shaft only slightly smaller. Below, his balls hung large and tight as two furry peaches. After removing his boots, he shoved his trousers the rest of the way down and turned to her. "Turn over, Jane, so I can remove your corset."

She turned over and bit her lip as he tugged loose the strings to her corset. Her heart pounded wildly. She wanted this. She wanted to be his and his alone.

"Stand up so I can push it down." She did so, gripping his linen-clad shoulder. As he tugged the corset over her hips, her gaze followed his hands. At the top of his thigh below the hem of his shirt, his mark shown. Her hands traveled down his stomach and grasped a fistful of linen and then pulled the garment up and over his head, watching his stomach muscles jump under her touch.

Her gaze snapped back to the adornment. The red shape of a bear, stretched to full height, covered the top of his thigh to the crease of his hip bone. Her shift covered her sight as he pulled it over her head.

As she reached out, her fingers grazed over the design. He growled. "Explore me, Jane. We have all the time in the world."

"Do we? I feel urgency for you to join with me."

Her face grew warm.

"Do you?" He reached out and grabbed the sides of her breasts and pinched the flesh, sending waves of pleasure through them to the tips. He continued to rub, and they blossomed, growing heavy under his touch. "The design was marked on me when I reached adulthood. The one on my back when I . . . joined with my first woman."

"Turn about." He did so, and Jane's eyes widened. The adornment on his back was of great claw wounds outlined in black. Jane's fingers wandered up the raised flesh. "Who did this to you?"

"One of the relatives."

"It must have hurt horribly."

He laughed. "I was in the throes of my first spend inside a woman. I hardly noticed. After, it hurt like the devil."

What a strange thing to say. People had watched while he shed his innocence! Her touch ran over his entire broad, muscled back. She traced his shoulder blades. Never had she seen such an expanse of male naked flesh. Every muscle was toned and a light tawny color. His body shook, and he turned. He pushed her back onto the bed; he pinned her to the soft mattress.

"Jane." He tilted his head to the side and stared at her with intensity. "You are my world, Jane." Chills raced across her skin, and her eyes rimmed with tears. Her lip trembled, and she snagged it with her teeth to stop the waver. Sweet mother! Her heart ached.

"I—I love you, Martin. I know it is so soon, but. . . ." She looked up into his eyes and gasped. The emotions on his face spoke of devotion, caring, and overwhelming faith in her.

"Jane."

A tear leaked from her eye and ran down to the bedspread. He parted her legs with his knee. "I had hoped but didn't dare dream to hear those words from you on this night. I love you, dearest Jane."

She put a hand on his chest. His heart pulsed just below her touch. "Your heart is mine, Martin, and my heart is yours."

He settled himself between her legs; the hot head of his prick carressed her folds. Creamy fluid trickled from her, coating his prick head. He pushed in bit by bit, and the lips of her sex parted, the tip sliding in her opening.

Oh! She wanted him to fill her. Her legs trembled and jumped, but he kept up the maddening, slow pace. Her flesh stretched and stretched until he completely filled her. Her hips arched up to meet his.

He ground his hairs into her mound, and the erotic tension coiled deep in her belly, building and building the pleasure. His hips pulled back, and his long phallus slid; every inch of his prick stimulated the walls of her pussy. The crown of round head pulled her skin taut as he pulled back through her opening. Her womb sparked with heat, quivering, needing his motions to bring her his gift.

"More, Martin, more."

He hissed and pushed back in. His arms shook as he held his large body away from her. Her fingers traced the straining muscles, feeling their power as her eyes fluttered shut.

His prick slid back in. Each beat of his heart resonated through the hard flesh, pulsing her inner core. She arched and wiggled, reaching for his body to touch hers in that delightful place that tingled.

His hips met hers with a groan. He pulled back out. His body shook, and he lunged back in and rolled. Wrapping his arms about her, he squeezed her tightly, pressing the air from her lungs and holding her body entirely motionless above him. She was as languid as a rag doll. He controlled her every breath.

His hips jabbed up, and he plunged his staff into her. Restless and with restrained motions, all she could do was receive his onslaught.

She opened her hip's joints, spreading her legs farther apart so that her sex lay fully open to him. The muscles about her torso shook violently and held her absolutely still. He hissed and howled, slid in and out once, and flipped her again.

Her breath heaved and her body trembled with intense heat and pleasure. The delight was building.

He stopped. His eyes wild, he stared at her, rocked his hips once, and grunted. His long, burly staff pulsed inside her. The feel of his seed tickled her womb and tightened her muscles.

Her hips jiggled as she rubbed herself against him. Her body shook in surging bliss; her legs clamped tight to him as she screamed in release.

Yet it didn't sound like a scream to her ears—it was more like a declaration.

He nuzzled her hair and loosened his grip about her body. She gulped in the smell of his arousal and their futter and groaned. She was a wanton! Her body was anything but sated. His hand rubbed her back.

"Not quite satisfied, dear Jane?"

Heat washed over her body in a twisted jumble of embarrassment and arousal. The cinnamon smell of his skin made her shiver.

His chest tremored in a chuckle beneath her. "No need to be embarrassed, Jane. Your body won't be satisfied until an Ursus grows in you. Give it time. In the meantime, I will do my best to keep pleasuring you."

Martin stared at Jane sleeping in his arms. His body was weak and drained from the last three days of nerves and worry. Never had he thought he would be settled at this age, but he wouldn't change it.

Jane. . . . He could smell his cub growing in her. The hairs on his neck lifted, and he sighed. This was what his life was meant to be.

Her eyes cracked open, and she gazed at him from under her lids.

"Martin, can you tell me? How did the Ursus come to be?"

His hand tightened about her breasts, and she groaned. "When our clan went into battle, we wore bear sarks that had been treated with magic oils and herbs to draw the power from the bear. Whoever wore the sarks drew the bears' strength and stamina to use during battle. Something happened during a battle years ago. . . . They say we were cursed by the clan we fought against, and the blood from the bear fur mixed with the blood of the battle and changed us for good. Strength and stamina are the main things we pulled from the bear, but over time other things developed, things bears did not have. We have ability to read minds and emotions, to use our strength not only physically but mentally, to move things. We all have these abilities in varying degrees. Devon, for instance, cannot move a thing with his mind. Well, maybe a feather. I, on the other hand, can move almost anything."

"The trees?"

"Indeed." He smiled at her. "I couldn't let you go."

She placed her hand over his heart. "And hearts."

He squeezed her. "I did not put a spell on you, Jane."

"I know that." She smiled, pushed up, and gazed down into his face. "Your desire for me is what won my heart, Martin." She leaned in and kissed his lips. The soft butterfly touch warmed him and sent gooseflesh along his skin at the same time. He raised his hand and cupped her chin; then he thrust his tongue into her parted lips. Intoxicating! He pulled back. "I love you, Jane."

Her lip trembled; before she could speak, he again kissed her hard, making their heads spin.

EPILOGUE

Tremarctos stood still except for the grunts and cries of mating that came from the room in which Miss Milton resided. It was good that he had left the castle. Devon and Martin were after that woman, and Mac, too, smelled her as a possible mate.

Mac wanted nothing to do with it. He could smell her Orsse even from this distance atop the hill, but he was safe. Martin had her. He smiled. He was happy for his twin, and he couldn't wait to find out what had happened with Father and Devon.

Miss Milton was a member now, and her cubs would be brought up at Tremarctos. The smell of her Orsse made his body shake.

Never would he take a mate again. Chills raced across his body. He would futter a woman once, and only once; then the urge would leave, and he could continue on.

His brothers could carry on the family. He would be a good uncle. He adored cubs, but never would he father a cub on his own.

MAC

1

Ursus Castle on the coast of the Gulf of Bothnia, 1801

"Which one, your highness?" Ann's small form appeared beside Rasalette as she stood at the edge of the circle and inhaled deep.

The ruby-encrusted chamber glittered in the tranquil torch glow but did nothing to soothe her nerves. Rasalette's hands shook, and she glanced about the room.

The celebration was well started. People reveled about, drinking and singing songs excitedly. Rasalette's skin dewed, and she cringed. Gracious! She wished she could relax enough to enjoy this year's Ursus gathering. But this year was different—she glanced at her brother's slight form sitting on his gold-and-emerald-inlaid throne. This year everything had changed.

A man passed her with a cup of sweet wine. The smell of cloves and comfort spices swirled in the air, and her mouth watered. A good glass of wine might help relax her nerves. No. That would not do. She needed her wits about her.

Rasalette sighed again and turned her attention back to the line of men her brother presented.

The gruff one with the beard was the only one who appealed to her. Would he be rough with her? Would he have the fortitude to uncork her brother if her brother came too close?

No.

Her shoulders slumped. Every one of these men her brother had selected because they would do as *he*, the new king, desired. None of them possessed the determination or will to be her true mate. Yet they all would smell just like one. Bumbelbroth. Her entire life relied on instincts she couldn't control. She had no say. She sounded like a spoiled child when she said such things, but she couldn't be a part of her brother's jests any longer.

"Try them on, spoiled dear. See if you like one." Her brother's detestable voice echoed, and the room dropped to silence.

Amazing. She ground her teeth, and the hair on her neck stood. They all listened to him. As they should, she supposed, but those three words made her skin crawl. *Try them on?* There was no choice. Her eyes narrowed, and her stomach flipped. She wanted to stomp her foot and lash out at him. Gracious! What had happened to her? *Rasalette, he is king now. He can do as he wishes, and you obey.*

She closed her eyes and inhaled a breath to give her fortitude. Indeed, she would give one of them a go for her dearest brother, king of the Ursus. "Why not give them all a go, dear brother?" The words chilled her breath as they left her mouth.

"Perfect, dear. So what will it be?" Her brother's eyes lit with merriment, and his smooth, clean cheek twitched.

Rasalette fought her lips to wipe the angry frown from her face. She wanted to slap him.

Her gaze swept along her possible mates carefully. He had

chosen them all specifically, so which one did her brother fancy most?

The first, Lord Arand, possessed a wealth of knowledge and connection in Spain. A week's worth of grease shone in his short, unwashed black hair. He probably had tried to increase his scent of anise in hopes she would be attracted. Anise was one of her lesser mate smells but a mate smell all the same. Chills raced her spine. She would have to allow him to touch her. The hairs on her neck stood, and she forced herself not to shudder.

The next man, Lord Franlish, by appearance would be the best of the three. His broad shoulders; long, dark flax hair and beard; and his scent of sweet honey appealed to her. His rounded biceps showed strength, and his high cheekbones and smooth, arched nose . . . a striking face. But she heard just last week his manor was filled with animals he'd saved from slaughter.

Not a trait she normally held against gentlemen, but the act showed his tender heart, and no doubt he would allow her brother to badger him into any request of her. Her jaw tightened.

That she could not allow.

Broken memories, fragments of images assaulted her—cornered in the hall, fingers pinching her nipple as warm, drunken breath wafted over her skin. His detestable words—*"You will do as I say because I am king. I can have any part of you"*—pressed against her sanity.

He would never touch her again.

One of these men would never do. She glanced back at Lord Tremis, the third in line. His slight form and shy-to-a-fault demeanor struck pity in her. Not one female in the kingdom had bedded him, to her knowledge—Ann's nanny's sister was a mistress and knew all the sexual habits of the men within the castle walls. He either was truly shy, as everyone thought, or he enjoyed the other sort of company.

Either trait would not protect her.

She didn't want to try on any one of these men. She closed her eyes again in hopes that when she opened her lids, the three would be gone. Fool! She shook her head and sighed.

Glancing around at the celebrations and the hundreds of Ursus in the room, her only hope remained that at this festival, surely one of the hundred large men would be willed enough to stand against her brother. Most of the men here she'd never laid eyes on before. Had her true mate come to the celebrations, brought by instinct back to his place of origin?

A small flame of hope heated her breast. She would be cursed to a lifetime of dealing with her brother if she began Orsse with one of the sots he presented. But what could she do? Tradition in her family dictated that the king could use the females in the line for their own advantage. She closed her eyes. What did he gain from any of these men besides access to her?

She glanced about and bit her lip. Her maid, Ann, hand-brushed her hair over her shoulder. "I have the sandalwood oil, your highness. You could try masking your scent on these men."

Rasalette's heart sped. *The sandalwood oil.* She turned her head slowly, not daring to believe that her maid had found the potent scent. Her stare met Ann's clear green eyes in desperation. "You are sure it will work?"

"Yes. My sister used the scent so her master would not smell her as a woman he could toy with in his house. She said the fragrance worked quite brilliantly. He never approached her, because the complications of futtering a potential match was too great. And she is quite handsome."

"Indeed, she used the scent for the opposite effect, to smell as a mate, but would fragrance work to not smell as one?"

"Quite so, your highness. Sandalwood is powerful not only in scent but also in its mystical qualities of masking identity."

Rasalette turned back to the men standing before her. They all knew she was a mate from prior introductions. Blast! The oil would not work on them. She snagged her lower lip between her teeth once more. She would have to allow them to touch her.

"Would you like me to rub on the oil, your highness?"

"No, Ann, the scent will need to come after, when I am done. I will use the sandalwood to find my mate on my own." Warming flutters of hope spread through her belly. Without her brother knowing, she could use sandalwood to try on any new men in the kingdom she fancied. She could see if they fit her needs, and her brother would never suspect, because the men would not know her scent.

Yes. After this round of her brother's suitors, she would spend the rest of the night doused in sandalwood. "Indeed, after this, Ann, when you wipe me down, have the cloth covered in the scent." She held in a grin of hope.

"Yes, your highness."

Rasalette's lungs tightened, and she swallowed hard. She had never done anything so outwardly devious, but this was her *life*. She would have only this night to do so. Her brother did know her scent and would grow suspicious if a new potential match was presented on the morrow.

She glanced around the room. Her chosen mate was somewhere, mingling in the revelries. Goose pins of excitement primed her skin. She would find him this night.

She straightened her shoulders. First she needed to prove how unsuited this batch of approved suitors was.

She glanced back at the three and swallowed hard. "Very well, brother." She didn't turn toward him. "I will test each of these men's tongues. The one who brings me to spend will be considered."

She never reached bliss from being orally frigged, so this should prove her point. "Drop to your knees."

Servants scurried, bringing pitchers, towels, blankets, and pillows. Each man knelt on a pillow on the floor, awaiting her instructions. Rasalette rolled her eyes and sighed. This was her duty for being born to privilege.

On shaking knees, she strode forward. The cool marble floor beneath her bare feet shot icy spikes up her calves, and her heart chilled. *No, don't let this act dissuade you, Rasalette.* She straightened her shoulders, drawing all her fortitude from deep within her animal self, and then leaned down in front of Lord Tremis. This act would pleasure her primitive side, and she would concentrate on the pleasure and not why she felt it.

Her coal-black hair spilled in loose ringlets off her shoulder and onto his back.

The muscles down his spine flinched.

Rasalette's eyes widened. He feared her. She reached out her hand and touched his bowed head; his short, bristly hair prickled her fingers. "You, Lord Tremis, shall be first, followed by Lord Arand and then Lord Franlish."

She walked down the line to Arand.

His brow furrowed, and he sniffed the air. "Delicious."

A shiver of fear raced Rasalette's skin, goose pins rising in panic's wake. Her stomach clenched. He smelled her, and her body would respond to him as well. She inhaled a deep breath that did nothing but pull air into her lungs. She could do this.

She glanced at her brother as a young servant girl sat on his lap. His hand dipped down into her bodice and pulled out her small breast. The girl squirmed. He whispered in her ear. Her eyes widened, and she visibly relaxed. The white of her skin was snowy in pureness, and her red hair only accentuated her look of innocence.

His hand pulled up her skirts, displaying fiery sprigs covering her mound of Venus. She was young, the kind of dally her brother preferred when he wasn't trying to corner Rasalette. His hand spread the girl's thighs wide and then dipped into her core. The girl tensed. Obviously a virgin. Rasalette's teeth ground together at her brother's tastes.

He remained fully occupied.

A spike of relief relaxed Rasalette's shoulders, but how horrid of her to be glad the young girl devoured his attention! Yet if he did not watch Rasalette entertain these men, he would never know if she enjoyed herself or not. Her stomach churned hot and acrid as anger sliced through her.

She hated him.

He had every right to force her to marry one of these men, yet he didn't care one grain of salt if she would be happy with any of them.

She turned back to Lord Tremis. "Lord Tremis, come to me."

2

Mac strode into the royal dining chamber, pushed his long brown hair over his shoulder, and glanced at the arched gold ceiling. Five gold and ruby candelabra hung suspended from chains. The highly polished marble floors thudded under his feet, yet the room roared, filled with constant laughter, chatting, and song.

"Sir Macedon Ursus."

The announcement into the hall of his arrival went unheard as the joyous banter echoed off the walls. He smiled and excitement brushed across his skin like a woman's tongue.

Years had passed since he attended the Ursus gathering. By damn. It was good to be in a room where all equaled him in size. Even the women, though smaller in stature than the men, possessed plush, round curves and amazing presence.

His eyes settled on a woman as she laughed and thrust her well-endowed breasts at a tableful of men. All Ursus exuded sexuality. He would not have to hold back who, or what, he was this week. His muscles relaxed as if a pail of warm water had washed down him. Indeed.

By the end of the evening, women would be dancing upon those chandeliers as raucous men watched them strip bare before fucking in a mass orgy on the tables and floor.

His cock stretched at the memory from his time here as a sprig and the memories of Jenny—the one time he and his brother fought, truly fought, over a woman. Jenny had also been a possible mate for Mac. To this day, Martin never knew. Mac's heart pinched in his chest.

Mac had fallen in love with her. She'd done her duty of being his first woman in the marking ceremony and walked away. Mac's instincts would not turn away from her. Just the thought of her sweet gardenia scent stirred possessiveness. If only he hadn't disgraced himself by chasing her. Milksop. He would never chase after a woman again, no matter how badly he wanted her, if she didn't want him. . . . He shook off the memory.

Duty required he say, "Good day," to the king. He would have to make his way to the royal throne. Announcing himself was only polite before taking liberties with any of his royal wenches. Even if he didn't respect the bon vivant, he fully intended to have his fill of the king's women this night, no matter his thoughts on his leader's tastes.

The brutal sea voyage to the homeland had drained him. He needed to find a willing woman who didn't stir his mating instincts and would futter until he sated his need and then fall into bed and sleep.

His jaw clenched as the smells of ale, wine, and women flooded his senses. He'd had enough of the mate smell and what the scent could do to his family from Jane, his brother's new life mate. Orsse had turned out well in the end, but he would not tolerate any more lack of control this year.

He rounded one of the circular tables, and a nicely plush woman thrust a chalice at him.

He smiled. "Thank you, ma'am." Clutching the gold cup in

his hand, he raised the glass to his nose to sniff. The sweet smell of red wine soothed his head. His tongue touched the warmed metal and traced the rim of the cup; then he sucked the thick liquid into his mouth.

He glanced at the woman across the edge of the cup. He feasted on her round, generous hips and the slightly plump swell of her stomach.

"Ye like what you see, milord?" His gaze jumped to her face, and the side of her mouth quirked up.

She looked for a good time. Nothing more. Perfect. He stepped closer, and his blood thickened at the smell of rich thick rose. She smelled of mate. He frowned. He would have to find another.

"You are an extremely pleasing sight, ma'am. Though I have no wish to bed a mate this night." He bowed his head to her.

"Ah, m' loss, milord. I am sure ye are a wonder to tumble." She winked.

His smile broadened. "Thank you, ma'am."

He turned and made his way toward the king. Pushing his way through the crowd, a moan of such sweetness stopped him in his tracks. He searched through the crowd for the source of such ecstasy.

His sight locked on an ebony-haired woman sitting in a chair. Her round, quivering legs were up over each of the chair's arms as her thin gauze skirt, fisted in her hands at her waist, shimmered with each jerk of her body in the torchlight. She no doubt was one of the royal court.

A fair-haired man, who possessed a slightly smaller build than Mac, conducted the delightful yet strained sound of her pleasure. The fair one's mouth frigged the goddess's cunt. His head bobbed up and down with each lick of his tongue, eliciting the birdlike song Mac couldn't resist.

Nowhere but in the homeland was a sight like this possible.

His mouth watered, and he licked his lips, wanting to be the one tasting her sweet, sweet spend.

But did she identify as a possible mate?

He inhaled, willing her fragrance to come to him. The smell of his wine flooded his nose.

Damn! With so many new smells in the room, her aroma was impossible to tell at this distance. He would find out.

Images of her scratching his back as he pressed her up against a wall, of his hands yanking up her skirts so he could taste her, hear her moan and scream for him as he drank her nectar, hardened his cock.

Mmmm. Indeed, he would bed her. She tempted him in a way he craved. She held in all her desire by not letting go . . . and he would make her fly. He didn't care if she was a mate.

"Time!" a small servant yelled as she approached the woman seated in the chair.

Mac's head jerked back, shocked. She had timed him? The man stood, wiped his hand down his mouth, clenched his beard, and then licked his lips. He bowed his head to the woman. "Your highness, I am sorry I did not bring you the joy you sought."

She was royalty. Not merely a member of the royal court, she wanted to come in a certain amount of time. He closed his eyes. The games the elite played amazed him.

She sat up straighter, and the piece of gauze clutched in her hands fell onto her thighs. The fabric, the same color as her pale legs, shimmered with silver-threaded glitters. She stood, and the fabric fell to the floor but concealed absolutely nothing. Damn! If she wore that gown at a public affair in England, they would have her committed.

The dark patch of curls at the apex of her thighs drew the eyes to the contrast in color. The peaked, circular flesh of her breasts poked at the thin covering, begging to be sucked and bitten.

He swallowed hard, and his stomach muscles tensed.

No doubt he could bring her to spend in under whatever time constraints she'd set for this fair-haired man. The small servant kneeled before the goddess, and with a cloth, starting at her feet, began to wipe her entire body of any sweat or scent left by the other man.

He would request an introduction . . . but from whom? He glanced around in search of a familiar face. Would he recognize any of his friends from childhood? No, they had all changed too much since being marked; images rose of him futtering Jenny as another Ursus placed deep claw marks on his back, the pain and exhilaration of his first spend forever outlined in black. He turned back toward the chair where the goddess stood. She had disappeared.

Where had she gone? His gut twisted, and panic pounded through him like a torrential windstorm. He needed to find her. He couldn't let such a vision go without tasting her offering. Pushing through the crowd of massive bodies, he alighted upon the exact space she had stood a moment before. The towel the servant had used on her lay on the floor. He inhaled deep and sniffed her scent. . . . Sandalwood clung to his lungs. Sandalwood. Not a mate match for him.

He sighed, and his shoulders rounded, half in relief and half in disappointment. He shook the possessive thoughts from his mind; he could bed her all week and have none of the pull, the desperation that came from joining with a mate.

He spun around. The servant who had wiped her down stood staring at him, the towel that had lain on the floor was now clutched in her hands.

"Pardon me? Where did the lovely lady go?"

The servant's eyes lowered to his shoes; then she pointed to a large wooden door.

"Thank you." He pushed past her and grasped the gold-inlaid handle. A twist of the knob, and the door clicked open. He slid through.

He paused to allow his eyes to adjust to the dim light. He stood in a hall. Arched windows lined the wall across from him, a solid wall with torches set in iron brackets on the other. Where was she?

He glanced to the left; a couple engaged in futter pressed up against a window ledge down the hall. He squinted at the woman; her hair glowed gold in the torchlight. Not his ebony goddess.

He turned to the right. Empty hall stretched before him. Damn. Nothing.

He shut the door and headed down the hall, away from the engaged couple. Their moans filled the hall as they joined, pleasuring each other in a deeply carnal way. Each note reached through his body, coaxing his desire, his need to futter. Enflamed, his arousal possessed his nerves. Where could she have gone?

Along the hall, another door stood on his left. He strode to the door and reached for the handle. The door clicked open before his hand grasped the knob. He lowered his hand and stood calmly as the door opened and his goddess walked straight into him without looking. Her plush curves connected with his hardness, and his carnal yearnings leaped to feast on her.

Rasalette shrieked as she slammed into a solid, broad chest that smelled of heavenly cloves. She inhaled deep, allowing the scent to curl in her body. Her head tilted back to take in the possessor of this warming scent. A startled breath caught in her throat as she beheld a man of presence. Wild, curly brown hair reached to his shoulders, and his crystallized, emerald eyes shone with predatory intensity.

The hair on her neck stood. Gracious! He uneased her. She

didn't know whether to turn back around and slam the door in his face or wrap herself in his severity. She had never sighted a man such as he before.

"Pardon me, your highness." His eyes lowered down her body to her chest. Her breath jittered. "I was watching your timed game and was so enchanted by your song." Pools of deep jade captured her eyes again. "I decided I must hear you scream."

Her muscles wound and shook in sensual bliss. Scream? Oh, indeed! His stare alone shot erotic pleasure down her spine. She could spend just from his gaze. "Scream? Why . . . in what way, sir?" My! He was delicious.

The corner of his mouth quirked up, and mirth danced in his eyes. "As you spend and spend in rapture, your highness."

Oh, indeed. She wished that. *Remember your plan, Rasallette.* "I am sorry, sir, but I don't know you. Please step aside." *Please let him stay in his steady.* She wanted this. He was a mate, and she needed to see if he would stand his ground for her.

"Your highness?" His hand lifted, and with his forefinger he curled a lock of her hair about the digit. Each twist of his finger pulled the lock taut.

Her gaze jumped to his deepening green eyes and stayed locked as her heart pounded to each wind of her hair in his grasp. Chills of hope washed through her, and her skin fevered in dew.

"I don't believe you want to go anywhere, do you, your highness?" He tightened the hair in another twist of his finger, and pins shot through her scalp. Pulling on the strand, her head arched back against the pressure. She closed her eyes, savoring the tingles erupting in her womb. "I think you want me to fuck you."

My gracious! His words . . . Wetness coated her pussy. Indeed, she wanted the act, but she still could not give in to his will this easily. She needed to see more. More of his magnitude.

His lips connected with the column of her neck. Heated tingles trickled down her body, and she moaned.

She raised up her hand. She trembled. She had never in all her experience trembled when a man kissed her flesh. Her breath hitched, and the smell of sandalwood assaulted her. She tensed. The sandalwood. He . . . he thought her a nonmate, and yet she was.

Be calm, Rasalette. This is what you wanted. Try him on. See if he has the determination to stand up to your brother.

Her hand stopped midair as she headed to caress his hair. She pulled back her arm, opened her fingers, and swung.

Crack!

The flesh of her palm stung as she slapped his ear. The loud popping noise echoed down the hall.

He growled, and his teeth bit the flesh of her neck. Her body jerked, and lightning shot to her cunt, flooding the walls. A groan bubbled up as he bit again, harder than the last. Her body arched into his, as she rubbed her hips, her mound against his large, firm thighs in a call for him to join with her. *No, no, no, Rasalette.*

"Step away from me, sir. Instantly!"

He chuckled at her. "Are you sure, your highness? Your body seems to say otherwise." The words warmed her ear, and his tongue slid into the cup. Wetness she could smell slid down her legs. She could not deny—she desired him. She needed to use another tactic to see how determined he was. She would be his torment, a tease.

"Very well. Then do as I say."

"No, your highness. You will do as *I* say." Her hair pulled, and the rest of his fingers snaked into her locks. "With your hands, undo the buttons on my waistcoat."

She bit her lip and raised her hands to comply. Her hands shook terribly as she tugged each fabric-covered button and slid them through the holes.

He held back her head at a precise angle. She could not look at him nor his chest. Her fingers slid the last button free, and her body shook, wanting him and this.

His breath deepened, and the rise and fall of his chest beneath the fabric told of her effect on him. She wanted to lower her hands to see just what kind of endowment he possessed. Her fingers slid lower, trailing the smooth cotton to the cool silk ridge of his waistband.

"No." He jerked her hair and pressed his body against hers. The cold stone at her back and his massive, hard warmth at her front pinned her. As she was unable to move, her heart thumped like a drum she swore she could hear.

His long, thick prick pressed against her soft stomach. The thickness at the tip tapered to a long, equally thick shaft. His sex was as solid as her wrist.

He rotated his hips. The pressure . . . delightful. A gasp elicited from her lips. She bit down on her lips, trying to hold back any further encouragement, and moaned through the torment of his teasing.

He chuckled. "Indeed, you want me. Want my phallus sliding in and out of your pleading cunny. Pull my shirt from my waist and touch my chest."

Her hands shook as she grasped the crisp cotton, and the dampness of her aroused skin clung to the soft fabric as she slid it up. His muscles jumped as the hem pulled from his waistband.

His heat . . . his smell . . . sweet and earthy. The tang of his arousal wafted about her, invading every pore. She trembled with need to touch him.

Her hand slid beneath the crisp fabric. She flexed her fingers, and her nails skidded along a rib, slightly digging into the skin. He shook.

Interesting. He liked that.

His hand reached down between her legs and pushed the fabric of her slip between her thighs. His finger probed her entrance through the fabric, and she slid her thighs apart. Her creamy, slick juices clung to the fabric as he rubbed them into her sex.

Oh! She thirsted for more of his touch. Her hands clutched at his chest, scratching his skin.

He sucked in through clenched teeth and then exhaled.

"What are the rules of your game, your highness?" His hand stilled and pressed, cupping and holding her sex and mound. He held her there, and the heat of his palm against her sex made her hips press, rubbing, trying to get him to move. "Your highness?"

"My—my game?" Her breath quivered as his fingers flexed. The fabric's rough texture tugged her swollen skin in a subtle, torturous pleasure. Oh! How she wanted his touch deeper, probing all her delicate recesses.

"Yes." His breath tickled her cheek as the warm wetness of his tongue trailed to her lips. "I witnessed the fair one only for a few moments before your servant yelled count."

He thought she played a royal game when she positioned for her future. She swallowed the lump lodged in her throat. Quite correct, in a sense—she did play them, and him. "I—I told them whichever man's tongue could bring me to spend in less than forty licks would be considered as a possible husband to me."

She felt the curve of his lips form into a smile just before they touched hers. Delight slid through her. He tasted of wine and tobacco. Luxurious tremors massaged the walls of her womb.

His tongue traced her lips, and he pulled away. His nose, his intense jade eyes held her. She shivered at the intimacy and desire pounding through him and her. The blacks of his eyes engulfed the brilliant green. Gracious! Had a man's stare ever affected her so?

"Very well, then. Forty licks, eh? You will spend in five."

"Five?" Her brows drew together. No one could make her spend in five licks. No one had made her spend with his tongue yet.

"You think my statement false?" His tone hung hard and challenging. "Two to wet and spread your rosy-hued nether lips." His tongue traced her bottom lip and then the top. Her mouth opened, and she sighed.

"One to satisfy my taste for your honey core." His tongue plunged into her mouth, swirling and dancing to the beat of her heart. Her chest tightened, and prickles of ecstasy peaked her nipples; her body arched into him.

He pulled back a breath's whisper. "One to swirl and tease your bud." His tongue swirled the left corner of her mouth as if licking a sweet morsel of food she'd just eaten. Her legs shook and quivered against his thighs.

"And one long, slow, firm lick from bottom to top. You will spend, your highness, hard. And I will drink every bit of the cream you produce." Every word he stated caressed the flesh of her sex as if he finger-frigged her. Her core wept for his caress.

He raised her arms and wrapped her fingers about the iron bracket holding the torch above her head. "Don't let go, your highness." He dropped to his knees before her.

Her mind spun.

Five licks.

Never. She had never spent this way. He surely jested.

Lifting her bottom, he hooked her knees over his shoulders, and pressed the fabric of her skirt between her thighs. His head pressed between. The silken caress of his hair touched her sensitized inner thigh, and she jerked.

"Stay still, your highness." He blew a long breath onto her sex, and her muscles relaxed as if spiced wine infused her veins.

He tilted her out from the wall; his mouth was level with her sex. The hot, wet tip of his tongue touched her opening at the base by her bum hole.

She quivered, her arms shaking as she held herself up.

The lick traveled up the left ridge of her pussy, pressing to her bud before lifting.

Warmth and tingling spread down her sex to the opening and then speared deep into the walls of her cunt. A moan, bordering on a scream, forced from her lips. *My gracious! Never!* She tossed her head to the side and bit her lip. He would do it.

The tip of his tongue connected at same spot, at the base of her opening, and her hips jerked. The caress traveled up the right ridge of her cunny, coaxing every nerve in her body to his attention. He touched her button, and the same intense warmth stabbed her womb.

She gritted her teeth, caging in the scream deep in her throat. Blissful tension twisted, churning deep in the walls of her sex.

His tongue speared into her opening, and her legs and buttocks shook. The scream erupted from her mouth as his tongue swirled and danced in her sex.

Her chest tightened and her toes curled as speckled lights popped and fluttered behind her lids.

His tongue circled her bud and then lifted.

Her legs strained, hips jerking against his head and face, hidden beneath her mound.

The tip of his tongue pressed to the base of her opening and flattened. Creeping up the length of her sex, he did not enter her hole, but teased, pressing her lips wide as juice from her core combined with his saliva and drizzled down her bum. *Oh, God, oh, God.*

He continued the intensely slow pace up her sex. Bit by bit, her body wound tight the bliss she wanted, coming closer and closer into her grasp. She'd never spent this way, and, oh, how she wanted to. She tried to part her legs farther to get his tongue to penetrate her sex, but his grip on her legs tightened, holding her prisoner to his will.

She squirmed and shook. The bracket she clung to bit her hands as she gripped and reached for the wave.

His tongue reached her button, the lick so slow, so painfully delightful, her body broke. Pleasure erupted from her cunny, overflowing onto his face, dripping down the curve of her bottom and onto his hands as she shook, her body pulsing with each hard contraction.

His fingers parted her bottom, and as her body continued to quiver, he pressed his finger into her bum hole. Bright red lights flashed as blinding spasms speared through her body, and she screamed, uttering words of passion she knew not.

He slowly lowered her bottom, her legs slipping from his shoulders.

Her gaze fixed to his predatory stare. "Indeed, your highness. I believe I have earned a spot in your bed this night."

She swallowed hard. Bed, yes. He had earned a great deal more than just one night. He could very well end up her life mate. Her body tremored. "Yes, indeed, I believe you have." Her legs trembled, and she put weight on them to stop the unease. "But we will futter here first."

He grinned, and laughter flashed in his eyes once more. "Indeed, your highness. We shall." His hands brushed up the back of her arms to her fingers clutching the bracket on the wall. The tips of his fingers delicately pressed each one open, his stare never leaving her eyes. He lowered her arms, and his thumbs rubbed each digit as the blood tingled back to the tips. "Turn around, your highness." He dropped her left hand so she could turn.

She lowered her stare to his full lips. His tongue slid out, and he traced the top and then the bottom. *Torment.* Her swollen sex spasmed, and she held in a groan.

"Turn."

Turn. She closed her eyes. Yes, she needed this. She would obey him. Pivoting on her heel, she spun as he requested. He raised the hand he still held and placed her palm flush to the cold stone wall. The tip of his finger traced and spread each digit. Sensations—a mix of tickling and sexual caress—trickled up her arm and down to her cunt. His path continued until her hand fanned out on the wall.

"Do not move. Not one of your fingers shall rise from this wall." His breath warmed her ear, and he touched her back, directly between her shoulder blades. Balmy desire glowed through her muscles, and she sighed.

His fingers wrapped about her other wrist, and he raised her right hand and fanned it out in precisely the same manner. "The same holds for this hand, your highness."

Goose pins pricked her neck, and her muscles jumped as his touch left her body. Why was he not touching her? His heat radiated all about her, but not once did his body connect with hers. A slight tug came at the fabric of her skirt, and the material rose, sliding up her skin.

Touch me. Touch me, her mind cried out in longing to him as she trembled.

The light silk reached the swell of her bottom.

Please. Please. She needed the feel of his skin on hers.

His hand harshly possessed her hip, and she started. The heat of his grasp soaked her skin, relaxing each and every muscle in her body. Her arms shook, and a finger twitched, pulling into an arch on the stone wall.

"What did I say?" The words were drenched in arousal, desire, disappointment, and command hung heavy in the air.

She pressed her fingers and palms hard against the wall. "N—not to move." Her voice shook, and her brow furrowed. Why did she care if she disappointed this man, a man she only just met?

"Indeed." The hands grasping her hip left her body.

She'd wanted this futter hard, fast. A quick coupling to sate her desire for his touch, for his smell. To soothe the ache in her womb for his seed. This would not do. Her need was too great. She twisted her shoulders, and her hand lifted from the wall. "Sir—"

His hand slapped hard on her buttocks. Her eyes widened, and her breath caught in her throat. *H—how dare he?* Pinpricking heat seeped into her bones, followed by hazy arousal wetting her cunny lips. She'd no idea. She struggled with the urge to fight him—appalled that he had just spanked her—or stay rooted, absorbing this new, unexpected sexual heat.

"No, your highness." His hand grasped her wrist and slapped her palm to the wall in the same location. Turning her body back to the original position, he pressed his hand over hers. "Do not move." Intense arousal and command filled the words, a warning and a sexual flint all at once.

Her heart pounded as fear, lust, and arousal shook her body. What would he do to her?

He blew out a tense breath.

The breath told her he struggled with his desires for her, yet he didn't know why. Her scent was wrong. Yet his body knew she was a fit. The knowledge spoke in his hesitation before he touched her. How could she do this to him?

His fingers snaked into her hair, jerking her head back in an arch toward him. Wetness primed her nether lips, and her mouth dropped open on a groan. All thought fled her mind except for the need of him. She would do anything to please him, to feel his hard phallus sliding inside her.

"Indeed." Humid desire dripped from him.

She trembled, and his hand slid between her buttocks and into the slickness of her sex. She wanted to shift her stance, to spread her legs and press back into him, but she didn't dare. Legs trembling, she bit her lip.

His fingers wiggled in her crack. "Oh. Yes, please," burst out in a begging whimper.

The tip of his finger nestled into the opening of her cunny.

"Please."

"You want more, your highness?"

She nodded her head.

"Spread your legs, shoulder-width apart. Do not move any other part of your body."

Her legs weakened as she slid them apart. Wavering, she leaned slightly against the wall to hold herself steady.

"Too much, your highness? I presumed you could take a whipping and not falter. If you grant me more time in your bed, you will see just how much I can stir and arouse you."

Damn! He already aroused her. He could do more? She inhaled a tight breath as her heart controlled her breathing. She wanted more. Yes, indeed, he would do. He would not back away from her brother, and . . .

She desired him.

His hand came down once again on her bottom as the fingers of his other hand thrust harshly up into her opened cunt. Wetness flowed from her with each hard press into her bereft flesh. She flourished, her body coming alive in a way it had never come alive. His fingers thrust into her increasing wetness, and the same stinging contradiction of his hand slapping warmed her bum. The pleasure mixed, swirled with roughness.

Such sharpness. No one had ever dared treat her such.

Delicious. This was as she always wanted, as she dreamed of being taken, by a man. Him controlling her, not the other way around.

"Good girl, your highness." His hand held firm on her stinging flesh, and his fingers disappeared from her cunt. Arousal vibrated through her. His words—*good girl*—floated in her mind, relaxing her as she drifted like flower dust in the breeze, not knowing where this encounter would lead but knowing it would lead her to new places, new beginnings.

The tip of his prick touched the wet folds of her cunny, spreading them. His hardness was like nonesuch she had ever experienced before. He rocked back and forth, wetting himself on her juices. A groan burst from her lips as the hot head of his cock pressed against her button.

His hands possessed her hips, and he slid all the way in. Her flesh stretched along his length and tightly sheathed him. She cried out as her body racked about him. The stars shifted in the sky behind her lids as she spiraled toward the sun.

He pulled out. The ridge of his thick cock head spread her lips; then he stilled. His hips rocked in small motions against her bottom; the ridge of his sex peaked her opening and then slid in a fraction.

Her nerves sprouted, absorbing the heat of his hands on her hips, his sweet clove smell, the humid crash of his breath on her neck as she trembled. He thrust harsh into her dripping pussy and fully claimed her womb. She screamed.

"Mmmm." His hands slid up her body in a rampant conquering of her flesh. He grasped her peaked nipples. She whimpered. The frenzied bliss stabbed through her body in rippling ecstasy. Her cunny spasmed in waves about his stone-hard cock.

His hips rocked against her buttocks, and his long, hard cock slid out of her tingling flesh and back in. He groaned.

Leaning forward, his weight pressed her to the wall. "Better, your highness?" Her arms gave out, and his hands wrapped about her waist, pulling her up and against his chest. "Indeed, I see you are sated. I am not. You will keep up with me, your highness. Will you not?"

She trembled against him as his cock twitched deep within her. "Yes, indeed, sir. I am not sated. I am relaxed and ready for more."

3

Mac's hands slid to the woman's plush breasts, and his arms locked her to him. He would spend soon, and he wanted a bed to relieve himself in. Her head arched back, and the humid tip of her tongue circled his earlobe. *Mmmm.* "Where are your chambers?"

The woman stilled in his arms, and then her tongue flicked his earlobe.

"Down the hall." Her tongue swirled into the cup. "Through the double doors at the end, sir."

He slid his cock from her creamy, velvet clasp, and she whimpered. Just a few moments and he would be back futtering her to a delicious spend. He wrapped his arm under her bottom and cradled her small, curvy form against his chest.

Her plush hip gave slightly against the hardness of his chest. Her curly mass of ebony-black hair touched and danced against his body as he traversed the hall. Heated chills of desire raced, standing his hairs on end. The sensation thrilled him.

The hall grew more opulent and refined as he traversed toward the floor-to-ceiling doors towering at the end. Two footmen, dressed in red, stood to either side of the hall. Large bears in the fighting stance, teeth bared and claws out, cut the wood on each of the paneled doors. His gaze settled once more on the footmen's dress. The royal insignia was embroidered in gold thread on the chests of their attire.

The woman he carried lived in the castle; she was not one of the blood who arrived at the homeland for the celebrations.

His brow pulled tight. She was from the royal family, but who was she? Princesses Gloria or Ann, the past king's sisters? Or Princess Rasalette, the current king's? He walked through the doors into a bedchamber.

Deep pomegranate, translucent silk hung from the walls and ceiling, framing an enormous oval bed. Gold candelabra encrusted with amber stood in the corners of the room, casting a warm, rich glow.

The room was fit for a queen. He inhaled a deep breath, and the smell of pure lily bubbled through his senses. He tensed. This couldn't be her room. The pure lily smell identified as his strongest mate. He leaned in and brushed his lips against the skin of her shoulder, and the scent of sandalwood overwhelmed him.

"Whose room is this?"

"It—it is Princess Rasalette's room, sir."

He walked to the bed, shouldering aside the pomegranate-colored curtain, and set her gently on the red-silk-pillow-covered bed. Indeed, this would be *the* princess's room.

Damn! The princess was a mate for him. That would shock his father. But something was amiss. His jaw set. "And who are you?"

He stared down at her ebony hair as her face tilted up to his. Her deep brown eyes, large and full of desire for him, stared straight to the animal living inside.

Her hands wrapped about his cock, one at the base and the other about the tip. She placed her mouth on the crown and slid her tongue through her grip, drizzling saliva on the taut skin.

He jerked.

Her hand worked the moisture across the head and, pulling his skin taut, she slid down the shaft.

It didn't matter whom she was—futtering a nonmate held no consequence. She would make this one night he would never forget.

Her lower hand circled his balls and pulled lightly, tugging the marbles away from his body. Her upper hand twisted, and squeezed, pulling his pego until the tip swelled and turned crimson.

The muscles in his stomach bunched, and she placed her lips on the tip. Pushing her head toward him, his crown popped through into her mouth, and the firm pressure of her lips gave way to a cavern of warmed honey and the sweet feathery flick of her tongue. The cascade of her black hair covered her back and her face from his sight. He groaned, wanting nothing more than to see her lips cresting as she slid him farther in.

He clenched his buttocks, arching his hips forward and sliding more of his pego into her slick hole.

She didn't hesitate or flinch. Her tongue massaged the underside of his head, and tingles followed in its wake.

"Good, your highness." He reached for the mass of hair concealing her face from the sight that set his pulse roaring. Sweeping the black locks from both sides of her head, he placed the strands in one of his hands and twisted, pulling her hair tight. God! He needed to be in her. The smell of lily in the room called to primal desire. The scent confused him; it overwhelmed him into a powerful raging flame.

He increased the pressure of the tension on her locks, and she withdrew to the tip of his pego. As he jerked the strands, her head arched back, his cock slipping from the warm haven of her mouth. Her eyes widened, and smoldering embers of black caught his as her throat twitched and she swallowed hard.

"Good. Are you ready for me?"

Her pink tongue slid out and traced her still wet lips. The embers in her eyes ignited to blazing flames. "Indeed."

He leaned in, his body pressing to hers, and pushed her down on the bed. Never mind the clothes. He would fuck her this way . . . once, hard. Then take her again in the morning before he left for his own rooms.

She spread her legs to the sides of his hips, pulling herself up and opening her core to him.

Need pulsed through him. His cock pressed to the steaming wetness of her cunny, and his hand turned her head to the side. His eyes feasted on the skin of her throat and the throbbing beat of her pulse beneath the thin layer of alabaster.

His mouth watered, needing to taste her skin and feel the throbbing beat of her desire beneath his tongue. His lips pressed harshly to the dewed velvet flutter, and he feasted on her. Flexing his hips, he slid fully into the warmed glove of her cunny. The muscled, slick walls sucked and massaged his hardness in a series of oiled ripples.

His cock twitched, and his balls sparked, tightening to his body. She shook about his invasion as he pushed harder, grinding his groin against her bud. The steaming velvet of her cunt grasped his cock, her passion, her ecstasy pouring through him as she squirmed. He bit down on her shoulder at the base of her neck as his weight held her still. The slick flesh of her cunny slid down his hard cock as his pego grew, filling her, pressing tighter and tighter against the spongy flesh of her womb.

Blood pumped through his prick, and sweat scalded his flesh. His muscles strained. He inhaled, and the mixture of lily from the room and the smell of this luscious woman, her soft curves quivering in waves as he thrust into her open body, pushed him.

His lungs expanded in flashing heat as his shoulders broadened. He growled and hissed through the bite of his teeth. His lips snarled up as the slits in his knuckles unsheathed, his bear claws sliding through the skin.

The pleasurable sensation of allowing this transformation to occur during mating . . . amazing.

He released his bite on her shoulder, wanting to see her, to gaze at what state her expression beheld.

His lust-hazed gaze feasted on the pulse of her neck, which beat wildly beneath the thin pink skin; then his gaze moved to her mouth. Her lips were parted, swollen and shiny from her tongue, which constantly licked and wetted the surface. Her eyes remained closed, the pretty fan of her dark lashes resting on the skin of her cheek.

He arched his hips, pulled back to the tip of his cock, and stilled. He needed to see her bear eyes, to feel her mind's connection to him, not just her body's pleasure in this act.

Her head tossed to the side, and she grabbed at the cloth of his shirt, pulling him, wanting him to push back in.

He held steady. . . . *Open your eyes.* His emotions reached out to hers, willing her to feel his desire without saying the words.

Her lids opened, round as a bear's, and her animal's soul leaped at him. Raw passion swam in his mind. The call of pure animal lust wrapped about him and infused his veins.

She growled. Her teeth bared, and he slid back into her. The buttered silk walls of her cunny spread, sliding down his cock, gripping him. She arched. Her nails pressed and then dug, clawing up his back. The fabric of his shirt tore. The sound spun into pain as his flesh gave way beneath her claws.

He hissed, and pleasure shot through him; his cock erupted from the intensity. Sliding back and forth with each forceful blast of seed, he growled.

She shook, her entire body shattering in bliss as his seed coated her walls. Her hips arched, and she rubbed and rubbed her button against him.

He settled his hips against her, pinning her motions to the bed. Her hips and cunt swam with his seed and her own juices as she slid along his length. She screamed; her body jerked beneath him.

He rolled and pulled her with him onto his back. She sprawled across him, and he instantly fell into deep slumber.

Mac awoke to the warmth and weight of a woman sprawled across his chest. He glanced about the room. He couldn't see a bat even if the night vermin swooped down and plucked him in the head. How bloody long had they lain like this? Not that it mattered.

He inhaled, and the smell of sandalwood, lily, and his clove aroused him. The smell confused yet inflamed his desire. His cock hardened and grew to full length, pressing against her side. Ebony hair, soft plush curves, and brown bear eyes swam in his mind . . . the woman who slumbered against him.

He didn't know her name. His body dewed, and he growled. He wanted her again. Now! The desperation overwhelmed him.

This need arose from the lily smell in the room.

Indeed! The smell of pure mate so strong in the room pushed his need to frenzy for a woman he could never claim as his. Would that scent alone be enough to fool his body? He glanced down at the slumbering woman entangled with him. Futtering an Ursus female fueled his inner animal.

He knew, if he so wished, she would fight him, wrestle and play until they collapsed, futtering on the floor. His cock twitched, and warm, sticky wetness smudged the skin of his stomach. Tomorrow afternoon he would return to her and do just that.

He slid her still, slumbering body so that she lay fully upon him. The weight of her body soothed him and entangled his emotions, pulling at deeper primal possession. Her animal appeal enticed him much stronger than Jane had, and she was a possible mate. The smell in the room . . .

He nuzzled his nose up against the pulse point on her neck, smelling sandalwood once more. The smell puzzled him deep down. The hair on his neck tingled. But why? Smell was the only way they determined if another's seed was compatible.

Her legs slid along his sides, straddling his hips. The wetness of her cunt pressed to his stomach and cock, and his lungs locked.

"Mmmm." She gently shifted her shoulders and nuzzled his chest before returning to deep slumber. He wiggled his hips, placed the tip of his cock into the swollen flesh of her sex. The lips of her cunny fondled the tip of him and then yielded. His pego slid into her oiled warmth. Fevered chills raced his skin. His desires, his animal wanted more. Who was he to deny them? Futtering her again would be blissful.

He thrust his hips up hard and seated his cock fully in her. She tensed and pressed her palms against his chest.

"Wait!"

Slowly she sat up upon him, grinding her dripping pussy against the hairs of his sex. Her body arched, and he leaned up, bit the flesh of her breast; then he licked a trail to the puckered skin of her nipple.

"Wait? I think not," he breathed just before sucking the hard point into his mouth.

She rose up on her knees, clenching her spongy walls about his hardness as she pulled to the tip of him and sank back down again. "Gracious, I can't deny you."

"I would hope not."

Delightful twinges speared through his belly straight to his balls, and a warm opening sensation bloomed in his sac. By damn! What did she just do? His hands gripped her hips, and his sac grew heavy.

Amazing. He bit her nipple, and his hands steadied her. He thrust up hard, hitting the head of her womb. She cried out and dug, clutching his shoulders.

He sucked the puckered tip of her breast into his mouth and bucked his hips up again, and then again. Each time, his sac tingled, the pressure built, the sensations of her wet flesh glided down his hard length in wave after massaging wave.

Lightning flashed before him, and he saw her. Black hair fanned out on the grass as he fucked her in a garden. The gargoyles above the arches of Tremarctos loomed close above them.

His eyes shifted, and his fingers dug into the soft, padded flesh of her hips. A vision. . . . He would have her again at his home.

By damn! He wanted that.

She squirmed and clamped her cunny muscles harder on his length. In the dim light, her head tossed back, and she whimpered; fingers clutched into his shoulders.

By damn! The smell of lily overwhelmed him.

He bit down harder, sucking her nipple farther into his mouth.

"Ooh—aah!" She quaked upon him, and he slid back into her shaking flesh. She screamed! The sound, more wonderful than the noises she'd made in the main hall, shot down his spine, and his sac burst, blooming fully, and he gushed into her. He hissed and groaned at the relief of the spend. His heart constricted, and his emotions flew.

The intensity shook him. The fuck had by far exceeded his most energetic spend of prior experience. More so than the first time he'd buttered an Ursus female, years ago.

His tongue circled the swollen, extended tip of her nipple, and his hands held her still on his length.

Nestled to her womb, his cock continued to tingle in little blissful eruptions. He rocked slightly out of her; the sensation shot straight to his toes. By damn. He shook with pleasure and thrust back into her oiled warmth, a large, thrilling spurt bursting from him.

She fell forward and nestled her head against his shoulder. Wetness caressed the curve as she licked and then kissed the swell. She wrapped her arms and legs about him, clutching him to her. He groaned. His eyes fluttered as he floated in a dreamy haze. Delightful twinges of ecstasy continued to caress his sac and cock. From her or from him? He didn't know.

He closed his eyes; a blissful, contented feeling of being matched and sated stirred his mind. His eyes felt heavy, and he yawned. He inhaled the sweat-soaked hair at the base of her neck. Lily. He smelled lily stronger than any other scent in the room.

Mac started, awake. Lily. She smelled of lily. Darkness still reigned in the room. He inhaled, and cloves—his scent—was all he smelled. A dream. He shifted and rolled his wonderful goddess to the side of him.

Stretching, he pushed up to sitting and swung his feet over the side of the bed. He turned and tucked the covers tightly about the woman he'd just futtered twice. A sense of pride, of possession swirled in his gut. His brow pulled tight together. He stood and then turned and stared down at her curvy form. His emotions swirled and reached out for her. Contentedness and slumber radiated from her.

Damn! Confusion. That is what he felt. Who was she? And what exactly had happened in the middle of the night when they'd fucked? Was this night all a dream, or did she truly smell of lily after they futtered? The hair on his neck stood. He'd always been exceptionally good at reading others' emotions, yet he had trouble deciphering his own.

He reached forward and touched her cheek. Erotic energy shot up his arm, and his cock jumped and hardened. He wanted to fuck her again and soon. He nodded. Indeed. She would be the woman he fucked this entire celebration and possibly longer. No doubt about that.

4

Rasalette awoke to the sound of her wooden brush handle sliding across marble as her maid straightened her dressing chest. She stretched and smiled; delightful twinges filled her womb—the beginning of Orsse, the sexual ritual for claiming a life mate. The *opening* had started. Her womb was prepared to hold an Ursus cub. She would need to tell her brother whom she'd chosen. She would need to tell . . .

She sucked in her breath. Who was he? They'd never exchanged names.

"Pardon, your highness?"

"I found my life mate, and I don't know his name."

"Pardon?" Puzzlement hung in Ann's voice.

"We—we never exchanged names." Her heart flipped in her chest, and tears welled in her eyes. She would never find him, not with all the men and women who ventured here for the celebrations. The tears fell in a heated trail down her face.

"That's all right. He will be drawn to you with a force he cannot deny. You will see." Her maid wiped the tears from her cheeks. "The sandalwood worked well. I could still smell the fragrance this morning."

"Yes." *He has no idea I am his. He thinks I am just a woman he took pleasure in.* She swallowed hard. "How—how do I tell him?"

"Oh, your highness, what man would not want you? You are the princess. And beautiful. He obviously fancies you. You may not need say a thing to him; he will be connected, your highness. He is a man of knowledge. He may already know." Ann picked up Rasalette's brush and, starting at the ends of her hair, began to brush. "And if he doesn't, you will tell him, and I am sure he will fall at your feet."

Rasalette squeezed her eyes closed. No. No, he would not fall at her feet. He would be angry. Even though she didn't know his name, all his actions from the night before shouted control of everything he did. She knew that. His mastery was part of his great attraction.

He would not be pleased that she had deceived him, no matter the reason why she'd falsified her scent. She needed to figure out how to deal with this. To make him see this was her only way and that she wanted him no matter how she obtained his protection.

Gracious! She did want him.

Did her craving from him come from her primitive self or from the princess she was raised to be? She frowned. She didn't know. The desire possessed her; it did not matter which part of her hungered for his touch, his presence, or his protection.

Protection.

A chill tapped up her spine, and the hair on her neck stood. Her brother. He would be livid with her for going against his orders.

"I need to speak with my brother. He needs to know I have chosen." *And he can no longer advise me.*

His livid face came to her. His jaw was set, and then sudden shrill laughter burst from his mouth. The chills racing her spine engulfed her body.

She could do nothing. He could do whatever he wished. *Take a deep breath, Rasalette, and calm yourself. Your fear of him is influencing your imagination. You did not just see a vision of your fall.*

She inhaled a shallow breath and exhaled the cold air slowly. The man didn't know her name . . . but deep in her gut, his possession of her soothed her. . . . He would not leave her. He would claim her.

Indeed, think of him. Think of how he will make your life better. She'd wanted to tell him to stop the night before when he'd slid into her sleeping body and begun the ritual. . . .

She'd almost confessed.

She closed her eyes. The want to concede all before he started *opening* stabbed at her soul. She couldn't bring restraint upon herself when she desired the joining and his protection so desperately.

Please! Don't let him shun her for the lie. *You simpleton.*

Punishment . . . indeed, she expected punishment. Her backside tingled as she remembered his spank in the hall last night. Scenting herself was a trick of the lowest form of Ursus. Once she explained, though, surely he would realize that dousing herself in fragrance was for the correct reasons. No matter, she would do what was necessary to show her devotion and comprehension that she did was wrong.

Ann finished her hair; she stood and walked to the window.

"Clove is a nice strong scent, your highness. Are you pleased with your selection?"

"You can smell the change?" Cloves. . . . She sighed. A warm smell that reminded her of spiced fall cooking. She cringed. Mooncalf!

If her maid could smell her, any male surely could. She

needed to inform her brother before anyone else smelled her, and preferably here in her chambers, where the danger of passing men was minimal.

"Your highness, your brother won't see you here. He is already in the main hall enjoying . . ." Ann shifted her stance and stared Rasalette straight in the eyes.

"A woman." Rasalette rolled her eyes. Well, he wouldn't corner her when he futtered another. "Very well, Ann. You will escort me to my brother."

"Your highness?" Her maid's eyebrows pinched in worry.

"Yes, Ann, you." Rasalette stood, straightened her red silk slip, and walked to the door. "Ann, if any male comes toward me, I wish you to inform me even if you feel I have noticed him." Any possible mate could come at her and try to claim her. She'd heard the horror stories, of course. The Ursus duke had fought to claim his life mate in the most scandalous event of her knowledge. He'd killed his brother to claim her. She shuddered, though she was the princess, and one yell would have the servants running to help her plight.

"Yes, your highness."

Rasalette pulled open the door and walked out into the hall on shaking legs.

The usual servants scurried about, but otherwise the hall stood free of any of the celebration revelries. Her heart pounded as fear pressed on her mind. What if she didn't find him in time? His presence massaged her skin. He stayed in the castle. Her instincts sensed him. She would arrive in the main hall momentarily. Hopefully he already resided within.

She traversed the hall, trying not to show any of her discomfort on the outside. Holding her head high, she smiled but not too brightly. She turned the corner and passed the door in the hall against which her mate had possessed her. She closed her eyes, seeing his body pressed against her.

His words—*don't move*—traveled through her mind. A

twinge pricked her lower abdomen, and wetness puffed the walls of her core. Thick and sticky, the honeyed arousal tickled the lips of her sex. Her knees weakened. Orsse. Her womb was now ready for his seed. Or anyone's. *Stop such destructive thoughts, Rasalette.*

She shook her head and reached for the door handle to the main hall. Please, let him be waiting on the other side.

"Your highness, a gentleman approaches."

The smell of anise flooded her nostrils, and her stomach twinged. The man was not him. Rasalette stiffened but didn't pause. She pushed through the door, Ann close on her heels.

The hall stood full. Peers sat at tables and sang. Royal court men and women draped across the chairs at the head of the room. Some appeared not to have left the hall since the night before.

Her gaze darted through the crowd in search of her mate. Her senses reached out for the newly forming connection between them. No. He was not in the room. The hair on her neck rose in fear. She would have to tell her brother alone.

Her brother was fucking the petite redheaded woman on the king's bed in the front of the hall. She closed her eyes. . . . She hated disturbing him when he was leaving her be, but the situation was urgent, and they had interrupted each other before.

She cringed as memories returned of him shouting at her—his face the color of a cherry—fingers wrapped about her neck as she squirmed and struggled to breathe.

Not a favorable outcome. This was not ideal.

She approached the large rectangular cushion that was big enough for ten people to fuck on, and her chin quivered. Tears threatened to push to her eyes. She inhaled deep and watched her brother tease the woman. Her stomach twisted and jumped.

Ann stepped beside her. "Mistress, you are pale."

Rasalette's hand spread across her belly, and she turned to face Ann. "My stomach is twisting."

Ann's eyes widened. "Press your tongue to the roof of your mouth, and breathe through your nose."

"Quite so! I had forgotten the teachings, Ann. Thank you."

She did as her teachers had instructed her about Orsse symptoms and approached her brother.

The redheaded young woman's eyes settled on her briefly and then closed as her brother bit her neck; her body arched off the cushion into him. He growled in appreciation. She inhaled; the smell of sex and arousal from everyone in the room dripped in the air.

Maybe her brother wouldn't smell the change or the *opening* fluid clinging to her womb. Foolish. He would smell, as everyone in the room would . . . eventually. Her heart sped. Deep in her gut, her instincts pressed her to leave the hall. She trembled in fear. No. She needed to do this.

She stood still, waiting for her brother to finish with this woman. His eyes darted to the side and stared at her; his lips turned up into a sinister smile, and his hand slid down the woman's stomach and caressed her mound as he readied the woman for his mounting.

No. She closed her eyes. . . . He would make Rasalette wait. She ground her teeth together.

Of course he would.

She shifted her stance. The smells in the room quickened her pulse. Cramping pain pinched the flesh above her mound once more.

Her eyes widened; she sucked in a breath, and the smell of her cunny made her shake. She swallowed hard—she would end up fighting for her life as other possible mates smelled her. If another male forced himself on her, he would be her life mate no matter his station. Her arms shook, and the hair stood in stiff icicles. A guard passed an arm's length from her, and her gut churned.

Damn her brother! She glanced around the room and hoped

to catch a glimpse of her future. The man her body so craved was not present.

Men inched closer to her, positioning themselves. The three men she'd allowed to touch her last night were among the gathering crowd. Her brother's chosen few. All eyes stared at her, and gooseflesh raced her skin. Gracious. They smelled her. How could they not?

She couldn't wait. She swallowed the panic burning up her throat.

"Dearest brother. I fear I must talk to you. Now." Her hands fisted at her sides, and sweat tickled her brow. She glanced around at the men standing, awaiting the opportunity . . . the circumstance to claim her.

"Well, well, spoiled dear, you will just have to wait. I am occupied. Take a seat in your chair, and when I am through we will discuss your smell and the scent of your folly."

Mac arose from a deep, hard sleep. He stretched; his cock stood straight up from his stomach as thoughts flooded his mind and emotions.

His goddess.

Her essence pounded strongly through him. He closed his eyes. Panic and fear swirled, icing his veins. He shook himself. They—they had connected.

Last night he had floated in a dreamlike fog, but the spend in the middle of the night . . . beyond anything he'd experienced. When he'd left her room, the shift in the smell of his scent should have told him . . . Orsse. The hair on his neck stood.

She had tricked him.

His jaw locked as his teeth ground. The emotional flow that was now coming from her, and possessing him, brought him to his knees. The connection could only be explained by the ritual.

Damn. He threw his legs over the edge of his bed and signaled to his valet.

He frowned and closed his eyes. "Damn. Damn. Damn. Damn." His head bobbed with each word.

How the hell had this happened?

His valet helped him dress. Her emotions were coming from the main hall. The connection to her twisted his gut. He could now track her exact position; if he completed the act, he would have that same ability for the rest of his life.

He paused as he slid his arms into the dark green silk coat his valet held up for him. Her ink-black hair tossed back, and her screaming out in passion the night before, clung to his mind, and goose pins caressed his skin.

Seeing her in ecstasy for eternity would be a treat, not a punishment.

But she'd lied!

He was no one's noodle. She needed to be taught to respect him. He pushed his feet into his tall black boots and headed straight for the main hall and her.

The hall to the main chambers went on forever. Last night this journey had been anything but. He quickened his pace. What did the fear in her connection to him indicate?

As he entered the main hall, everyone was turned toward the royal court's platform. Her essence hit him in the gut, stopping him in his tracks. Panic and fear sliced through his chest and stole his breath.

By damn! She stood surrounded by men. Other Ursus who in one move wished to claim her. This was the one instance he wished he possessed his brother's ability to use his mind.

Mac felt. He could read a room's emotions in a glance or concentrate on the one he wished, but he could not change people's thoughts, as Orin could, or move things simply by concentrating on what he wanted, as Martin could. Right now his goddess feared.

He strode forward and worked his way across the crowded marble floors to the royal platform. His majesty, the king, stretched out on his public bed, languidly fucking a woman who at first glace appeared to be a child.

Mac had heard stories in his adolescence of Prince Kodiak Ursidae V. As a young man the current king possessed fierce tastes in the female flesh, rivaling any man of any age, but that was not surprising, considering the ease with which he could have what he wanted.

The rumors Mac found interesting entailed Prince Kodiak craving younger, untutored women.

Mac heard accounts of the old king removing his daughter from the castle, when she reached her womanhood, so Kodiak couldn't touch her. That juicy bit of gossip had occurred on Mac's last visit to the homeland over eight years hence. By damn! Mac's father loved to grab on to any bit of information putting down the royal family.

Kodiak's father, King Ursidae IV, had sent Mac's father to England and then asked him never to return to the homeland because of his scandal. The king had never forgiven Ursidae.

The sister had always been a vague reference . . . Princess Rasalette.

"Whose room is this?" Mac's words from the night before burned his ears.

Princess Rasalette's.

Princess Rasalette's.

He had fucked his goddess in her room last night.

Princess Rasalette's.

Her glorious black hair, and the smell of lily mixed with his clove when he'd left this morning.

Princess Rasalette's.

His goddess . . . the princess Rasalette. They were one and the same.

Chills raced over his skin, and he reached out to feel her emotions once more. Fear sliced straight down his spine and pierced his gut, making him crunch over. His nostrils flared in rage, half at her, and half at whatever she feared.

How dare she join the two of them without his knowledge? The princess.

How dare she cover her scent?

Who dared frighten a princess? Who dared frighten his mate?

His mate.

Indeed, she was his mate. He couldn't deny that. His eyes shifted, and his claws unsheathed. Mac groaned, his arms shaking as he tried to pull back his emotions. To wait. Charging in would gain him no favor.

He needed to see what was afoot. Rash actions would not serve him in claiming her. However, telling his beast to prowl would never do. She was his life mate; his primitive side raged and churned like a ravenous dog with a steak set just out of reach.

But . . . punishment for her folly, her deception, sadly would ensue. She could not believe he would be made a fool for the rest of his life. Princess, indeed. . . . Her title meant nothing to him and his family. She would know that deception and lies of any sort were not to be tolerated. She needed to offer herself to him in truth.

Holding all his instincts in check, he slowly moved toward the platform. His eyes locked on to her.

She stared directly at him. Her beautiful long lashes closed and fanned her creamy cheeks. Relief washed down her and through him. Her stance relaxed just a fraction.

By damn. Her beauty stole his breath. Black, wavy hair fell

over her shoulders, catching the sunlight, streaming through the windows in the curls' depths.

Her eyes jumped to her brother and then to the crowd of men and women who had gathered around them.

Mac stood at the back, willing himself to hear any one of her thoughts. Closing his eyes, he concentrated and, clenching his fists, reached out . . .

Nothing.

Damn it all! He swallowed and sniffed the air. The smell of his *opening* fluids filled the room. He inhaled again, and the scent of her Orsse blazed in his gut. His cock swelled. The aroma clawed at him. His instincts, raw and primitive, to claim, to own, to make sure no one else was entitled to her, raged. His jaw locked, and he shook.

No! Pull your instincts together, Mac. What do you need in this situation?

Her.

Indeed. But he needed to know what itched up his spine. She feared more than ending up with a mate she didn't choose. But what did she fear?

He blew out a tense breath and reached out for the emotions of the room.

That's it, Mac. Control this. . . . Work on her plight logically.

The men and women around them all exuded excitement at varying intensities. Two males, who stood off to the side close to Rasalette and to the king, also showed nervousness.

Mac's brow stooped, and he considered them. Silk breeches, well-fitted waistcoats, and expertly polished boots spoke of the moneyed. Gentlemen. The nervousness didn't fit them. Something was amiss.

The hair on his neck stood, and his will to protect Rasalette made his hands shake. He inched closer, needing to place himself as close to her as possible. As he reached the edge of the bed, the emotions shifted. The king motioned for another woman to join him and the redhead on the large mat.

The woman, a slim, fair-haired waif, knelt. Shifting to her hands and knees, she wiggled as close to the king as she could. Once there, she lay on her back, her hands sliding out to caress his majesty's thigh and the breast of the redhead he futtered. She parted her legs; the king released a hand from the redhead and slid his fingers into the new woman's cunny. She arched her back and squeezed the redhead's breast.

Mac vividly tasted Rasalette's tart cunny on his tongue. His concentration was fully on her as she sat in the chair at the side of the room. Waiting . . . waiting . . .

The king pulled from the redhead. "My spoiled, dear sister, please come forward."

Rasalette's eyes widened. She glanced around the room and locked gazes on Mac. Mac stiffened; his claws extended fully. Her fear churned in his stomach and shifted to terror. His vision hazed, and his chest rose and fell at a rapid speed. He couldn't breathe. His rage won.

"Lord Franlish, you too come forward."

"Yes, your majesty." Franlish striped off his coat and waistcoat and unbuttoned his breeches.

Lord Franlish radiated unease, smug excitement, and a sense of pride. Mac didn't like this one bit. What was the king up to?

"Come now, spoiled sister. Did you think I wouldn't know what you would do?" The two women who lay next to the king fondled each other as his fingers continued to frig the fair-haired one.

Rasalette stood. "Pardon? What do you mean?" Her hands trembled, and her panic made the hairs stand on Mac's back. *Calm, Mac, calm.* This was not good. His shoulders broadened. He would not hold back much longer.

"Why, dearest, that if I presented men to you, you would

find your own and start the ritual." He smiled a satisfied smile. "And you, dear, did exactly that. Now the man I wish to be your mate will finish Orsse."

Lord Franlish pounced in a streak of white cotton and fair hair at Rasalette. Mac froze as Franlish tore up her skirt and pushed her back against the wall. White-hot possession blinded Mac. He surged; his coat and breeches tore as his size shifted into protection form. The will to protect his mate forced his transformation.

He had no idea how he cleared the king's mat or landed on Lord Franlish's back, but he tumbled. His fist hit Lord Franlish's face as if he hit a feather. His claws cut a trail of blood down the smaller man's cheek.

Franlish grasped Mac's coat sleeve and yanked; the fabric gave way. A hot gush of blood sprayed Mac's face. Bloody hell! The rogue had cut him.

He slashed and slashed at Franlish. His fists hit in a flash at his flesh.

Rasalette screamed.

Mac tore his gaze from Franlish and focused on Rasalette as she whimpered. The other man who had showed nervousness was forcing Rasalette down onto the king's mat.

Mac shuddered as his mind tried to shake through the animal instincts possessing him. What was going on? He was a pawn in a plot the king was playing out against his sister. Rage at the king for not only this but for the way he had treated his family for generations flooded him.

Mac's gaze pierced the king. The king showed smug triumph. Mac pushed from Franlish's grasp and staggered back. Franlish's head jerked back, his eyes wide in shock. He thought he had won.

Franlish's predatory gaze jumped to Rasalette and pounced on the other man, knocking him from Rasalette's body.

Mac stared at the king; his muscles and bones ached from each hit he had made, and the cut on his arm began to throb.

The bloody milksop would make amends. Mac grasped Rasalette by the waist and yanked her against him.

"I—I'm sorry." Her entire body shook as she sobbed and pressed her body to him.

"Not now. Your actions will be discussed, but not now." He picked her up; her legs straddled his hips and her face buried in his chest as they pushed through the crowd. Franlish and the other man did not notice Mac walk away, their prize in his grasp.

"Get him, you fools! He is getting away with her!" The king leaped to his feet and ran toward Mac.

Everyone parted, allowing his majesty access. Mac turned toward the king and stopped. "Your brother will take you if I do not finish the ceremony here and now."

Rasalette trembled. "Yes, yes. Please don't let him take me from you." Her fists grasped his coat in a panic.

Mac grasped her waist, spun, and sat her on a table; the people at the table didn't budge from their conversation or drink.

He separated from her slightly and freed his cock. Grasping Rasalette's thighs, he slid them apart. His phallus glided along her humid flesh, and he thrust his hips; her cunt opened, sliding his pego into lavalike warmth.

She arched against him. The smell of her Orsse and his aggressive animal state collided in him. This needed to be quick.

"Stop them!" The king's voice echoed close in Mac's mind.

Hands appeared from all about them. The people at the table caressed Rasalette, pinching her breasts and massaging her stomach and legs.

Other hands tickled and wrapped about Mac's legs. They caressed and rubbed both of them to ensure the process happened quickly and without interference from the king.

A feathery touch caressed his sac as his cock slid into Rasalette's honey-coated walls. The fingers tickled and rubbed his marbles, timing the presses with the stroke of his cock into her slickness.

Damn! The sensation was exquisite. His seed twisted, rising fast. Fire spread through his stomach, and his cock exploded as he emptied all his will into her, claiming her as his life mate.

Rasalette screamed, crunched her stomach, and then slammed her shoulders against the tabletop. Her legs trembled and shook about his hips. The bond formed steadfast as his seed joined the flesh of her womb.

Rasalette's eyes shot open, and she stared at him. Tears fell uncontrollably down her face. Mac's eyes narrowed. Why did she cry? He reached out and rubbed the palm of his hand along her cheek.

She turned her face into the palm of his hand and sighed.

"Let me through! Move aside!" the king's voice shouted from the left of him, just beyond the crowd of people who had gathered.

5

Rasalette shot straight up at the sound of her brother's livid voice. Her fists clutched at her mate's sides as she buried her head against his chest. The hands of the other people dropped from about them.

The beat of this man's heart beneath her chest soothed her. Each breath he made pulsed through her body. His cock, still slick in her womb, connected them with more than just his seed. Their souls intertwined.

She quivered, inhaling his scent mixed fully with her own, and sighed. His powerful arms wrapped about her shoulders and shielded her from her brother's view. She would be safe.

"Step away from her now!" Her brother pushed up to the table.

A deep warning grumble came from her mate.

She didn't know his name.

She gazed up at the harsh angle of his jaw and rounded contour of his chin. "My sir, lover, and mate, what is your name?" she whispered.

Her brother snarled. "Why, spoiled dear, you could not have

chosen a less appropriate Ursus. I will kill him, and you shall choose another."

"No!" Her eyes widened as fear sliced a jagged cut through her belly. Her hands tightened on her mate's shirt, and she pulled herself as close as possible to his body, his heat, and his protective embrace.

Her mate leaned toward her brother so close their noses fairly touched. "You will do no such thing, your majesty." His gaze traversed her brother's form and then pierced his eyes once more. "My father already has issues with you and your . . . habits." His voice dropped in tone to a damning hiss, sending shivers straight down her spine. "If you dare come near me or mine *ever*, you will regret your actions."

Her brother's narrowed eyes jumped to one of his guards, who was standing just off to the side, and his hands fisted at his sides. "Regret? I think not." His gaze then settled back on her. "This is not done, dear sister."

Her mate reached out and snagged her brother by the robe. Rage shook her mate's arm, and Rasalette's eyes widened. The searing-hot fury engulfed her body. Her skin turned icy cold, and her muscles tightened.

"Yes, it is." Her mate pushed her brother backward, releasing the robe as her brother stumbled out of reach. Her mind spun. . . . Her brother had met a man he had no sway with.

Her mate's hand returned to her. Long, lean fingers squeezed the flesh of her thighs, and he pushed her legs together down the front of him.

He clutched her upper body to him and lifted her; his cock pulsated deep within her. Her full length pressed to his chest and legs. Every bit of her was possessed by her mate. His arms and his engorged erection held and caressed her body, soothing the deep yearning to be one. His actions toward her brother had calmed her fears of ever being harmed or humiliated by anyone again.

They pushed through the crowd and headed toward the door that led to Rasalette's room. "Your servants will pack for you, and we will leave the celebrations this night."

Rasalette trembled at his command. She had never trusted anyone with her own well being. She smiled. He would never let harm come to her. "Yes, sir." His cock twitched inside her, tickling her womb. She bit her lip and jerked slightly with pleasure. "What is your name?"

They pushed through the door leading to the hall that connected with her rooms. "I am Mac Ursus. The Duke of Tremarctos is my sire."

She inhaled a startled breath. One of the duke's sons. They had a fierce, wicked reputation. A shiver of shock, fear, and excitement slid through her. The hair on her neck stood. No one would ever slight him or his family. Including her devious brother.

"Which . . . which son are you?" Her eyes never left his face.

His lips curved into a smile. "It thrills you to be part of the scandalous family, I see."

Her tongue slid out and wet her lips. Indeed, it did, but for reasons he wouldn't fathom.

"I am Mac, one of a set, second born to the duke. Martin, my brother, is the other half of the matched pair."

A twin and son of the infamous duke. "Indeed. I chose well for my mate."

"That, Rasalette, remains to be seen. You deceived me. The deception cannot go unatoned for. You have not pleased me."

She tensed in his arms. Yes. The moment he'd touched her in the hall, the control over his life, and how easily he'd possessed her, indicated his will. Her actions had not pleased him one whit.

"I—I understand. I hoped you may understand my situation, but I knew you would not be pleased that I grasped the bull in my hands." She inhaled deep and tried to steady her growing unease at his displeasure.

She should be thrilled that she possessed the exact type of mate she wanted, but every bit of anger that washed through him was warranted. The footmen opened the doors to her chamber, and he shifted her in his hold.

"*You deceived me.*" His words shamed her. No, her actions did that deed. Gracious! She should have thought this through a bit more, but she didn't think any man would object to her. He could have, and did, hold her at fault for her actions, so why didn't he turn and go?

"You—you, sir, could have chosen to walk away."

A smile flickered through his eyes, but his lips did not curl. "Indeed, I could have. So, Rasalette, why didn't I?"

He lifted her and slid his cock from her body. The pull of her flesh as his hardness left her still hungry cunny sent tingles of heat up her stomach. A moan rumbled deep in her chest. Her feet touched the ground, and her legs wobbled. His hands about her waist steadied her. She glanced up over her shoulder at him, and soft green eyes stared back.

"Why didn't I?"

She had no clue. A man of his power and determination could have turned the moment he walked in the hall and smelled her swimming in his fluids. Or could he? Had she locked him to her last night because his pure animal would not let another near her while she was in Orsse?

That was the question she needed the answer to, but at this moment she would do all she could to make up for her wrong and follow his orders or . . .

She could offer herself to him, offer herself in punishment. His hand smacking her bottom the night before in the hall and the erotic pinpricking heat created in her returned. Her pussy twitched, and her breath deepened.

"Put together a small satchel, and we will leave." His voice was hard yet soft. How could that be?

"Ann, please help me."

"Yes, your highness." Her small maid appeared with satchel in hand.

Mac watched as Rasalette instructed her maid on what she needed packed in her satchel. The way she moved in pure grace brought him to his knees. If he had ever wished for any mate, it was she.

The moment he had seen her in the chair being pleasured by the fair-haired man, she had called to him in a way no other woman ever had. Indeed, she exuded beauty, but, no—it was more than handsome looks that had pulled him to her. She had needed him, if only to protect her from her bloody brother, and Mac had not been *needed* by anyone before.

He sighed a tense breath that shook his body. She had deceived him, and he didn't bloody well care. Strife had filled her plan. She wanted protection, but she had bent the truth to get it in the most base and lowly way.

Her plan had not been wise.

He strode to the settee by the windows and sat; his gaze never left her. A man who lusted after the status she would provide him, and nothing more, could be sitting here instead of him.

In his mind, a dog would prefer the side pocket over what her bloodline ensured him or what her money could provide him.

The king's sister.

The hair on his neck rose. Without looking at her or having touched and breathed in her true animal, the notion chilled him. His father would have his head about this.

Her innocence and fear, the fact that she needed him for protection as well as guidance—those qualities brought her close. So close to him, there was no way he would let her go.

He closed his eyes again as his blood thundered in his veins. Images of their futter the night before, of him pressed to her as she trembled against him in the hall, tapped through his brain. Yes, indeed. She infused him and made him stronger.

It was unfortunate that her apology in a more sincere way was necessary. He wanted only to hold her and push away her fear. He frowned as she pointed to the ribbons on her stand. A presentation of herself to him in honesty, not just because they were now fully connected, needed to happen.

She suddenly stilled and looked at him. Sadness, relief, and guilt swirled in her eyes. He closed his, not wanting to see the remorse she felt for deceiving him. Would she trust him and give herself to him, letting their relationship move freshly forward? He hoped they could do so and leave this incident fully behind them. A door opened and closed, and he opened his eyes. The maid no longer resided in the room, and Rasalette lowered her head.

"Sir, I wish to make amends for my deception." Her voice, deep and lust-filled, thickened his groin.

Intriguing. Could she read his thoughts? No. No Ursus woman held any special power. Her statement was not at all what he expected.

"What is it you wish, Rasalette?"

She sauntered toward him. Her hips swayed as the tips of her nipples poked through the thin fabric of one of her celebration gowns.

Would she change into proper clothing to head to the boats? He hoped not.

Standing in front of him, she kneeled, her skirts billowing out about her. She depicted the goddess she knew she was as she stared up at him with sadness, remorse, and lust in her eyes. His pego hardened. A truer woman he had yet to set eyes on.

"Sir, I wish for your punishment for my wrong. For you to set my disrespectful actions to right, so we can move forward on equal standing." Her hand rose, and she pointed to the sofa next to him. "May I, sir?"

His punishment? What was she up to?

"Indeed. You may rise, Rasalette." He held out his hand to

her, and she wrapped her fingers around his and stood. Lifting her skirts, she displayed to him rounded thighs, swelling to a firm yet plush bottom, and a glistening thatch of black curls. He inhaled deep and savored the smell of her lily mixed with his clove, of her tart honey coated in his seed.

She lifted her leg and then knelt beside him on the sofa. The rounds of her knees butted up tightly against the side of his thigh. "My Lord, may I?"

It hit him like a thousand erotic women's swaying hips. He swallowed hard. She wished for him to spank her. . . .

Punish her for her wrong. He laughed outright. Punish her in a similar fashion as he had last night when she'd moved in the hall. By damn. Indeed, he would spank her.

He swallowed hard, and his cock pressed against the soft fabric of his pants. He wanted that. It would be an erotic, pleasurable spank. Corky in tone yet filled with words so she understood that they stood equal and that he was no pawn in her play.

"Indeed, please do, Rasalette."

She leaned across him, hands planted firmly on the outsides of his legs.

His left hand gathered up her skirts and slid them up onto her back. His right hand pinned them in place. The swell of her dove-white bottom in the bright daylight was enough to make him drool like a dog at the dinner table.

She wiggled her hips slightly, and he fought to hold in the chuckle punching in his chest. His lips twitched. My God! The pluck she possessed!

"Be still." His fingers tapped, tickling the bend of her knee. Her muscles tightened, and she sucked in a sharp breath but remained still. His touch feathered her calf down to her petite feet. The skin of her heels was as soft as any silk he'd donned; it amazed him. He circled the edge and then dipped down into the arch.

She squealed, and her legs jerked. He grinned, and his heart warmed through. She was ticklish. Oh, this could be lots of fun.

"Do not move, Rasalette." His finger continued in light butter-fly swipes down the arch of her foot to her toes. Each one of his fingers tapped her dainty pads as if playing a piano.

His hand lifted, and quickly, in a flurry of small whisper-light pets, he tapped—

One, two, three.

One, two, three.

—along the hollow of her foot.

"Oh! Stop that!" She giggled and then full out laughed as she tried to squirm and pull her feet away from him.

"No, Rasalette, I will not cease."

His right hand snagged her hair and pulled the locks, arch-ing her head back. He continued to tap at her ticklish feet but held her firm.

The murmuring sweep of his finger along her feet made her body quiver deliciously. Her back arched, and her hips spread wider and wider.

The tart aroma of her dripping as she extended her hips spun his head. Her taste on his tongue the night before was so fresh in his mind; he licked his lips and moved his ministrations north up her calves to her knees, swirling his finger into the dewed crevice.

She moaned and thrust her buttocks out. Indeed, she was ready—ready to be tasted and spanked. His hand left her knee and slid into her crack. The heat of her bottom, of her cunny, warmed him to his soul. His fingers dipped into her drizzling flesh, and she rocked back, inviting more.

"Hold still." He thrust his three fingers harshly into her pussy in three quick successions. With each finger frig, her hips arched farther back, her breath jerked, and she gushed fluid onto his hands.

So wet, so wanton, so ready for him, and he hadn't spanked her yet.

He removed his fingers and smeared her butter around her crack. He paused at her puckered bud. Would she allow him to penetrate her with his cock? His brows drew together, and he curled his index finger, applying pressure against the muscled hole. She didn't stiffen but moaned.

By damn! His blood hammered through him. He certainly would try. He continued the trail he'd first sought, wiping her cream about the crack and then straight up her back; her flesh rippled and shivered in his touch's wake.

After her spanking, she would be more willing to allow him to penetrate her puckered rose. His sac pulled up close to his body. An age passed since he had buggered a woman; in England, ladies saw the act as evil. He adored the feel of tight, silky muscles about his pego; he knew his brothers did as well.

His right hand released her hair and wrapped about her stomach from underneath. Soft and warm, her belly quivered as he gently braced her for the first of her spanks.

His hand rose into the air, and he bent his fingers, creating a cup. His muscles tensed, and he inhaled. One, two, three.

He swung.

Whack.

The flat of his hand hit her bottom at the curve of the round swell. Pinpricks tingled his hand, and a strangled whimper burst from her mouth.

His hand held that spot, allowing the heat to infuse not only his hand but her bottom. He wiggled his fingers, gently tugging the flesh of her bottom to expose her crack.

She arched her bottom back up to him.

"You shall never again deceive me, Rasalette. Do you understand me?" He paused as his words seeped through her aroused fog.

"Yes, sir. Never, never again."

"Good girl, and I shall never deceive you. Truth and honesty always, no matter how painful."

His hand raised again into the air, the red imprint of his slap cooling on her flesh.

"Indeed, sir."

His hand descended through the air and hit her flesh in the same spot—

Whack!

—and then quickly retreated to add another spank.

Whack!

Her body tensed, and then she groaned. The sound was the same sweet music he'd heard from her in the hall the first night. A primal sound of arousal, enjoyment, and pleasure.

His cock strained against his trousers. Removing his hand, he dipped into her honeyed crack, the hot oil of her sex dripped from her opening and onto his hand.

By damn! She enjoyed this. He pulled his hand back until the tip of his finger found the crinkled ring of skin nestled between her buttocks. Slowly he pressed the tip of his finger against the muscled opening.

She strained her muscles against the digit and then succumbed. Her anus opening to him; the tip slid into the velvet inferno. He stopped; she gasped, ragged and long, trembling at the penetration and then moaning.

The sound of wanton pleasure in her moan thrilled him. His cock jumped in his trousers, and he sucked in a breath through clenched teeth. *Just finish the lecture, and you can have her, Mac.*

"We are equals, Rasalette. Our society rank and money hold no sway in our relationship." He withdrew his fingertip from her bum hole and rushed on. "You will never wield over me, and I shall never over you. Your opinions and emotions will always be listened to and held in consideration to any decision. As will mine. Do you understand?"

"Y—y—yes, sir."

"Good. Don't ever treat me as a pawn in a ploy again."

His hand rose into the air once more and flexed. His eyes fixed on the swell of her bottom and the red handprint already burning her flesh. His hand descended and hit the swell of her bottom.

Whack—whack—whack!

She cried out, shaking and trembling, as honey from her cunt speckled the fabric on his lap. His hand stung, but his heart beat in triple time as his loins screamed out for him to plunge into her watering cunny.

He lifted her pliant body from his lap and placed her knees on the seat cushion; her hands were on the arched back. He stood behind her and undid the buttons on his trousers. The flap fell free, releasing his heated erection.

His hands grasped her hips, and he arched his hips. Pushing forward, he slid his long length into her overflowing cunt.

Her flesh clasped him, and he shook. His balls tightened, and seed rose rapidly. He inhaled and stilled, not wanting this to end too soon.

She groaned and pushed her hips back against him; her flesh quivered in waves about his flesh. He withdrew from her cunny with full purpose.

He would spill his seed in the tight ring of her buttocks. His heart beat in his throat, and he glanced down at his cock; the flesh glimmered with her juices. Placing the tip at her tight rosebud, he pressed forward. The ring of puckered flesh gave way, and the band of his bulbous head popped into her molten core.

She gasped, shuddered, arched her back, and pressed her bottom up to him. He leaned forward, and his breath puffed against the skin of her nape. "Rasalette."

He licked her sweet flesh. Tightening his stomach muscles, he pushed bit by bit into the slick, silky warmth of her bottom.

His face, level with hers, absorbed every whimper and quiver, every gasp of pleasure as he seated himself in her fully.

She was so tight; every inch of his phallus was caressed by her snug channel. His sac contracted, and he groaned as heat speared his gut.

He reached around her body and found her nipple, the tight bud of flesh puckered and hard. He circled the peak as his other hand trailed down her stomach to the slick folds of her sex. He traced the outline of the eye of her sex, and his palm rubbed her nubbin as he pinched her nipple and thrust his finger into her cunny.

She screamed, spending hard against his finger. He pulled his hips back and thrust into her quivering bottom again and again. The shocks of her spend pulled the seed from his sac with each erotic clasp along his tool. The sensations collided with emotions, and liquid bliss exploded into her, burst after burst spilling from his insides. By damn! His muscles shook, and he wobbled. Leaning his weight upon her in exhaustion, he sighed.

"Rasalette."

She trembled beneath him. He reached out for her emotions and touched raw pleasure so intense his skin tingled. She'd enjoyed him as much as he had her. He grinned. They had a good chance of a long, happy union.

Rasalette intently glanced across her shoulder at her mate as he dressed after emerging from the tub. Immaculate was the only word she could think of to describe him.

Broad shoulders, a narrow waist, long brown hair, and green eyes that sparked with desire whenever he sighted her. She was indeed lucky to have him.

"My sir, I am so sorry I deceived you into being my mate. I was not looking to trap you but to find my own freedom."

He stared at her eyes, which were hard yet filled with compassion.

"I know, Rasalette. I know what your brother has been rumored to do. My guess is the actuality is worse in many aspects and total lies in others."

She lowered her eyes from him. "Indeed." She licked her dry lips.

"I will learn all in time, Rasalette."

She nodded her head. "Because of him, I needed to make sure my mate held no fear in uncorking him, if need be."

"You chose well, then. I won't let the rogue near you; besides, you will be coming with me to England."

Her eyes widened. England. "Mac, will I fit in there? I was raised here with strict Ursus values."

"Indeed, and I find those values delightful. You will be just fine. We will have to dress you a bit different, but you can wear what you have on any day for me alone." He grinned as his gaze swept her sheer gown, and her cheeks grew warm. "Indeed, I like that idea immensely."

He was correct. She would be with him, and she would be far away from her brother. Two blessings. This man had managed to touch her heart. The loving emotion was small but growing with each moment in his company. The warmth in her heart gave her hope. She had faith that they would be happy. But did he feel the same?

"Mac, I need to know how you feel beyond the life-mate bond. Do you care about me?" She closed her eyes and shook her head. Simpleton, they had only just met.

In two strides, Mac stood next to her. He knelt down before her and placed his hands on her thighs. "Rasalette, I don't know how to explain this." His tongue slid out and traced his lips. His head tilted a bit to the side, and his gaze caught hers and held it. "You have made me feel needed and wanted in a way no one ever has in my life. My father and mother were happy, but how they arrived as life mates was beyond scandalous and has clouded our existence. Hell, my first brother doesn't know who his sire is. Everyone in my family has their own needs, their own powers. My powers are trifling in comparison."

Her eyes widened. "Your powers are less than . . . than theirs? But you are so strong and so . . . so . . . intimidating."

"Indeed. Our family was banished because what my father did threatened society's values."

"I understand, Mac." She bit her lip. "What is your other power, Mac? I have been trying to figure it out, but it has eluded me."

He inhaled a deep breath. "My twin, Martin, can use his mind to shift things, move things, to read people's thoughts. It is quite amazing. He moved the earth to stop his life mate from fleeing in fear before he had explained things to her. I wish my power was more, but, alas, I simply read emotions. Just by staring at people, I know how they are feeling, no matter how they try to hide it." He stared at her.

"You are reading my emotions? What am I feeling, Mac?"

His eyes didn't leave hers. "Excitement, awe." His lip quirked. "Tiredness." His eyebrows wiggled. "Desire and . . ." his eyes shifted around, "love."

Her lip quivered, and tears sprang to her eyes. "You . . . you can see that." How mortifying. . . . He knew she had begun to love him. After only one day! She tore her gaze from him and stared at the window past his shoulder.

"Rasalette." He shook her knees, and she turned her gaze back to him. "We are equals. No secrets. I would never hold loving feelings above you. Besides, I have adoring feelings for you, too." He winked.

"Oh, Mac." She threw her arms about his neck and squeezed. "I did pick well. Extremely well."

"Indeed, Princess, you did well."

ORIN

1

Sudhamly, England, 1817

"Lord Ashbey cuts a dashing figure, does he not?"

The leaves crunched beneath their steps down the trail through the woods, and Wilhelmina sighed. Why did all her friends find her future husband so . . . so handsome? She could barely look at him without the hair rising on her neck. A chill raced down her spine at the memory of his cold lips hurriedly brushing across hers in a nervous caress as he'd left her father's estate two nights past.

"Marie?" Wilhelmina stared down at the rocks and brown earth on the path they traveled. The women's silk skirts swayed back and forth with each step. "Haven't you ever wanted . . . well, something—someone different?"

"What do you mean, Mina? Like the stable boy or someone unsuited?" Marie giggled. "I have always found your stable lad enchanting." Marie's smile broadened.

Wilhelmina shook her head, and an unruly curl of red hair sprang into her vision. *No, someone . . . intense. . . . A man who didn't sit on his buttocks all day and play endless games.* She frowned. "Not unsuited, Marie. Ashbey is just so . . . Well, he is uninteresting, as is every other suitor who has come to my father's door."

They turned the corner in the bend of trees, and the path opened onto a field filled with gently swaying blue and white flowers. Wilhelmina stopped still as the warmth in the beauty of the scene curved her lips into a contented smile.

She loved this field, this walk, and Sudhamly. A sigh pushed from her chest. That was part of the problem—she didn't want to go to Surry to live at Ashbey's estate. Seldom would she see this field filled with cheery flowers. Her heart twisted in her chest.

"Oh, Mina, I am so not like you. I just want a nice, suitable man who will take care of me. Nothing more. You have always . . . well, you have always been the eye of the ball. Is there a gentleman who has caught your interest?"

"No. I—I know it is silly of me to want more than what Ashbey could offer me."

"Pardon?"

They turned and continued down the edge of the field. The earth shook with hooves, and ahead of them a deer burst into the field. Wilhelmina's heart leaped as the sleek brown coat of the deer rippled, its nostrils flaring.

Marie screeched, and Wilhelmina grabbed her friend by the pelisse, pulling her back into the woods just a fraction. She covered Marie's mouth with her kid-gloved hand. Marie's breath warmed through the leather as the earth continued to shake. The sound of thundering hoofbeats and . . . a flapping leather saddle grew near.

"Shhh, feel the shaking. . . . A horse approaches."

Marie nodded her head, and Wilhelmina dropped her hand from her friend's mouth.

They stood in plain view of the field, tucked off to the side in the shade of the large tree branches, as a large black steed jumped through the trees in pursuit of the deer. The deer weaved and cut across the field; the horse and rider were a blur as they gained ground.

Wilhelmina's breath caught in her throat. The man was enormous. His black boots, shined to a high polish, reflected the sun. The blood-red fabric of his coat stretched taut across a muscled back and then tapered, flying out about him.

She stood frozen, mesmerized by his masculinity. He didn't wear a hat, and his unfashionably long, mink hair swirled and thudded in a queue down his back.

His horse, a beastly black draft horse with tufted hooves and a long flowing mane turned as his rider shifted his weight slightly to the side.

They truly rode as one. Wilhelmina bit her lip. The rider handled that beast with ease.

He transferred the horse-sweat-slick reins to one hand. The motions of his horse's head slipped the reins back and forth within the man's gentle, flexing grasp.

Oh. Her chest tightened. What would his calm, confident grip on her fingers—as he lifted her hand to his lips—be like? Her hand trembled, and she puckered her lips in an imaginary kiss. Heated prickles raced across her skin. Indeed.

His beast came alongside the deer, and the rider sprang from his saddle. His chest hit the buck's stomach hard, and he toppled the deer to the ground.

The deer squealed and thrashed beneath the large man as he effortlessly sat back on his knees. His eyes widened and his jaw set as he held the deer. His breath was so loud as he exhaled it sounded as if he growled.

All the hairs on Wilhelmina's neck stood, and her corset grew tight against her breast. She couldn't tear her eyes away from him.

The deer continued to thrash in his hold. The man's fingers

flexed on the deer's coat, and the buck stilled, teeth chattering in a steady clatter.

The gentle caress of his fingers against the deer's neck had soothed and calmed the beast. How had he done that?

The man stood and set the deer on the ground. The deer didn't move. Wilhelmina's eyes widened.

He grabbed the antlers, one in each hand, and jerked his arms, twisting them. A crack of bones pierced the air.

Wilhelmina jumped and screeched, covering her mouth with her hand a moment too late. He had killed the deer with nothing more than his hands. He possessed gentleness, power, and control. Her heart pounded, and she swallowed hard.

The man's head jerked back, and round eyes settled on them. Round eyes?

He shook his head, and his hair loosened from the queue. He unfolded to full height and stared at her.

No. She was wrong; his eyes were normal. How could a man so beastly affect her so? She licked her lips, wanting to kiss him and compare the masculinity in his actions to Ashbey's dandy caress.

"Mina . . . Mina . . . come, let us go. I—Impossible to believe we just witnessed a man killing a deer with his bare hands. I don't want him to approach us." Marie's hands clutched and dug into Wilhelmina's arm as she pulled back in the direction of Wilhelmina's father's home.

Approach them. . . . Would he?

Her heart skipped in her chest, and her skin tingled with excitement in a way it never had before in her life. She wanted to meet him. Needed to know his name. She needed to know what such a man's touch was like.

"Who is he?"

The man wiped his hands on his gray leather breeches and spun back toward his mount.

"I'm not sure, and I don't want to find out."

"Truly, Marie? He is fascinating. Doesn't he excite you?" Her nipples grew hard beneath her corset and pressed uncomfortably against the tight restriction. She wiggled her torso, trying to dispel the discomfort and prickles circling her breasts.

"Fascinating? Exciting? I think not. Daft in the attic is more likely." Marie continued to pull at her arm. "Please, Mina. Let us go."

Wilhelmina shifted her stance but did not take a step.

The man pulled a length of leather rope from the saddle and turned back to the deer.

My poppies, his hands engulfed the thin deer's legs! What would those hands appear like on her wrist? She swallowed hard, imagining his large hands covering her entire stomach. A featherlike sensation shot from between her legs straight up her belly. The flesh of her sex tingled, and a gush of moisture leaked out.

She sucked in a breath.

The sticky moisture did not result from a need to relieve herself or from her monthly. Her cheeks grew warm. He affected her that way. Amazing. She watched him wrap the deer's legs with the rope and secure them. Her legs trembled as if his fingers brushed along her ankles.

Tilting his head back, the man closed his eyes and inhaled. His head fell forward, and his wide and intense stare pierced hers and held.

"I'm going, Mina." Marie's hand dropped from her arm, and she turned.

She should go . . . indeed, she should retreat, but she couldn't tear her eyes from him.

Marie's footfall on the leaves behind her stopped. "Mina, I can't leave you alone. Come with me, please."

The sound of fear and unease in Marie's voice broke through the sensations pulsing through Wilhelmina's body. Indeed, Marie was correct. Wilhelmina should leave. But . . . "I need to know his name, Marie. I shall be only a moment. Please, please wait here while I find out."

"Mina!"

Wilhelmina stepped from the shade of the trees and out into the sea of blue and white flowers. Her legs shook with each step toward the enormous man. He was immense.

A lump formed in her throat, and she swallowed. She felt the sensation of a feather tickling her skin; it increased the closer to him she stepped.

He watched her approach. She licked her lower lip as he stood a mere arm's reach away. She tilted her head back and stared up into his face.

"Sir? I am Lady Wilhelmina, and you are?"

He inhaled, sniffing the air again, and closed his eyes.

He didn't answer but turned, bent down, and lifted the deer from the earth. Turning back to the horse, he laid the buck across his horse's haunches and slid the leather wrapped about the deer's hooves through loops in the saddle. His enormous hands worked with a deft preciseness.

Amazing how his large fingers worked a string so small. She glanced at Marie standing at the edge of the field. *Get his name, Wilhelmina, and go!*

"Sir?" Wilhelmina's tongue dragged across her dry lips again as he moved to the other side of the horse and secured the front hooves.

The black steed stood still. The man came back around to the side of the horse where she stood; his gaze slid down her body, trailing her body in dew. Wilhelmina gasped.

"My lady, you do not wish to know me or anything about who I am." His gaze settled on her skirts about her hips. He closed his eyes and inhaled so his chest stretched taut under his superfine waistcoat; then a deep growling sound vibrated in his chest.

His eyelids opened, and he stared her directly in the eyes.

His jaw set in a firm line; he licked his lips. "I suggest you remove yourself from my company."

The heat pouring off him wrapped her in a warm blanket she couldn't remove from herself, even on this tepid day.

She straightened her shoulders. "Not until I know your name, sir." She smiled at him, and her knees weakened as if like butter. Her determination had left her. No, her fortitude had not fled. Excitement. Indeed, a heightened frenzy had turned her insides to custard.

A smile curved one side of his lips, and something deep and vigorous spiraled in his eyes.

The name of the intense emotion that lay shimmering in his depths eluded her. Her chest rose and fell, yet she gasped for air.

"Lady Wilhelmina, if you do not remove yourself from my grasp *now*, I will bury my wick in you . . . here in this field in front of your friend."

"Pardon, sir?" What did he mean by his wick? Another gush of wetness slid from between her thighs, and her cheeks blazed with heat. My! What a delicious sensation, and all caused by simply standing near him.

He inhaled again, his body shaking as he fisted his hands at his sides. Tearing his gaze from her, he peered over his horse's saddle. "Leave now! I am not jesting."

His words cut with disappointment yet titillated her in an intriguing way. She couldn't walk away and not know his name. She glanced at Marie, who stood watching in the shade of the trees. Marie stared at them intently. Then Wilhelmina turned back to the man.

"Tell me your name, sir, and I shall leave." Her lower lip trembled. *Please, please tell me. I—I can't leave without knowing who you are.*

His hands grabbed her waist and branded her through the muslin and thin petticoats. Every fine hair on her arms rose, and she swayed, light-headed as if in a fit of vapors that never came. Oh, my. . . . Exhilaration pulsed through her every nerve.

His lips came down hard and harsh on hers. His tongue thrust into her mouth, and she moaned at the invasion, not knowing what else to do but feel his touch.

Maybe *wick* meant "tongue."

She sighed, and her head spun. He could take this liberty with her anytime. No matter how shocking. "Mmmm." She relaxed to him and gently moved her lips, mimicking his motions along hers.

His lips pinched and pressed hers. The moist cavern of his mouth and tongue tasted of coffee and anise. Oh, this was what a kiss should be—sweet, spicy, and filled with passion. She swayed into his arms.

"Mina! Mina!"

Her friend's yell cut through her haze. Marie couldn't let her friend enjoy a single adventurous, scandalous kiss.

He pulled back from her lips and stared down at her. His warm gray eyes swirled with pain, confusion, and longing that jolted her soul. Her heart ached for him.

"Go now." The words were growled through clenched teeth. "I will not stop if you do not."

Indeed, sir, don't hesitate. Wicked, adventurous thoughts. A jolt of heat seared her face and chest. She wanted him to kiss her again and again, to run his hands along her hips and touch the ache in her breasts.

She opened her mouth to speak, but a moan bubbled up from her throat instead of words.

His hands squeezed her hips harshly, pulling her slightly toward him, and a warming pain shot through her flesh. His arms jerked, and his fingers released her as if he grasped what he wanted and hated all at once. His head shook, the long, inky brown hair sliding loose over his shoulders, and he swung up onto his mount.

Gray eyes—filled with need and desire—stared down at her, wrapping her body and mind in an invisible rope of hunger from which she was unsure she wanted to flee.

"Go!"

She stepped toward Marie but refused to break eye contact with him. She wanted this ... whatever the emotion was she had just experienced. Her soul needed it.

Click-click. His tongue clucked as he spurred his mount in the sides and galloped toward the trees.

Wilhelmina stood, unable to move as she watched him disappear into the woods.

Who was he? Who was he? A mind-maddening kiss and she didn't get his name.

"Mina. Oh, Mina, are you well?" Marie stepped in front of her, and Marie's gaze darted all around her face. "Oh—oh, Mina! Look what he did to your lips!"

Wilhelmina's hand rose, and she touched the swollen, moist surface. Her finger slid along the lower puffy lip. *My poppies!* The skin felt just like silk. She gazed back into the forest where he had disappeared. "It—it was amazing, Marie. I didn't know a kiss could be so intense."

Marie giggled. "It looked harsh, Mina."

"Oh, Marie, that kiss ... I have never experienced another like it." She sighed. "I still don't know his name." She dragged her gaze from the trees and to her friend's face. "Do you have any idea who he might be, Marie?"

Her friend ran her hand down Wilhelmina's arm. "No."

Blast! She grasped Marie's hand and raised her finger to her lips. "Touch my lips ... they are amazing."

Marie's fingertips glided along Wilhelmina's swollen lips. "Oh, Mina, they are soft, softer than the finest silk."

"Yes." She breathed as her body tingled in a delicious haze. "I—I have to know who he is."

* * *

Orin sat astride his mount and watched the lovely, innocent Lady Wilhelmina as her friend ran a finger across her angelic lips.

He groaned.

No. Orin, you will not allow another encounter. She is too pure to get tangled up in a quick couple with you.

He would destroy her in every conceivable way if he touched her again. Thank the Ursus she'd not been alone and her friend was susceptible to his mind sway. Two implied thoughts to her friend, asking her to call out Lady Wilhelmina's name, and she had bent to his will. Even if he had threatened to take her in front of her friend, he did have a bit of honor, and he would never ruin a titled innocent as another stood and watched.

He should have used his mind to erase his presence all together. He sighed. *Fool, Orin. Another frivolous interaction with a non–Ursus woman.* His only grace would be if she walked back to her home and promptly went on with her life. The life of a duke's daughter revolved around parties and friends. She would indeed forget him. He sighed.

What a blundering blockhead.

Lady Wilhelmina.

He blew out another sigh that did nothing to help relieve his tension.

Daughter of the Duke of Coltensley.

Their fathers' lands had bordered each other for years, yet their families never spoke. Until today. He would make sure he never conversed with the pretty, red-haired, green-eyed angel again. She would be their downfall. His downfall.

He turned his horse toward Tremarctos. He would lock away Lady Wilhelmina's soft, trembling lips and plush curves in his mind and throw away the key.

2

The cold earth pounded beneath her feet, and she shivered as bumps spread like tickling fingers across her skin. She spun about and about. Nothing.

Nothing but the darkness of the woods surrounded her. Her heart pounded in her throat.

Whoot, whoot.

She jumped and screeched, her hand flying up to cover her mouth. *Calm down, Wilhelmina, the sound is simply an owl.* The hairs on her neck prickled as though she was stared at from behind. She turned about. Lord Ashbey stood behind her.

He held his thin arms out wide for her. "Come get warm, my lady."

She stepped forward, shivering, and into his embrace. His arms closed about her, barely enough to hug her, and the coldest ice of winter blew up her spine. A tremor shook her limbs.

She pushed against his chest and back from him. "No. No, this is wrong; you are not the correct choice."

A growl came from over her shoulder, and Ashbey dropped his arms. Wilhelmina spun about to face the intruder who had made that noise. The man from the meadow stood at the edge of the woods.

His gray eyes flashed as an animal's flashed at night in the torchlight. The heat of his presence engulfed her body, and the shivering stopped. She glanced back over her shoulder; Ashbey had disappeared.

Gone? W—where did he go?

She turned back to the man in the meadow, and he, too, dissolved into the night. How odd! His warmth remained, radiating about her. Her nipples tightened to hard points, and the smell of anise swam in her lungs. She closed her eyes, and his lips closed on her left nipple, the moisture sticking her shift to the skin.

His teeth pressed and dragged, biting the peak. Pleasurable pain curled like a corkscrew through her body, opening her thighs and wetting her sex in her wine. She jerked, and her eyes fluttered open.

She lay in her bed, legs spread open, nipples poking straight to the ceiling. Her thick feather covers were kicked to the foot of her bed, and no man from the field was biting her flesh.

She frowned and gathered up the blankets, snuggling into them. Closing her eyes again, she smelled anise. The scent clung heavy on her covers. The flesh between her thighs gushed with dampness once more.

Why did he affect her so? Her hands pulled up her nightshift beneath the blankets, and her fingers traced down her belly to the crisp curls of her sex. She squeezed her eyes tightly closed. *You shouldn't touch yourself, Wilhelmina, it isn't proper.* She didn't care. Her fingers parted her folds and slid through the honey. Tingles of heat blew up her body, and her hips arched into the intense pleasure her touch created.

Oh! Oh, my! Her touch firmed on her sex, sliding around the rim of her entrance and back up to the hard nubbin of flesh.

Stars sparked behind her lids, and her leg muscles strained as she pointed her toes.

Indeed, I want you, Lady Wilhelmina. The man from the field's voice flooded her mind but not her ears.

Her fingers worked her flesh as more and more moisture coated her nether lips. She moaned into the darkness, the pleasure entwining her nerves in delight, cutting deep into her belly.

Would you . . . would you allow me to touch you as you are now—but more?

Her middle finger pressed into her opening, and she trembled. . . . "More, yes, more." Her chin wobbled, and she pressed farther into her channel, glorying in the spongy, drenched texture and the delight of being inside herself.

More, indeed. But I cannot offer you softer emotions. . . . His breath . . . oh, my . . . humid, and laced with port, heated her neck. *Slide your fingers in and out of your sopping cunny faster, and pleasure will be yours, Wilhelmina.*

Faster?

Her hand rocked back, pulling her finger out of her, and then slid back in. Oh, my poppies. . . . Her entire body arched, pressing her hand harder against the flesh of her sex. Her lungs locked, and every nerve tingled in erotic sensations.

Her middle finger wiggled and wiggled, her toes curled, and sparks flashed as her body shook. The flesh of her channel grasped hard about her finger and then released it in waves.

She panted for breath as if she had hiked to the top of the lookout on her father's property. Oh! That had been the most blissful pleasure she had ever experienced from touching herself.

Oh! How she wanted him—the man who had been flooding her every thought since this afternoon—to touch her sex in just such a way.

Yes, indeed, Wilhelmina.

Hmmm, but he is not offering himself to you, Wilhelmina. He is only offering to touch you with passion, not give you his heart.

"No ... I want your touch, like you did in the field, and more. I want you forever," she murmured aloud. She wanted to feel the way she had in the field today on a never-ending basis.

Then it cannot be. I would destroy you.

She opened her eyes to the darkness in her room and stared at the ceiling. Did he truly believe he would harm her? The memory of his fingers squeezing her flesh then jerking back, letting her go, came fresh to her mind. Indeed, he did. But why? His size was not what he feared. There was something deeper, something primal he wished her not to see.

Sitting up in bed, she stretched her sated limbs. She needed to know his name, and she had no idea how to find that out.

Wilhelmina stood at the side of the road in Sudhamly and stared through the glass at the ribbons as Marie spoke to the shopkeeper.

Wilhelmina sighed. Ten days had passed since she had lain eyes on the man in the field. Her dreams at night floated with vivid depictions of him. His gray eyes and long, curly, deep chocolate hair. His hands on her hips as he had passionately kissed her.

Though, mainly, his thoughts swooped in on her night visions. The memory of his voice spoke to her. *I am unsuited for you. I will ultimately destroy the desire you have for me if you don't forget about me.*

Yet each morning Wilhelmina awoke fevered, the flesh between her legs throbbing as her hands rested between her thighs.

Her nipples peaked beneath her corset as the vision of him from this morning—her lips quivered in search for his kiss and her body arched in the bliss her fingers had brought—came back to her.

She closed her eyes and chewed the inside of her lip. She'd gone mad. Proper ladies didn't have such thoughts, didn't do such things. Did they?

Marie exited the shop and walked toward her. "Mina, come here." She grasped Wilhelmina's hand and laced her fingers through hers, pulling her slightly to the left. "Look in the shop."

Wilhelmina peered through the paned window, and her eyes widened. A large, finely dressed man gathered up a package and turned toward the door.

Her heart wrapped about her lungs and squeezed all the breath from her body "I—is that him?" Wilhelmina squeezed her friend's fingers and her hand trembled.

"No, it is not him."

Her heart sank just a fraction. "He must be related," she said and stared at her friend, filled with hope. She may finally know the name of the intense man from the field.

"Yes. Yes, indeed, I believe so." Marie's eyes danced, and a smile curved her lips. "There cannot be many men in this vicinity his size. He is coming, Mina."

The gentleman who had walked out of the shop had similar features but was not her gentleman. Loose, fair hair brushed the blue fabric of his coat, and crystal-blue eyes caught her stare.

He inclined his head toward her.

This is it, Wilhelmina. Ask.

Her tongue grew thick in her mouth. *Now, Wilhelmina. Ask him!* "Sir? Pardon me, sir?" Her words rushed together, and her cheeks grew warm.

He stopped still and turned toward them. Her eyes widened as a full smile spread across his face. "How may I help you?" He gestured with his hand toward them.

Oh! "I am Lady Wilhelmina."

"Ah." His eyes danced with mirth. "Lady Wilhelmina, indeed. How may I be of assistance?"

"Well, sir. Who . . . who are you?" She shifted her stance,

and Marie wiggled her fingers in her hold. His gaze slowly trailed to their intertwined hands. She still held Marie's hand like a nervous, fresh-as-grass schoolgirl. She squeezed Marie's hand tighter for added reassurance.

He laughed out loud, and two dimples danced in his cheek. "My, you are not what I would have expected for an English duke's daughter. Devon Ursus at your service, my lady."

Get this done with as soon as possible before he thinks you are without breeding or class. She raised her chin and stared him directly in the eyes. "Sir, do you have brothers?"

He laughed again and stepped toward her. "Do you have an appetite, Lady Wilhelmina, that only one gentleman can sate?"

She sucked in a shocked breath. How dare he! She wanted to turn and walk away but held firm in her stance, unmoving, when propriety said she should turn away when spoken to in such a manner.

Devon grinned, and his entire face lit up. He jested with her.

"Sir, I feel I met a relation of yours, though I never received his name."

His lips flattened into a line. "I do have brothers, Lady Wilhelmina. Three, in fact, and seeing as you have approached me thinking you know one of us, you probably do. Possibly carnally. What did this relation of mine look like?" He closed his eyes and inhaled, sniffing the air. "Anise."

She bit her lip to hold in a confirmation. Indeed, he smelled like anise. How did Devon know that? She held in her desire to sniff the air in return to see if she smelled anise, too.

Kind blue eyes stared at her.

"He had long, dark brown hair, held back in a queue, and rode a black steed," Marie stated from beside them.

Devon's gaze diverted to Marie and then back to Wilhelmina. "When did you meet?"

"We met ten days past, sir." Wilhelmina's hands shook. Torturous. "Please, sir, his name?"

Devon Ursus's fingers scratched his chin, and he glanced back at Marie. "*Blood*-red coat?" His lips quirked, and he winked at Wilhelmina.

"Indeed, sir." Marie's voice held a note of excitement.

He enjoyed toying with them. Wilhelmina frowned at him.

He raised his eyebrows at her as though shocked by her impatience. "Well, that can only be my brother." He turned back to Wilhelmina, and his eyes deepened to a sapphire blue. "The Marquess of Arctos."

Marie sucked an audible breath. "The—the Duke of Tremarctos's heir."

Devon smiled. "Indeed." His gaze never left Wilhelmina, and he dropped his volume to an intimate whisper. "He is nothing to fear, my lady. If you have had a connection to him in any way since meeting him, please consider him."

Wilhelmina nodded. *Consider him.*

"I must be off." Devon Ursus abruptly inclined his head. "Have a good day." He walked away.

Marie wiggled her fingers in Wilhelmina's grip once more. "What kind of connection could he possibly mean?"

Connection . . . Nightly visions is more like. "I—I'm not sure, Marie." It was horrid lying to her friend when she *was* connected to Lord Arctos somehow. Her dreams possessed more than any dream she knew.

They were him.

Him speaking to her. Warning her not to get close to him.

But why?

Why contact her at all if he didn't want a connection to her?

She was perfectly suitable, and from what she'd witnessed of him both in the field and in her dreams, he was intense but by no means mad. He simply needed a bright spot in his life. She intended to be that. . . .

His peace and laughter.

3

Orin trotted down the lane astride Beelzebub, his black draft horse. The secluded cliffs were well worth the rutted road to get there.

He had journeyed to his favorite place daily since meeting that blessed girl.

He growled deep in his chest, and Beelzebub tossed his head, jerking the reins in Orin's grip. He could not shake her. Her fiery red hair and sparkling green eyes pulled at his gut and at his groin.

He groaned as his prick swelled. The earthy, musky smell of her arousal, with hints of rose . . . the sounds of her wetness as she fingered herself in her dreams . . . The devil.

No wonder his words held no sway in convincing her to leave him be. He had no resolve in staying from her hidden mind.

He had used all his will to pull himself from her body in the field. Her friend would have been appalled if he had lost control and diddled her right there. He would have been shot as an animal, or, worse, she would have been forced by her family to wed him. He inhaled a tight breath.

His wife . . . his life mate.

His lips turned up into a smile. Indeed.

No, Orin! He shook his head. *You will never subject a human woman to your appetites.* His gut twisted. She was too innocent, too precious. His teeth clenched. His mind was fully engaged in the logic, but his instincts wanted her. To hell with honor.

He rounded a bend in the road, and the smell of earth and roses tightened his chest.

She was near. Someplace in the woods.

He yanked Beelzebub to a stop and closed his eyes. *Go home. You are on my land. You are not welcome here.*

His eyes remained closed, and her heart beat through him. Her pulse quickened, realizing he was close. Arousal, thick and desperate, wet his tongue. He wanted to be inside her, fucking her hard as he bit and tasted her flesh, her virgin's blood.

He growled and hissed. His cock pushed against the soft leather of his breeches and the hard, cold saddle beneath him. *Turn around, Orin. Go in the opposite direction. You know this will only end up bad for her.*

He opened his eyes and pulled on the left rein to spin his mount. She stood in the road behind him, mud six inches up her lace hem, her hair windblown and her cheeks flushed from the wind, sun, or him—he was not sure. The sight of her before him, *alone,* licked at his soul. Pure angelic innocence.

He clenched his teeth, trying to hold in the monstrous animal clawing beneath his flesh, wanting to break out and be free to destroy her, feast on her until only bad resided.

She stepped toward him. *Move, Orin. Spin Beelzebub about and leave her.* His hands clenched the reins, but he couldn't pull them. *Stay calm.* He inhaled deep. *Mistake. . . .*

Her essence, her thick cream flowed from her sex and down his throat. The animal within feasted, wanting more than the minuscule bit of her floating on the breeze.

Her green eyes stared up at him as she stood within his reach but not close enough. He wanted her body crushed to his as he pleasured her and made her scream before . . .

No, Orin.

"Lord Arctos, I—I need to speak. You see, I feel I have gone mad with thoughts of you. Dreams of you speaking to me." She swallowed, and his gaze fixed on the column of flesh and muscles as she licked her lips and swallowed again.

"Go home, Wilhelmina. Now. I will not warn you again. I am not for you."

Her brows pulled together. "How do you know what is for me? I don't know you. You don't know me. I wish only to know you." She paused, and her lips turned into a frown. "I want to see you smile."

Orin's mouth set in a frown, and Beelzebub shifted his stance, stomping his foot. Smile?

He sighed. "The smile from your face will fade if you get to know me. I would rather know that you desired me than have you taste desire and have that ravenous worm eat you from the inside out."

"In my dream, you asked me if you could touch me, but you offered nothing more. I—I wish to feel your touch, to know where the sensation you create in me leads." She fidgeted with her hands. "Even if *this* is all it can be."

Orin's heart pounded in his ears, and his vision grew hazy. . . . Those words, he had not expected. He blinked his eyes to clear them and stared her hard in the eyes. "Are you positive? If I touch you again, I will not stop until I have spent my seed in you. . . . I will not offer you more."

His chest locked on the idea of never seeing her again, of not seeping into her dreams at night. *Stop, Orin!*

"Yes . . . yes, I know what I am saying."

"Do you know what I am? Do you know what seed is?"

"No, on both counts, Lord Arctos. I want to learn all. I want to know all of you."

He closed his eyes. *Orin, you can't do this. She is an English duke's daughter. If you do, you will break her heart and soul.*

"No." He swallowed the lump in his throat and then opened his eyes to behold an angel's stricken face.

"No," she breathed, barely audible. "Why?"

Why? He closed his eyes. *Because if I take you, I may not be able to stop. I may need you again and again.* The heat of her hand pressed to his knee, and he tensed. All the cells of his being jumped to life with fire, desire, and need he could not deny.

He slid a shaking hand down his thigh and covered her hand. Her palm flattened against his flesh. The devil . . . His large cudgel dwarfed her wee fingers. He would smash her.

He opened his eyes, and the haze of his lust fogged all but her standing next to him. An angel looking up at the devil. He swallowed, bit his lower lip, and squeezed her hand.

Her muscles tensed, and her hand pulled and tugged against the pressure of his grip.

His eyes narrowed. "Not so sure, Lady Wilhelmina? I do not know what gentle or tender is."

"No. I—I want you."

His hand released hers, and he grasped her round chin. As he turned her head up as far as her neck would allow, the flesh of her neck strained, but she didn't resist. Her flesh at her pulse point fluttered like a hummingbird's wing, and he released her chin.

Swinging his leg over the pummel of his saddle, he slid down to stand before her on the ground. Her head came to just below his chest. She tipped up her chin to stare him in the eyes.

A pink tongue slid out and traced her lips, leaving a slight sheen on the puckered surface. He focused on the delectable glimmering flesh and licked his lips. Her sweet taste from the kiss in the field flooded his mouth in anticipation of tasting her once again.

Her hand rose, and the dewed flesh of her palm touched his cheek. Fingers flexed, softly grazing the stubble of his beard, her hand then cupped his harsh features.

He closed his eyes and absorbed the gentle caress, which was filled with compassion and desire, everything he ever wanted or needed but didn't dare let himself have.

"Indeed, Lord Arctos, touch me, kiss me. Do whatever you wish."

His vision hazed, and his tongue grew thick. He absorbed every bit of her. The fire in her red hair pinned in curls atop her head. His gaze slid lower. Her lips quivered and parted against his eyes' caress. Her pulse at the base of her throat beat wildly, and the smell of her . . .

He growled, a sound of pure animal lust deep in his belly, as his skin ignited with need to complete the act, to take the innocence she offered and consume them both.

He stepped forward. She stepped back. In unison they crossed the lane until he pressed her firm against a large oak tree on the side of the road and dropped to his knees. The cold, hard earth registered for an instant before he grabbed her skirts and pulled them up. She gasped.

The smell of her sweet cunny coaxed his desires from deep within.

His cock strained, and he could taste her earthy scent on his tongue. He gathered the cotton petticoat and the muslin of her skirt in his hand. "Hold up your skirts, Wilhelmina."

Her hand wrapped about his and the fabric. The warmth in the small caress tore at his hold on the fiend, deep in his soul, that wanted to possess her. Twisting his wrist, he slipped from the grasp. Her hands trembled as she held her skirts up to her belly, exposing smooth, freckled skin stretched across nicely padded bones. He drank in the soothing milk of her. She delighted him.

Needing to feel the heat of her pulse under his bare touch, he unbuttoned his gloves and tore them off. His hands grasped her hips as he had in the field on the day they met.

She moaned and arched her hips toward him in a primal invitation for more.

An invitation he could not refuse.

His right hand slid, tracing a line of freckles to her curls, and then rotated and slid between her legs to cup her sex. He parted the folds with his middle finger and slid into drenched flesh. The devil . . .

She clamped her legs together about his hand.

"Change your mind, Wilhelmina?" He raised his eyebrows at her.

"N—no." Her lips parted on a sigh of pleasure.

"Spread your legs."

Her legs jumped and then slowly slid apart. The heat of her core opened on his hand, and his heart flipped in his chest. He wished his hand was the curl of his tongue as he tasted her thick oil. He would bring her to a delightful end before ruining the act as his beast unleashed and spent his seed. Her legs quivered on both sides of him, and wetness spilled from her hole onto his hand.

"Mmmm." He wiggled his finger in the folds, and she moaned with him. "You do want me."

"Yes," she breathed in a whisper.

"Then you shall have me."

He glided his finger up into her balmy channel. *So tight.* His eyes closed, and he savored the spongy, slick walls giving way to his probe. She would bleed, no doubt. His pulse thundered as he imagined the tight ring of her pussy popping over the small apple-sized head of his cock as he stilled and then thrust into her slickness. Soon his demons would claim her. He swallowed hard. He couldn't allow himself to slip into the carnal passions he possessed. Not with her.

His lips came down on the silky, rose-scented flesh of her belly, and he kissed and nipped as his finger, slick with dew, slid out and thrust back in.

She squirmed and moaned, spreading her legs farther and farther apart for him, her desire for him displayed in her actions and in every sound.

His kiss hardened and slid lower on her belly with each caress. His mouth watered. The devil, he wanted to taste her. The additional saliva on his tongue drizzled a line to the springy curls of her sex.

His finger slid out of her cunny, spilling her essence onto his tongue as he pushed into her folds. He growled. Tart, earthy sweetness primed his tongue. My angel: she tasted as she smelled.

Sweat tickled the hairs of his neck, and his eyes hazed, his bear checking his will. He licked and laved her slit and button with increased adoration.

Her hips arched into his mouth with each pass of his tongue. "Mmmm," he hummed, vibrating her pussy lips. Her free hand snaked into his hair and clutched for support. With her legs shaking, her knees gave.

His free hand reached up and cupped her bottom, her full weight now supported by him. He added another finger and thrust into her weeping cunt, spreading her channel wide.

She cried out, the slick walls grabbing in waves at his fingers. Her cunny juiced, squirting a beautiful spend on his hand and tongue. He licked her Venus button again, and her hips continued to rock as her muscles spasmed.

He leaned back slightly and slipped his fingers from her dripping flesh. So wet. Thoroughly aroused, she would have no problem accepting his size or his rough bucks into her.

His hand undid the buttons to his flap, and he pulled free his stone-hard cock. He gripped the shaft in his hand, released her bottom, and stood.

Her eyes slit open; the pupils engulfed most of the brilliant green. A pleasured grin spread across her face, and his skin pebbled from the erotic energy that simple smile pulled forth. His angel had tasted him and wanted more.

Her lips parted, and her tongue traced the surface. He leaned in and kissed her. His tongue speared into her mouth, tasting sweetness mixed with tea and her musky cunt, still lingering on his tongue. He nipped and then bit her lower lip, and she sighed, giving herself to him completely.

Why she did so, when he would only hurt her, he couldn't comprehend.

His hand wrapped about her waist, and he lifted, pinning her between his massive body and the tree. Her thighs spread wide about his hips. His tongue traced her lips again, and the head of his cock brushed the lips of her cunt, drenched in her steaming oils.

She moaned and tossed her head back against the tree trunk. His mouth traveled from her lips to her neck, his tongue feasting on the column of flesh as he found the strong flutter beneath the flesh. He circled the beating point with his tongue, and his vision hazed again. He needed to be inside her, the beat of her heart pounding about his cock as she wiggled and moaned. Yes, indeed, he needed to fuck this sweet, sweet woman, tasting all she offered him.

She trembled with need in his arms. He would join their bodies as one.

He stroked his cock along her nether lips, coating the length with her juice. Bending his knees slightly, the tip of his prick found her pussy opening and nestled firmly into the hole.

With his pulse thundering in his ears, the slits on his knuckles crested open. His teeth pointed, and his jacket stretched to the point of fraying as his back broadened.

He dragged his tongue along her neck and flexed his hips. The tapered head widened her farther as he slid into her heated core.

She moaned and whimpered, and her hands grabbed at the fabric of his coat. His tongue flicked her pulse, and he bit—not enough to puncture but enough pain to distract—as he harshly thrust into her welcoming body until their curls meshed as one.

She screamed, and her entire body locked tight. He held still in her tight, gloved warmth, licking and licking her neck and the indentations he had left on her skin, until her body relaxed.

"L—Lord Arctos," she breathed, and he pulled his head from the crook of her shoulder to look in her eyes.

Brilliant, passion-filled green shone back.

A smile curved up one half of his lips, and he rubbed his pubis into her curls.

"Oh, my." She closed her eyes and groaned, her cunt gushing oil down his cock.

"Indeed, Wilhelmina, you are mine." His lips came down on her swollen ones, and she quivered beneath him.

He pulled out and bucked back into her. His body expanded, the bear in him set free to feast on his mate. He bit and squeezed her flesh, unable to get close enough, to hear enough of her pleasure.

She moaned, whimpered, and screamed.

A wave of bliss erupted from her as her cunny clamped hard to his length. "The devil!" His balls contracted and twisted, knocking him to his knees with euphoric contractions as he spilled his seed into her womb.

He pumped and pumped into her, the tingling sensation in his balls subsiding. He lay panting on his knees, her legs wrapped about his waist, and shook.

He held her fast to him and inhaled her rose scent. He wanted her . . . again and again . . . now and forever!

No, Orin! No more. You know what will happen. He inhaled deep and jerked as he reined in his desires.

He opened his eyes. She lightly slumbered in his embrace, eyes closed and body limp.

Thank the devil she did not see him—eyes round, shoulders broadened, and three-inch claws extended from his knuckles. She would fear him.

As she should, Orin. You are a beast. A demon who has no idea who fathered him. She deserves so much more.

His eyes focused back on the divine woman in his arms, and his heart sank.

She had swollen and slit lips, the flesh of her neck red, scratched, and bitten. *The devil.* Those marks would no doubt bruise. His stomach flipped, and he closed his eyes. Gentlness.... There was nonesuch with him. *You fool.*

No, he could never allow this to happen again. He swallowed hard and slid his cock from the warm cavern of her body.

She whimpered, and he lifted her. Placing her gently on the grass, he pushed her knees wide to inspect her cunt and give her the required gift for allowing him to mount her.

The lips pouted open, his seed, mixed with raw blood, lay ready to slip from her womb. He leaned in and tasted the buttered flesh.

His frame shook with each lick, the desire to have her for his only rising in his veins.

No!

He would not claim her. His throat closed, and he swallowed hard. He would give her the gift as required, for giving innocence to a boar, and then send her back to her world.

Her Venus button grew hard, and his tongue swirled and then traveled back down the wet flesh and thrust into her cunt.

Her hips arched off the grass and to him. He sucked and licked his tart, stingy seed mixed with the coppery taste of virgin's blood and musky cunny.

Blood flooded his cock, hardening his flesh. He groaned, the need to start the ritual Orsse his only desire. His sac swelled with the potent opening juices. He wished to make her his forever.

Orin, no. Bring her the gift and leave. Leave while you can.

He inhaled a deep breath, smelling nothing but her tangy cunt. Growling, he shook his head.

To the devil and back again, Orin. One more time.

He couldn't stay . . . but she deserved this served pleasure, for letting him mount her so violently.

His tongue flicked the bud and then tickled the opening of her pussy. Her hips arched higher as he stroked her, reaching for the gift, wanting the release more than anything.

His lips closed on her peaked flesh, and he sucked. Her legs clamped his head, and she shattered, screaming. Her body trembled violently in passion as oil spurted from her womb.

Orin closed his eyes, his heart in the pit of his stomach. He frowned and leaned back to observe her.

She lazily smiled at him and then drifted to sleep. He pulled his arms out of the sleeves of his red riding jacket and laid the garment, wrapped in his warmth, upon her slumbering body.

Leaning in, he kissed her forehead. "Good-bye, my angel." His feet stayed rooted to the earth. *Move, Orin. NOW! Before she awakes, before she sees you as the monster you are.*

He couldn't move. She should be delivered home, at least. He slid one arm under her legs and the other behind her shoulders and lifted her.

A deep frown, the expression etched on his face from years of practice, returned to his face. He wanted to bathe her, to rub her limbs and make sure she stayed well.

His chest tightened, and he swallowed hard, choking down years of longing and hurt. He was the devil's jest. He would never be different, and gently caring for the one he cherished . . . A scream of pain ripped from his throat, and he crushed her slumbering body to him. That could never be.

4

Wilhelmina awoke to the sound of horse hooves shaking the earth as they faded into the distance. She shot up. She lay alone on the freshly cut lawn of her father's back cricket court.

"*No!*" Her voice cracked. "No! No!" Tears ran down her face, and she trembled. He hadn't woken her.

Indeed, Wilhelmina. You are mine.

He had said those words but then left without another word, his first statement to her holding true. "I will not offer you more."

Would he hold true to those words? Would he stay from her mind at night? She didn't want to know. The desire to go to his estate and force him to speak to her sped her heart and choked off her tears. She needed him to verbalize why.

As she pushed herself up onto her knees, the muscles in her body throbbed and ached. The flesh between her thighs tingled, and pain shot through to her womb. My . . . oh, my. . . . She closed her eyes and bit her lip.

She needed to soak in a bath for a good hour before trying to decide what to do. Her gaze focused on the trees bordering the lawn.

He had left her.

Wilhelmina's lower lip quivered. She had thought so much more of him. She pulled his thick jacket around her shoulders; the garment could have wrapped about her twice or more.

Her hands had fisted in this same fabric as his large frame had pressed her firmly to the tree behind her and he had joined their bodies in bliss and pain.

She inhaled, and the scent of anise wrapped her in a cocoon of warmth and pleasure, grabbing and massaging her skin. She trembled. He had made sure she remained well. His presence infused his coat, which was oddly strange—her brows drew together—and delightful. A part of him, she knew not, had remained in his coat and comforted her.

Deep in her mind, her soul saw the peculiar truth.

Standing, her body shook and ached as she walked toward the back servant's entrance to her father's home. She hoped no one saw her enter.

Wilhelmina's heart fluttered, thinking of the marks on her body. Her fingers ran along the thick velvet choker she adorned for the dinner party and ball at Marie's. The reddened patch on her neck beneath the velvet was a reminder of her joining with Lord Arctos.

Her father stood next to her in the line of guests waiting to be announced into the ballroom of Marquess of Quinten's home. She straightened her shoulders and pushed to her lips her always present smile.

She didn't feel like smiling tonight. How could she smile when she wanted more than anything to be back in the woods pressed up against a tree as Lord Arctos diddled her? Would she truly never see him again? His presence in his coat had faded when she'd entered her house. Coldness had seeped in to her gut.

"Mina. Lord Coltensley." Marie's eyes lit with excitement as she saw them.

Wilhelmina's smile broadened in true pleasure; she always adored spending time with Marie, and she had so much to tell her, even if the experience remained hard to tell.

"Marie." She held out her hands, and Marie grasped them and winked.

"Come, Mina, I have a surprise for you."

Wilhelmina's brows drew together as Marie led her farther into the ballroom.

Marie leaned in, and her breath warmed Wilhelmina's ear. "I sent an invite to the duke's home for the ball tonight."

Wilhelmina's heart pounded in her throat. She had what? Her gaze darted through the crowded ballroom. He was here.

"Your marquess did not come. The fair-haired brother we saw in Sudhamly did."

"Oh." Wilhelmina's heart sank. Would she ever see Lord Arctos again? Mooncalf. Only half a day passed and her insides were tangled in a bumbelbroth, wondering.

"Are you not pleased, Mina?" Marie stopped and turned toward her.

"Oh, indeed, Marie. I only wish *he* came."

"I understand, Mina. But you can now converse with his brother and find out more." Marie's bows pulled together. "What happened to your lip, Mina?"

Wilhelmina's tongue slid out and traced the split skin on her lower lip. She shook her head. "I—I . . ." Marie's eyes softened. Wilhelmina couldn't lie to her. "I saw him, Marie. He kissed me again. Oh, Marie." She glanced around to see if anyone stood close enough to hear them and then stepped as close as possible to her. "He is so, so . . ." She could not think of one word to describe him. He was sad yet full of life; he possessed a strength she should be frightened of; but she simply craved more. "He is just delightful."

"What did you tell your father about your puffy lip?" Marie's hand started to raise to touch Wilhelmina's lip, but she fisted her fingers and then placed her palm flat on her chest.

Wilhelmina cringed. "I told him I ran into a tree branch while out walking."

"Ouch."

"I don't think he believed my story entirely."

Tingles raced up Wilhelmina's back, and she glanced behind her. The large male from the street stood staring at her from the doorway. His lips curved into a wicked smile, and he prowled forward. Every eye in the room focused on this man, who had never graced this ballroom or any other they had attended before. How could a duke live in Sudhamly and never socialize with his peers?

"Good evening." He bowed to them. "Thank you for the kind invitation. Unfortunately the rest of my family was previously occupied this night."

"Sir, Devon Ursus." Marie smiled at him.

"Quite so, my ladies."

Marie glanced around him. "Please excuse me. My father calls."

They both watched as Marie exited through the doors, so obviously leaving them alone.

Devon's blue eyes gazed at Wilhelmina. "Well, well, you smell of nothing but Orin." He inhaled again, and his eyes flashed with wickedness.

"Pardon me, sir?"

"And look at you. He has had you." Devon grinned. "I knew one day he would let go of his demons. From the look and smell of you, he has."

Wilhelmina's eyes widened, and heat raced through her body in a fevered blush. "Pardon me, sir? Who—who is Orin?"

He didn't have to answer. Deep down that name shone like the sun to her . . . Lord Arctos. The skin of her arms puckered.

He smiled a full-toothed grin. "Well, Lady Wilhelmina." His tone chided. "Do you want him?"

She bit her lip. Did she tell this man, this stranger, her innermost desires for his brother? Telling Devon seemed a social blunder.

"No need to verbalize your desire, my lady. Your expression and energy say all I need to know."

"Devon, where is he? He said he would never . . . never . . ." Tears welled in her eyes, and a sorrow so deeply rooted in her soul threatened to burst forth.

Devon's hand touched her shoulder. "He has no choice in this matter, Wilhelmina. We are ruled by our instincts. He can try to fight his attraction to you, and he may succeed. But eventually he will find a mate and settle down. He is the next duke, after all."

"He may succeed?" She breathed and closed her eyes.

"Has connection started?"

Her eyes shot open. "Um, I felt tied to him mentally and emotionally after the kiss for days. But since . . . since . . ."

Devon grinned at her discomfort.

The rogue. She wouldn't say "joining" or "diddle." "Since *then*, nothing."

"He is using his influence on you and possibly on himself." Devon frowned and then glanced over his shoulder. "Can you leave one of these events with ease?"

"Sometimes, yes. Why do you ask, sir?"

"I wish to try pushing him with you. If we could leave, would you be willing?"

Wilhelmina bit her lip. Was she willing? Quite so. Anything to see Orin again.

"Yes, sir. I will feign a headache and then send the carriage back for my father."

"Excellent! I will follow in our carriage and meet you on the main road."

"Very well. Half past eight, then?"

"Indeed."

Orin paced in the dining hall, the black marble floor reflecting his somber mood with each step. His mind block on her was not working. His emotions wrapped him in a bind he must break.

He wanted her, but her bruised neck and puffed lips . . . No, not what he wished for every time they joined. He ground his teeth together. *Three days . . . give it three days, Orin, and this need to claim her will pass.* His sac grew swollen as an image of her sweet, pouting cunt lay displayed for him to claim. His fist connected with the tabletop as he passed it, circling the dining hall for the fiftieth time.

He would stay locked in this house until this need passed.

He inhaled, and the strong aroma of earth and rose locked his lungs. Wilhelmina resided in this house.

He howled and sniffed the air again. Indeed, she was here.

"Wilhelmina!"

The windowpanes rattled with the force of his growl.

He ran for the front door, not thinking, not rationalizing his actions, as his Ursus freed himself. He turned the corner, and Devon stood in the middle of the hall, grinning.

Devon's eyes danced and shifted to the Ursus round. "Out for a joyous evening, brother?"

Orin stopped in his tracks and studied Devon. "What are you about, Devon?"

"Simply put, brother, I wondered if she'd broken the beast out of his cage." Devon's wickedness showed straight to his soul. "It seems she has."

"Where is she, Devon?" His heart pounded in his chest, and his lungs couldn't take in enough air. His mind spun as his instincts to possess her pushed him. *No, Orin. You will only hurt her.*

"*You* tell *me*, brother. Has she broken you?"

Orin growled and leaped, toppling Devon to the floor beneath him. His hand clutched Devon's throat, crushing his cravat. He straddled Devon's chest, pinning him.

Devon smiled up at him and then laughed, the act jostling Orin's body with each mocking note.

Orin jerked his hold on Devon's neck, releasing his grip, and then stood. "Where is she, Devon? I mean to send her home."

"Is that what you wish, Orin? To send away the one woman who has touched you in a way you need to be touched? You have capped off your instincts since marking. Why?"

"I cannot have her, Devon. She is a duke's daughter a human duke's daughter. I will destroy her."

"Do you not think leaving her after showing her who you are will harm her? She will long for a touch like yours forever, Orin."

"No, she won't. She deserves a gentle caress, not the beast who can't control clawing at her."

"You are only a beast in your mind, Orin. Ponder that thought. You are Ursus. You should be proud. Look how many of us through the years have successfully mated with humans. Look what our powers have done for our kind and humankind."

Orin blew out a breath through his nose, and then there she was, standing in the entranceway to the house, staring down the hall at him and Devon . . . his angel.

Orin's eyes widened, and he pointed at her from down the hall. "Out! Out of this house now!"

Orin shook, every fiber of his being holding his devil back. His mind ruled this situation. He could hold the monster back. Indeed, he could.

The tart scent of her cunny oils surrounded him, and his

eyes shifted round, his vision hazing. "No!" He spun about and ran for the dining hall, his heart sinking to the soles of his shoes. "Get her out, Devon. She cannot see me like this."

Tears sprang to Wilhelmina's eyes. He didn't want her here. She turned around and grabbed the door handle, yanking open the enormous door. The wind blew in large gusts beyond. A storm was coming, and not just one involving rain—tears and gut-twisting pain would be involved. She inhaled a choppy breath, holding back the deluge that would occur as soon as she was alone. Devon stepped up beside her.

"Sorry, sweet one." His hand brushed a lock of hair behind her ear. "He is in love with you and fears his instincts and his force."

"I—it holds no consequence. He does not wish to have me. I cannot do anything about that. I—I wish to go home."

"Indeed. The carriage is still here."

5

Round, silver eyes floated in a sea of ebony, rippling in the wind.

The cool, soft caress of the breeze pebbled her skin. Claws flashed in the moonlight, and she screamed. With her heart in her throat, she stood frozen.

A man, larger than any she'd seen before, emerged out of the mists. His eyes flashed as he drew closer. He growled the same deep growl Lord Arctos had as he'd pleasured her with his hands and tongue.

Her knees shook with fear, cold, and some erotic, pleasurable sensation she newly tasted. Her breasts tingled, and the nipples hardened to peaks.

The closer he prowled to her, the more the air shifted. The coldness of the misty night dissipated, wrapping her in soft, silky warmth. The atmosphere crackled with energy, running along her skin and tickling her sex. Her lungs tightened, and she panted for air, but didn't dare move.

The man did not say a word. He circled and circled her, out of her reach and concealed in the mists so she could not see his face. She wanted to move, to take a step forward and touch him, but traversing the distance between them was not hers to do.

This man's presence was Lord Arctos yet different. This man possessed great power; he was a man whose essence was purely natural, carnal, untamed. No restraint captured this man, but he held all control.

She sucked in a broken breath as deep-seated desire raced across her skin in goose pins. She wanted to be as natural as this man who stalked her, yet she couldn't move. A natural force within her held her absolutely still.

Her arms trembled, and she closed her eyes to the sight of him. She bit her lip, and his breath, warm and laced with anise and port, wafted to her nose.

Her eyes shot open to blackness. Where was he? His teeth grazed her neck and bit. My poppies! Her knees buckled, but she still couldn't move. She stood limp yet erect and unmoving. Nothing held her but the night.

His lips kissed and suckled the flesh and continued to bite. A growl of deep pleasure erupted from him, and her body shook, uninhibited. The warm, silky fingers of the dark traveled her skin and pressed her legs wide.

A tangy, earthy smell reached her nose, and the man who was behind her, yet not there, moaned. She twisted her neck to the side to see if he truly stood by her.

She shivered and swallowed convulsively. A flash of pure-white claws caught her gaze from the corner of her eye. She jumped, and dew sprang across her skin. The press of three sharp points traced her collarbone with the sound of tearing cotton. She screamed in fear, not pain.

"Shhh." The growl-like noise soothed her skittered nerves, and her entire body relaxed.

Her nightshift slid from her body, leaving only the air to

warm her fevered flesh. A blazing touch traced the crease of her bottom and up her hip to the small of her back; then it dipped into the crack of her bottom.

The caress was so intimate she quivered deep to her bones. The touch left her with a pained growl. She spun about to see the large man's eyes shift back to human. The eyes of Lord Arctos. She sucked in her breath and raised her hand in an attempt to touch him.

"Wilhelmina." The wind breathed her name in a whisper of longing, and she started awake. Lying in her bed, she stared at the ceiling; the gold and cream brushstrokes of sweet cherubs and clouds stared back at her.

He thought he was a beast, a monster, when—to her—he possessed all she wanted: a man who loved with all his being, no matter what that being was.

Orin yawned. He had not slept the night before. His mind fought his instincts, and he nowhere near won. He languidly strolled into the dining hall to find Devon, Martin, and Martin's life mate, Jane, settled at the table having morning repast.

Devon looked up at him with a devious grin, and Orin stopped still.

"Good morning," Jane said while pouring more tea into her cup.

He grunted his usual morning greeting back at them all and continued to his seat.

The footman brought him his coffee, and he sat, inhaling the strong scent. The devil—he needed this.

"We all wish to help you, Orin." Martin stared at him from down the table.

"Pardon?" Help him? There was no help for what happened to him. Besides, he didn't want or need their help.

"Indeed." Devon's eyes softened. "Orin, I saw how she affected you. I also saw the marks on her. What do you fear, Orin?"

Orin's eyes widened, and he sat, unable to move. What did he fear? He feared he would eat her alive from the inside out or the outside in. He frowned.

"Orin, it is all right. We are your family. We wish only to help you. From what Devon told us, you need our assistance." Martin stood, pushed his chair in, and then walked around the table and pulled out the chair across from him.

"What did Devon tell you?" Orin sat, shocked. His brothers wanted to help him. The family freak. The one boar who didn't know which father sired him. The one boar who freakishly, as a child, had influenced all of them into doing as he wished, even though he had never intended to.

He shook his head and stared at Martin—Martin, who looked so much like the duke. And Devon—Devon possessed their mother's hair, but the rest was fully the duke's, even his personality.

Orin possessed their mother's eyes, but all else remained their grandfather's features, meaning either the duke or his brother could have sired him, and with the scandal that had ensued, there was no way to know.

He inhaled a deep breath and sighed.

"Orin." Jane's soft voice came from down the table. "Do you want Lady Wilhelmina, Orin? She certainly is suitable in every way. You will be a duke. She is a duke's daughter, though English and human. I could not see a better match for you, bloodwise."

"I . . ." He stopped his thoughts from admitting his desire. No, he couldn't have her. His mind would not allow him to hurt her again. "There is no possible way, Jane."

"Why?"

"I refuse to subject a human to me."

"Pardon?" Martin's eyebrows rose.

He didn't want to have this discussion, but it remained obvious he had no choice. "I—I am rough. Too rough when I mount. Never have I been able to control my carnal passion. God—Devon saw her! She was attacked. Bruised, scratched, bitten." He swallowed hard and forced himself to go on. "She is an angel and deserves much more than a monster who could seriously injure her." Orin stared down into the thick black liquid in his cup as if coffee might have a solution to more than just tiredness.

No one spoke, and Orin looked up to see all eyes staring at him. The devil. He frowned harder.

"You love her." Jane's lips curved up.

"Does it matter, Jane? I think not. A worm loves an apple, but he eats the soft center from the inside out."

"Yes, *love* does matter, Orin. You would never intentionally injure her. You would go out of your way to make sure she was brought no harm."

Orin's teeth smashed together, and he growled. "You don't understand. I am *not* like the rest of you. I—I have seen my brothers mount women many times. Martin, you have seen me only once, and what did you see?"

Martin inhaled a deep breath. "Indeed, Orin, you are more primal, but being so doesn't have to be a bad thing. Did Wilhelmina complain, Orin? Does she want you still, Orin? Those are the questions you need answered if you truly want her. If she does want you, then you will make it work."

"No! I refuse to wake up each morning to a woman I bruised. If I choose a life mate, she must be Ursus."

Devon stared at him. "We have no choice in our life mate, Orin. Or, rather, we have only the slightest choice. If you walk away from this and the urgency passes, you will think of this woman for the rest of your life." Devon shifted in his chair and reached inside his jacket, removing a lock of fair hair tied with a ribbon. They all stared at the keepsake. Devon rubbed the lock between his thumb and forefinger, never taking his eyes from the curls of hair. "I have loved this girl since before marking."

Orin stared at Devon. Devon's eyes shone with years of longing for a woman no one in the family knew. The devil. Orin's eyes widened. "Devon, who—whose hair is that?"

Devon sighed and tucked the memories back in his pocket and looked up, the sadness effectively removed from his demeanor. "It matters not, Orin. What does matter is if you try to cage your beast, you will only lose. If not immediately, then down the road you will regret denying yourself tenfold."

"Orin," Martin said calmly. Orin turned his gaze to Martin. "Would the formal Orsse ritual help you?"

The formal Orsse ritual involved his chosen mate futtering him only after he had fought to get to her.

"How, Martin?"

"Well, if you feel you are too rough, if you released your aggression to obtain her, you may not be as raw when you join with her."

"The formal ritual does me no good, Martin. The ceremony would go well, but what about the rest of our lives?" He closed his eyes. "I can't do that to her."

Jane's small hand slid across Orin's. "Orin, your roughness may be because you have repressed your needs for so long. You may find that once you satisfy your desires on the basis they require, you are able to control them more." Jane glanced up at Martin.

"Yes, indeed, that is true, Orin. I have much more control over my instincts since I have Jane."

Devon snorted.

Martin and Jane both speared him with nasty glares.

"Sorry. I don't believe you can ever control the beast of desire. I sate mine quite regularly, and I am still obsessive and raw when I futter. Truth be told, Orin, I don't think you are as violent as you believe. From looking at Lady Wilhelmina, she simply looked well and thoroughly ravished. Not violently beaten and attacked as you have in your mind."

Was that true? Could his idea of what she looked like be all in his head? His brows pinched, and his frown deepened.

"You may have a point, Devon," Martin said from across the table.

"Well, I hope so . . . I am an Ursus after all and just as carnal as the rest of you."

Orin turned to Jane. "Jane." He glanced at Martin. "Jane, do you ever have bite marks or bruises on you from Martin?"

"Orin," Martin growled in warning.

"I—it is important, Martin. I need to answer him." Jane stared Martin in the eyes.

They communicated through thoughts again. Orin rolled his eyes, but he secretly envied them.

"Very well, but I am warning you if she is at all uncomfortable with this, Orin, Jane does not need to answer you."

They both turned back to Jane.

"Indeed, Orin, I always have marks. I am excited when I see them. They are a reminder of his passion for me and of what we did. . . ." Jane blushed a deep red, setting off her pale green eyes and fair hair.

"I will ponder all you have said." Orin pushed back from the table abruptly, having not eaten anything.

6

Orin stood outside the Duke of Coltensley's home. The rain came down in an icy spit, slicking off his greatcoat and hat. A glow radiated from the windows, but no heat radiated to warm him.

She could, in all truth, turn him away. He had never been civil to her in any sense of the word. His heart lay in the pit of his stomach as he stood on her back steps looking in on women and men drinking tea and eating lemon cakes. A tea party.

He couldn't have chosen a worse time to come raging out of his hell in hopes an angel could save him.

He concentrated hard on her beautiful smile and red hair as she conversed with her guests. *Turn to the windows, Wilhelmina. See me. See me standing here needing you with all my twisted soul.*

Her head turned, and she stared out the window. Her eyes widened, and her chest rose and fell quicker and quicker.

Indeed, I am here for you. Excuse yourself and come to me.

She blinked ever so slowly; then she blinked again. Her brows drew together, and she turned back to the conversation about her.

Orin closed his eyes. The devil. Would she come? Or would she make him wait here in the rain?

Waiting held no consequence. He was numb and would wait a moonfall or longer for her to breathe life back into him and fill his heart with the warming innocence she possessed. He needed a reprieve from his self-inflicted torture.

He opened his eyes, and she was gone. He spun about, the rain swinging from his coat and hat in a circular spray. Nowhere; she had disappeared.

He sighed and closed his eyes again. *Come to me, Wilhelmina. Come to me now.*

He stared off into the distant forest where they'd met. His skin tingled with lust and desire, with the need to make her his for a lifetime.

"Ahem."

Orin's gaze shot in the direction of the voice. A well-dressed butler stood in the rain holding an umbrella above his head.

"Lord Arctos, Lady Wilhelmina wishes me to inform you, if you wish to see her, then you must gain an appointment to speak with her father first."

Orin stood, unable to move. She wished him to speak to her father . . . and say what? *Good evening, Lord Duke, I have ravished your daughter, and I wish to make my actions honorable and complete Orsse with her.* Coltensley's reputation was a vicious loon. He would laugh in his face.

Orin glanced back to see the butler still standing in the rain waiting for a reply. "Do you wish to speak with Lord Coltensley, Lord Arctos?"

Orin sighed and clenched his teeth together. This was ridiculous! Did she mean to run him off? If so, why didn't she just say, *Withdraw your pursuit of me,* or ignore him altogether?

"Indeed, I will speak to the duck. I mean, duke." Orin closed his eyes. Bumbelbroth. She had tangled his stomach and whit into an unyielding labyrinth of knots.

The butler turned back toward where he'd come, and Orin followed, close on his heels.

He opened the door. Orin slouched beneath the door opening and stepped into the back entrance to the main hall.

The smell of Wilhelmina overwhelmed him. The main hall at the front of the house held two staircases that twisted in an arch to the next floor. Paintings of cheery flowers and fruit covered the hall. Orin frowned. Maybe he would smile more if fruit graced his hall. He silently chuckled to himself.

"This way, Lord Arctos." The butler led him to an open door halfway down the hall.

"Lord Arctos, my lord."

"Yes, indeed, please do come in." The man, seated in a large leather chair in front of the fire, stood. His gaze traversed Orin, and his eyebrow rose in the way Englishmen did when curiosity grasped them.

Orin sighed. "Sir." He strode forward and held out his hand. Lord Coltensley grasped his hand in a strong grip of which Orin took note. "I am here to discuss your daughter."

Lord Coltensley's lips frowned. He rubbed his chin with his fingers, and then he smiled. "Very well, then. Please sit."

Orin glanced at the leather chair and then at the slightly larger settee. He strode for the settee and gingerly sat his large frame on the brown velvet cushion.

He licked his dry lips and then stared Lord Coltensley in the eyes. *Give your daughter to me.*

"I am going to presume this is about Mina. Her actions of late have given me cause to believe she had interest in someone besides her betrothed."

"Betrothed?" The word had slid out before Orin could restrain it. *She will be betrothed to me.*

"Indeed. I see she did not inform you." Lord Coltensley raised a glass to his lips and drank a long swallow. He settled the glass on his thigh, and his eyes filled with challenge. "Have you ruined her?"

Orin swallowed the knot in his throat and found his head nodding before he had time to think. The devil. Why was his influencing not working? What was with this family and him not being able to persuade them to his will? He raised a shaky hand and ran his fingers through his hair.

Lord Coltensley sighed and chewed the inside of his cheek. "You wish to have her, then, do you?"

Orin's head nodded again.

"What do you have to offer this family?"

"Ahem," Orin swallowed again. "Indeed, sir, I am the heir to Tremarctos."

"And your title is?"

"I am the Marquess of Arctos, my lord. I will be the Duke of Tremarctos."

"A duke? *Not* an English duke. From what country does your family originate?"

The devil. Coltensley knew of Tremarctos. They were neighbors. Why was he doing this? "My family originates from a small country to the north, next to the kingdom of Sweden."

The Duke of Coltensley stood, and Orin stood as well. "My God, you're ridiculously large." Lord Coltensley stared up at Orin. "Visit tomorrow. I need to gather information about you; you can see Mina then."

Orin swallowed hard again. "Lord Coltensley." He inclined his head and strode out into the hall alone. Maybe he didn't believe Orin was a marquess. How could he not be? He stared down at his greatcoat and highly polished boots—look at how he dressed. Besides, they had lived next to each other for years. Coltensley knew his family was moneyed and of foreign good blood. This could not be good.

The smell of Wilhelmina so close made him hard as a rock.

His muscles tensed, and his arms tremored; he needed to be inside her.

"Lord Arctos." Her soft voice, barely a whisper, turned his head down the hall toward the back entrance.

Her hand emerged from a door on the opposite side of the hall.

He strode forward, making not a sound, and pushed open the door to the servants' stairs. She stood on the third step up, her smiling mouth at height with his.

Her tongue slid out and traced her lower puffed lip. He stared at the wet sheen as his eyes flickered. His monster clawed at his flesh in an attempt to pounce on her and take her on the stairs as he had against the tree in the lane. The devil, she was beautiful, red hair pulled up in ringlets on top of her head.

She reached out and wrapped her fingers around his hand. "Come with me."

He strode up the stairs behind her, not saying a word. Where was she taking him? He inhaled and held back a half groan, half sigh. How she moved him. He needed her more than anything in his world.

With each step he took, the stairs creaked beneath his weight, and she giggled softly. He smiled. The sound of her laughter lifted his heart from his stomach to beat like a hummingbird's wings in his chest. She was his. He would not leave here today without starting the ritual. Her father be damned.

They alighted the third story in the house, and she pushed open the door into a large, dimly lit room. He stepped into the room and instantly ducked his head and rounded his shoulders—the ceiling slanted at a pitch.

"Pardon, Lord Arctos. The eves is the only place I knew of where we could be alone for a bit."

He nodded. "Not a problem. I often have to crouch . . ." his lips curved into a smile, stretching the muscles of his face unfamiliarly, ". . . and pounce."

She laughed outright, and he did, too. He sprang at her. His arm swiping around her waist, he pulled her plush curves to his body.

"Lord Arctos." She breathed deep with lust.

"Orin." He stared her in the eyes. "I wish you to call me Orin."

"Or—Orin." He watched the beating pulse at the base of her throat.

"Yes. Say my name again." His lips came down hard on the beating skin.

She moaned and then shook, arching her head back. "Orin."

His hands busily worked on the buttons of his pantaloons. He folded back the flap as he tasted and bit her rose-scented flesh. His tongue traced the bodice of her dress down to her bosom.

Her hands grasped his hips, and he slid his fingers beneath the edge of her bodice to cup her full, round breasts. The touch of her fingers lingered on his waistband and then slid slowly to his sex. She gasped as her fingertips trailed the stiff flesh, wrapping about his erection.

He groaned, closed his eyes, and pinched her nipples. She was untutored in loving, and her hands simply held him, gently squeezing his skin back from the head. The pressure of her grip was just enough to tighten the skin about the head, maddening his desire. His prick grew thicker and longer beneath her caress.

His pulse pounded in the tip as his cock heated. The opening fluids tingled in his sac, and a small pearl of the fluid peaked at the tip, smearing on the fabric of her skirt and clinging the material to him.

He groaned. "Wilhelmina," he breathed.

"Or . . . in." The word shook from her lips as he pinched a nipple between his thumb and forefinger.

He fisted her skirts in his other hand and raised them.

"Turn about, Wilhelmina, and place your hands on the floor."

7

Wilhelmina turned without hesitation, presenting her rounded backside to him covered in a swath of silk and petticoats. What he planned to do to her in this position, she'd no clue.

Would he mount her like one of the animals in the fields? Her heart sped. Mmmm, indeed, that appealed. Was such a position possible with humans? She hadn't thought possible futtering while standing, and she now possessed and loved that experience.

His hands rubbed her bottom and fisted in the fabric. He hesitated, and his hands shook against her flesh. He held back, and she wanted him all.

"Orin, please be who you are. Be the man I saw in the field who primitively snapped a deer's neck. If—if I wanted a *gentleman*, I would have an English gentleman."

Her words hung unanswered in the small space of the room; his hand stopped the tremble of restraint, and with a jerk her skirt flipped up and covered her head. She could see nothing but the floor before her. Her body shook as his hands delved into the flesh between her thighs and slid. A light flashed behind her eyelids as they fluttered shut.

His finger found the opening of her sex and plunged into her. Her flesh stretched about him without hesitation. Oh, how delightful! She moaned and pressed back against him as blissful sensations speared up through her stomach to her neck.

"Wilhelmina." His fingers slid in and out of her.

Erotic fever washed her body in dew and a frenzied need to reach that place he had brought her to several times by the tree.

Her eyes squeezed tighter, and all she did was feel the curve of his thick fingers as they thrust into her and the stretching as they slid back out. They traversed the perimeter of her slick opening and sank back into her body once more. The heat of his thighs radiated off her bottom, and his tongue licked her skin at the base of her back. She shivered and bit her lip, wanting to ask him for more.

His teeth bit, pinching the flesh of her bottom. The pain tingled, and he groaned as his fingers moved more quickly and easily in and out of her. Her body trembled, sensations flooding her limbs and core.

Wet tongue traveled to the crack of her bottom and slid down, circling her bum hole. She tensed, and his fingers cupped her sex as the tongue pressed into her opening. She squealed.

What was he doing? An overwhelming pleasurable sensation boiled through her insides. *Oh! Oh! That feels good.*

His tongue wiggled, and her legs shook, sliding apart to open her sex to him. The flick of his tongue caressed her inner flesh and rosebud as his teeth scraped lightly the flesh of her bum crack.

The touch vanished.

She folded down onto her elbows to try to calm her shaking arms and jumped as the smooth skin of his sex slid down the crack of her bottom, parting her pussy lips. The tip nestled into her opening. His scorching, dewed hands grasped her hips, and he thrust his length—hard—into her. Her sex stretched to full, and she shook.

He growled.

Her heart raced as a rope of sensation wrapped about her lungs and stopped her breath. She struggled to breathe against the sensations assaulting her.

He pulled back out and bucked into her again . . . and again. The blissful stretching of her cunt built the urgency with each slick stroke of his cock. Spears of pleasure stabbed up through her being.

His hand grabbed her skirts and yanked them off her head. The coolness of the air shocked her, and she gasped as his thick fingers grasped the curls atop her head. Pulling her head back, he lifted her upper body off the ground.

His cock continued to slip in and out of her sex. The angle shifted with each increment that her body moved as he pulled her to the upright kneeling position, her back against his chest. His lips came down on her neck, and teeth bit.

She screamed.

The bite shot straight to her cunny muscles, and a blissful eruption of ecstasy poured from her body as wave upon wave of her sex clasped his hardness. He growled and then froze; his teeth dug harder into her flesh.

He pulled out of her and then slightly rocked in a series of small strokes, back and forth. Wetness dripped from her hole with each rub of his member. His cock head pressed to her womb, and prickles of heat possessed her inner core.

Her entire body shook, trembling uncontrollably. A tickling sensation, as if butterflies' wings caressed her bum hole and opened her pucker. She sucked in a startled breath as something pressed up into it.

His finger? Possibly.

It stretched her opening and wiggled as he continued to rock and rock in small motions. The gushes of seed had made her shake, and fevered chills raced her body. The liquid dripped from her and coated her legs.

His lips kissed and kissed the flesh of her neck.

"Wilhelmina. You are mine, Wilhelmina. Tell me. Tell me that is what you wish."

She trembled, and her heart swelled in her chest. "Indeed, Orin, I desire only you."

He sighed into her hair. "I am not normal, my Mina. And before we complete the joining ritual, you need to know all I am."

"Orin, I have seen. I know who you are. You have shown me in my dreams."

His tongue traced her neck to her shoulder as his breathing slowed. "Have I? What have you seen in your dreams, my Mina?"

She closed her eyes, and the images flooded back to her.

"Round eyes, claws, teeth. The height and breadth bigger than anything I have seen."

"Indeed. You are not afraid, my Mina?"

"No, I am not afraid. Curious. Indeed. But I do not fear you."

"I am Ursus. My kind was cursed in battle many years ago in the homeland. We possessed qualities of the bear. We all have little to no control of our mating instincts, but once we choose a mate for a lifetime, they are our only loves."

Her hand reached up, and her fingertips touched his cheek and then trailed a loving caress into his hair. He rubbed his head against hers.

"Your father does not believe I am heir to a dukedom."

"Pardon?" Her muscles tensed, and she tried to turn toward him. His grip on her held her pinned to him.

"Don't move. The opening fluids are still spending."

"Pardon?" *What were opening fluids?*

"Opening is part of the joining ritual for my kind. Taking a human or any mate once holds no consequence in my world. Twice, and Orsse starts. If you do not complete the ritual, both parties will go through extreme pain shedding the life that would have been."

Pain? She bit her lower lip.

"The third spend from a male Ursus is powerful and holds the cub you will carry."

"Pardon?" A child ... cub? The next time they joined she would not only be his for life but would then carry his child.

"You don't wish to be mine, Wilhelmina?"

"I—I do. I just hadn't thought about children. Well ... no, I mean, of course I have, but I had not thought of carrying one this year."

She wanted children, quite so. The information came with just a bit of a shock. Knowing all about Orin's kind, and what they possessed as a being, felt suddenly important. More so than it had a moment before.

"Orin, can you tell me more? I wish to know all about the Ursus."

"Of course, my Mina. You will learn all in time."

The stairs leading to the attic creaked, and Orin slid his throbbing cock from her body with a groan. He released her, and her skirt fell down about her. She pushed up off her knees and turned about, the flesh of her sex wanting him to join her again. He tucked his still engorged sex into his trousers and buttoned the flap.

He was so handsome. Masculine and ... hers. She smiled. He was hers, just as she was his. His gaze stayed fixed on her.

"I need to tidy myself and return to tea, Orin. When will I see you again?"

"Your father has requested I see him and you on the morrow."

Her heart leaped. She would see him in one turn of the sun. She grinned and stared at him behind lowered lashes. She . . . she was in love with him. Her heart soared.

He grabbed her wrist and pulled her toward him and the stairs. "Your smile lifts my heart from the animal who caged it, Mina."

Her eyes widened as he raised her hand to his lips and kissed the knuckles of her hand.

"Thank you, Orin. You are an amazing man."

8

Orin paced, waiting for Beelzebub to be brought about. The duke hadn't said what time he wished Orin to call this day, but noontime had arrived, and Orin could wait no more.

He heard horse hooves and the clatter of the Tremarctos carriage on the stones outside the stable. His father must be heading out. Orin's brow knit. His father never went anywhere.

The carriage pulled up in front of him, the black lacquered paint reflecting the sun into his eyes. He squinted and turned his head away.

His father stepped up beside him. "Ready to go, boar?"

"Pardon?" Orin's eyes widened in shock. "You are not going."

"The Duke of Coltensley put out several inquisitions to the community about who our family is. There is no possible way I am allowing him to poke further. You want his daughter? Then you have to deal with me for this day."

Orin cringed.

"You desire the girl. . . . She is suitable to your station.

Coltensley was willing to let us be until his daughter wanted you. Now he wants to know all about us. I will make sure no Englishman understands our true lineage."

Having the Duke of Tremarctos involved in any part of Orin's life was the furthest from what he wished. Having him involved in this . . . His eyes shifted to the round of the Ursus. "You will not touch her. Do you understand me?"

"Control, Orin. I am the master of this house, and you will be a good boar, as you always are."

The footman opened the door to the carriage, and his father waved his hand toward the open door.

Orin grunted and climbed up into the cab, sitting with his back to the driver. His father climbed up after him and settled into the leather seat opposite.

The carriage started on the short drive to the Duke of Coltensley's.

"Sir, what are you to say to Lord Coltensley?"

"That all depends on what he says to me, boar." His father rubbed his chin; then he stared hard at Orin. "Your mother would be delighted with your choice, Orin. She herself was a high-ranking Englishwoman. The daughter of a marquess. She always loved the English ways."

"I know, Father. Did you think I forgot her?"

"No." His father's voice softened. "No, I did not think you would forget. She, I know, loved you beyond . . ." His father turned his gaze out the window. "She loved you greatly, Orin."

Orin swallowed hard; the lump formed in his throat. He'd never asked. . . . He needed to know. "Sir, are you . . ." Perspiration wetted his hands, and he fisted them. "Are you my sire, sir?"

His father's gaze snapped back to him. Love and compassion filled his eyes. "How long have you doubted your origins, Orin?"

He swallowed again, not dislodging his discomfort. "Since I

was old enough to understand the rituals. Since marking, I suppose."

His father leaned across the carriage, his face a mere breath's whisper from his own. "Whose nose do you have, boar?"

Nose? "Grandfather Orin's, sir."

"Indeed. And whose chin?"

"The same. Grandfather Orin's, sir."

"Indeed." His father's hand pushed Orin's face to the side with a light slap. "And whose ears?"

Orin fought with his head and freed himself to look his father back in the eyes. "I have no clue, sir. Mine, I suppose."

"No, boar. You have my ears. When you were born, your face looked so much like mine. No doubt rose that you were my cub. Not your uncle's. Your mother swore to me, after she was mine, that your uncle never actually spent his seed in her a third time."

Tremarctos sat back across the seat from him. "Don't ever doubt who you are, Orin. You are my boar."

His father turned his attention back to the passing trees.

No one knew what had happened that night when the Duke of Tremarctos killed his brother to claim his brother's mate. No one dared talk about the scandal. All Orin knew was that he was the product of a sinful night.

He reached up and traced the outline of his ear with his fingertip—large, curved top, a few ripples as the flesh curved downward to large lobes.

He had never considered his ears.

His eyes traced his father's ear, the top hidden beneath his long gray hair, and Orin's finger glided along his own again. His ears, in the least, possessed similar shape.

In a simple two-minute conversation, the Duke of Tremarctos had swayed his fears. The fears Orin had carried his entire life. He sighed. Amazing. Was his life making a turn? Indeed, a major turn for the better.

* * *

Wilhelmina sat in her father's library, waiting. She straightened her skirts and sighed for the hundredth time.

"Mina."

She turned toward her father, and he held out a glass of port. She winced as a cramp tightened her womb.

"Yes, please. Thank you, sir." She grasped the slightly warmed glass and raised the rim to her lips. The thick, fruity flavor flooded her mouth, and she swallowed and sighed.

She and her father, in the years before her come-out, had done this same activity on rainy days. She would read her books, and he would attend business as they shared a glass of port.

"Mina, are you sure you want this man?" Her father's voice remained calm but filled with questions. "He is quite impressive in size, and—after all inquires—he does appear to be from real higher blood." He frowned. "There is a quality about him, though. . . . He puts forth a controlled front, dear. I worry what he is holding in."

Wilhelmina smiled, and a warm, fuzzy glow washed over her. "Father, I want him more than anything I have known. He is all a man should be."

"Hmph. You think, dear? Describe him to me. Through your eyes, maybe, I will understand."

She closed her eyes and pulled to mind the image of Orin in the field the first time they had met.

Orin bursting through the woods and out into the fields. "Masculine, intense, and filled with life."

Orin cradling the deer in his grasp and running his hand along the buck's neck to calm it. "Calm, soothing."

Orin visiting her dreams, trying to protect her from himself. "Protective."

Orin's fingers sliding along her skin and into her sex and making her scream. "He is loving, yet powerful. Yes, powerful."

She opened her eyes, and her father stared at her. "You are in love with him?"

Her lips curved into a beaming smile, and her heart lifted in her chest. "Yes, Father. I—I am."

"Very well, Mina. As long as he behaves himself when he arrives today, he shall have you in one month's time."

She smiled a smile that shot straight to her toes. "Thank you, Father. Thank you."

The butler knocked at the door and entered. "My lord, Lord Arctos and the Duke of Tremarctos."

Her father raised his eyebrows at her. "Have them enter."

Both men ducked as they entered the room; the two of them made all minute within the four walls.

"Lord Coltensley." The immense, silver-haired man inclined his head to her father. "We have lived in this area for more than twenty years, and we have never been introduced."

"Twenty years. Yes, indeed. Not for lack of my father and myself trying."

"No, Lord Coltensley, you certainly did try. I have always simply wished to be private." He smiled, and Wilhelmina forgot to breathe. The duke was absolutely striking, just as Orin and his brother Devon were striking—and there were more of them. Wilhelmina wanted to learn all about them. She would soon, very soon.

"Indeed, I can see why, with your size. Well, I will not keep you on your toes. Lord Arctos, you may wed my daughter in one month's time. Obtain your license, and I will order the bans to be read."

The bans, the license. All would be legal and proper. She stared at Orin. Desire and passion for her shone in his eyes and expression.

"Very well, Lord Coltensley. I believe my son wishes to speak with your daughter."

She heard the words but didn't dare turn her gaze from Orin.

"Indeed. There is no harm in them being alone for a few moments." Her father stood and walked with Lord Tremarctos from the room.

"My Mina." Orin strode to her side, and his deep silver eyes stared down at her. He inhaled and shook. "Are you faring well?"

"Mmmm, indeed. Very. A few twinges, but otherwise . . ." Her hand spread across her abdomen.

"The opening. I smelled the sweetness on the wind. It is why I shake. I must complete the ritual this night, Mina. Do you understand?"

Her eyes widened, and she stared up at him. He needed to spend his seed in her or she would not become his. "Yes, I understand, Orin. Where?"

"Come to the main road after dark. I will have a carriage waiting to bring you to me." His hand rose and snaked into her hair, tilting her head back. He growled, and his warm breath caressed her ear. "I cannot stay, Mina, or I will change form." He stepped back and dropped his hand from her.

She stood and pushed to her tiptoes, placing a kiss on his cheek. "I will be there, Orin. Tonight I will be yours."

He turned from her. She sat back down on the chaise and watched his broad shoulders stretch the fabric of his coat as he paused in the door to the room. Her womb tingled, and wetness leaked out of her sex to pool on her thighs and skirt. He glanced back at her, eyes rounded, and hissed; then he shook his head and left the room.

She picked up the glass of port and downed the last drop.

9

Wilhelmina skidded in her slippers as she traversed the path running the side of the drive to the main Sudhamly lane. The dark of night surrounded her, and her heart raced. She giggled. This path . . . She shook her head. This was the second time in a week she had traversed the dirt in the dark.

Tonight, in Orin's world, she would become his. In her world, them being together would take another four weeks. The bans were read weekly for three weeks, and then the wedding. She sighed. She wished she could journey to Scotland now, but she would hurt her father if she did so.

Until the bans finished, their relationship would be formal meetings and sneaking about.

Her skin skittered with chills, and Orin's glowing silver eyes emerged out of the trees. His arms wrapped about her waist and hoisted her into the air.

Her muscles tensed, but she didn't scream. She held no fear of him. This she wanted—him to take her with such an onslaught of passion she was left exhausted by his attentions.

His humid breath caressed her neck as he pressed her back hard against his laboring chest and stepped back into the darkness of the trees. She closed her eyes and shook as chills raced her skin. The fabric of her corset tightened about her ribs, and she struggled to breathe.

Not a word was spoken by either of them. He stepped back, foot after foot. Not once did he hit a tree or stumble on a rock or log.

He floated.

His arms clasped about her as he pulled them deeper and deeper into the blackness.

In her mind, images from dreams past, of seeing him in the woods, a presence of animal and human, of devil and benevolent being . . . Her pussy quivered, and wetness leaked down her thighs. She loved all of him.

His chest expanded against her back, and he growled. His tongue slid out and licked the flesh of her neck.

She groaned and arched her head back against his shoulder. A hiss erupted from him, and his teeth scraped along the skin of her shoulder and pinched the loose flesh.

Pain tickled her nerves, only to be soothed by the tingling of the crisp night air caressing the wet mark on her skin.

He stopped and lowered her. Her body slid along his hard front. His large erection pressed a trail down her body and sensations burned through her clothes, catching them on fire until the cold earth pressed to the bottoms of her feet once again. Oh, my. Somewhere in the woods she had lost her slippers.

Her eyelids fluttered. The glow of the moon shown through the tree limbs into a small clearing. This was the place. The spot in her dreams at which he'd shown himself to her, tangling her thoughts and emotions. This was the place at which she had come to know and desire this man.

He stepped around her. His round, silver eyes glowed like highly polished crystals in candlelight.

His jaw worked, and the points of his teeth poked out over his lower lip as he swallowed.

Her heart jumped into her throat, wanting the feel of his teeth dragging across her skin as he bit her flesh and joined with her. She closed her eyes, and her tongue ran across her teeth.

He laughed, a full-hearted, deep sound.

What was he laughing at? Her eyes shot open to stare at him. His hand raised, and fingertips trailed her chin, followed by the drag of cold, hard points. She inhaled a sharp breath and held still.

His claws!

"I will never harm you, my Mina." He curled his fingers under, and his claws drew lines down her neck to the edge of her dress bodice. "Hold, Mina."

She struggled for breath, not wanting to breathe too deeply. She trusted him, but, still, claws like his cut and cut deep.

His claws caught the fabric and trailed downward. The zipping sound of hard and sharp bone across muslin made the hairs on her neck stand.

A blazing need followed his claws as they dragged down her dress. Her legs shook, and sweat sprang across her skin. She inhaled anise and the fresh, crisp smells of the earth. Oh, how she loved the smell of him!

The warming in her womb burst to a roaring flame, and she moaned and whimpered. She needed him inside her. Her head lolled back, and she licked her lips. Mmmm. Indeed. Passion, need, and want, all in one.

She would do whatever he wished of her, no questions asked. Oh! How blissful. He reached her hips, and his fingers pulled back the fabric of her bodice, exposing her cotton corset beneath. She trembled as his smooth hands slid the fabric up and off her shoulders.

She wiggled her body, and the fabric slid down her arms and pooled about her waist. He stepped to the side and behind her. His breath caressed her shoulder blades, and her heart beat faster. Why did his breath on her skin excite her so?

His fingers slid along her back, from the center to the sides, and then down the curve of her torso to the swell of her waist. A tug came at her laces.

Thank goodness. She would be able to breathe now. Her body jerked slightly. Then another tug and another, as one by one her stays loosened up her back. The cold night air caressed her fevered skin, raising delicious bumps in its wake. She shivered.

His hands parted the cotton and bone and pushed her stays forward. The garment fell to the forest floor without a sound. A sigh pressed past her lips, and she inhaled a breath as if for the first time.

Warm fingertips slid around her waist, and her arms jerked. The touch continued up her stomach to her breasts, and his fingers gently circled the blossoming flesh growing ever so slowly in the centers. She sighed again, and her eyes fluttered as a cross between a tickle and ecstasy raced her skin. His fingers reached the tips, and his thumb and forefinger pinched and held the centers of the flat tips.

She inhaled a sharp breath. The pain spiraled from the puckered flesh and flowed to her womb, tightening all her muscles in its wake.

His tongue licked up the side of her neck, and her body shivered.

"Hold still, my Mina." His voice was hoarse with pleasure. He dropped to his knees behind her and slid her skirts over her hips. They fell to her feet with a swoosh of fabric. "Slide your legs apart, Mina."

"Orin." Her voice came out a hushed whisper.

She stepped out of her skirts and slid her feet apart. The cool air against her opened sex caressed her as if a second set of hands brought her bliss. His lips pressed to her bottom in steamy contrast, and his tongue dragged on her flesh in an openmouthed kiss.

The walls of her cunny clenched, remembering his tongue and the sensations of him licking her secret flesh. Oh! She wanted his tongue there, flicking her bud in long, sultry licks. She moaned. Such scandalous desires. . . . She grinned. She adored them.

The hard edge of his claws trailed up the insides of her thighs to her dripping flesh. Her eyes widened. . . . He wouldn't, would he?

The point of his claw touched her tender lips. She inhaled, and her breath caught in her throat. She shook. The hard claw gently separated her labia. *Don't move, Wilhelmina. He may accidentally cut you.* She bit her lip. The fingers of his other hand massaged her thigh, her buttocks, and her back, trying to relax her.

The hard tip disappeared, and the warmth of a finger curled and wiggled in her sex and then pressed up into her core. Oh, my! The subtle difference in the sensation, from hard, inanimate bone to flesh and blood, was powerfully intense. She pushed back and down with her hips, wanting more of him in her, wanting him stretching her with the hard width of his prick.

Warmth and cold tightened all her muscles, and light flashed behind her eyelids. He wiggled the curved digit in the eye of her sex.

"Oh, oh, indeed, yes, indeed," barely left her lips as her body jerked in spasms about his finger when the bliss she'd reached for rippled through her.

He pulled out the finger and grabbed her by the hips. The hot, tapered flesh of his cock head pressed between her legs and glided along, deliciously spreading her labia.

The tip nestled into her hole, and he pressed into her with

one long pulse. Her quim stretched greedily about him, welcoming his length and width. Her legs rocked back, and he cocooned his length deep within her belly.

His arm wrapped about her hips, and his other hand grabbed her breast as teeth grazed along the side of her neck and down her shoulder. He growled and thrust into her open hole.

The sounds of her moans and his hissing filled the night with harmony, egging on her lustful desires once more.

His body possessed her; his spirit flowed through her every pore as he jerked, licked, sucked, and nibbled her flesh. She answered each act by offering up her passions without restraint.

His tongue slid up to her earlobe, and the sharp point of his teeth grabbed the flesh and pinched. All motion stopped except for the beat of their hearts. A prick of pain pierced her earlobe, and he shuddered, his breath hissing in her ear. The throb of his heartbeat intensified in her womb, and his cock jerked; a warm gush filled her womb.

She cried out, and her muscles trembled about his hardness as his prick sprayed his seed within her.

His mouth sucked her earlobe, and he stumbled back, sitting down, dragging her with him. She sat in his lap, legs spread along the outsides of his thighs as his cock throbbed in her. The night air chilled her dewed and fevered skin in an agreeable caress. Her womb tingled, and Orin laid his damp forehead on her shoulder and sighed.

"My Mina. My angel. I adore you. My heart beats only your name."

She squirmed in his lap, wanting to see his eyes. He didn't move. "Orin, I—I could never have wished for a man more than you are. You are all to me. I have been in love with you since I first set eyes on you in the fields connecting our lands."

"You, my Mina, do not deserve a man like me. I am rough, gruff, a devil who will end up eating your emotions and leaving you hollow inside out."

Her hand reached up and slid into his hair. His lips caressed the side of her neck, and raw sensations of pleasure, love, and despair wrapped about her body. "Orin, you are no monster. You are a wonderful mixture of masculinity, love, and pure animal longing. I love the carnal man you are."

Warm wetness caressed her shoulder, and a trickle of tears ran down her collarbone to pool in the crevice of her throat. He cried.

Her hand stilled in his hair, and she closed her eyes, feeling all her love for him overflow. Tears welled in her eyes. "Orin, I love you."

His throat worked against her shoulder. "I . . ." *Ahem.* "I adore you, Wilhelmina. In your eyes, I am whole."

"Orin, you are whole. You are so much more than I could dream you to be or any other simple man could dream of being. Your unique qualities do not make you a monster, Orin. They make you extraordinary." She grabbed his hand and pulled it to her lips, sucking his fingers into her mouth. His cock twitched inside her, their wetness melding the flesh of their join.

"You are mine now, Wilhelmina. Always."

"Indeed, Orin, I am devotedly yours."

He squeezed her tightly and sighed. "I wish you to come home with me, Mina, but I know I cannot have you nightly for several more weeks."

A smile quirked her lips. Indeed, it would be a long, long four-week wait.

DEVON

1

Amanda walked down the dirt road in town, her hands fisted at her sides. She passed the butcher's shop and the milliner's.

"Good day, Lady Amanda."

She nodded but kept up her quick pace out of town. She cringed at the cheerful flute and fiddle music playing in the distance. My God. Her head hurt. She reached up, and her fingers grazed across the tender skin between her eyebrows.

The May Festival had begun, and all the young girls danced prettily around the pole as the men watched. Her heart beat faster than her legs could carry her as her stomach twisted in her gut.

The girls laughed and sang; the men of the town sat drinking mugs of grog and ale until they passed out, caught one of the maids, or tossed their crumpets.

It was vile and disgusting.

She needed to leave. She couldn't be a part of this celebration. All those poor girls believed in love. She knew the truth: only women possessed the ability to feel that emotion.

Her heart pinched.

Harold had enlightened her with that lesson. Futtering and drinking—those things, men craved. *"Love . . . love is for silly girls, to trick them into marriage, and marriage is for increasing one's wealth or bloodlines, futtering, and producing children. Nothing more."*

The first time he had said those words, she had thought them a jest. The second time she had thought the spirits had the better of him.

The third time . . .

Well, the third time he had said them, she'd burst into tears. Everyone in town said he was the catch, a wealthy merchant. To them, her title did little but grant her a "Good day" with a "Lady" attached.

She had seen very little of her family since her father had wed her to Harold for the sum of thirty-five pounds a year. And Harold, until five months ago—the day he had died—had treated her as his servant. A cat's paw, whom the only thing he had wished was the act of shame with him and his friends once a month.

She supposed futtering wasn't all bad. She did find pleasure in the act, and, on occasion, craved the touch of another. Futtering simply never lived up to her expectations, her fantasies. Maybe she simply disliked men. She rolled her eyes. That went a bit far. . . . She hated Harold and, well, most men in this town.

She turned up the path at the edge of town leading to the cliffs and Rye Harbor.

She watched the well-worn path as her kid boots peeked out from under her skirts. The sounds of the celebrations faded to the sounds of the sea. The sun still shone, and by the time it dipped down behind the land, the field she was crossing now would be filled with men as they futtered any woman in town they could get their hands on.

She stepped from the path and crossed the field toward her

favorite rock. Tucked back, away from the wind, the haven was where she had met her dream, and in one foolish adolescent act had had her longing taken away. The one man she still to this day could say she loved.

She put her hand on the stone and slid her leg over the edge. She dangled her body above the sea and imagined his large, firm hands on her waist as he had lifted her down to the little hidden cove in the side of the cliff.

Her body had slid along his broad chest, and she had let her fingers uncurl, releasing the rock in a quest for his hot skin. . . . She fell and the bottom of her kid boots hit the path below. The memory vanished, and she blew out a breath.

She cherished those moments, yet they were in all likelihood lies. My God! What a simpleton!

Men don't love. They lust. Women are a means to bring us to discharge, nothing more. Men have men for company, and women have women.

She shook her head.

Her mind knew that truth. How could she not? She'd spent the last twelve years with a man who'd tutored her thus.

She spun about and stared out at the sea. She was forever stuck in this little town. She sighed. No, that wasn't true. She could leave. She could journey back to her father's, but after not speaking to him since her wedding day, she didn't know quite how to approach him. Besides, they had never been close, even before she'd married.

Devon Ursus . . . his blond hair and blue eyes. His smile and his laughter. Her dream man. Well, really he had been a boy when they had met. She wished she knew where he settled.

He, in all probability, had wedded a pretty English rose. She smiled. He'd hated those simple girls who tittered and giggled. Amanda's striking looks and thirst for adventure had lured him to her—just as her fair hair and pale blue-green eyes had fetched her father a pretty sum from Harold.

She stared out at the sea; a ship with white billowing sails turned into the cove, heading toward the town. A new shipment from a far-off land . . . fabrics and lace from France, port and wines from Italy, or tea from China. One thing she'd learned in her marriage—imports could make you very wealthy. No doubt, the items aboard headed for the capital and the rich households of her long-ago peers.

London.

Aunt Bess had a house in Mayfair. Scandalous Bess. Her two highly visible affairs with the Duke of Carlisle and his son, both at the same time, had earned her reputation. Amanda giggled.

Her aunt was fond of futtering. Amanda herself found a bit of joy in the act, but she had never craved a man as her aunt did.

It would be comforting to see her again. Oh! She sucked in a longing breath. To sleep under silk sheets again and go to the theater. Indeed, an opera. She loved all sorts of entertainments, but the local tragedies played out daily by the townfolk were the only entertainment she saw in this little town.

London . . . Ten years had passed since she'd walked the serpentine. She would write her aunt a letter this night and journey back to her past in hopes of finding the passions she'd lost while living in this town. Besides . . . a change certainly felt due.

The sixteenth of May, 1818
Dear Amanda,

I am relieved you have written.

The entire family is sick with worry about you down in that small little town with not a soul and, now, no husband to take care of your other needs. Smile.

My gout is paining me awful, dear, and I am journeying to Bath to take the waters for one month's time. I

*have informed the staff of your arrival. Do as you please.
I am simply tickled in the knowledge you will be staying
with me.*

    I look forward to catching you in "the act" *on my re-
turn to town.*

Wicked Bess

2

London, England
Twenty-ninth of May, 1818

Amanda walked down the large hall in her aunt's Mayfair home. To her left, a bronze statue of a nude male. To her right, a painting of a woman lounging naked in a field. Simply being out of Kent brought Amanda joy. This house . . . well, this house was designed to heighten the senses. Indeed, heighten the sexual senses, which was a good way to say it titillated your wanton urge.

She wandered into her aunt's library in search of a book with which to sit in the garden. One week from this night, she would journey to her first opera in twelve years. She sighed. As a widow, she could go about town without a chaperone. The last time she'd been in London, she had been escorted everywhere by her father's sister to preserve her reputation.

She smirked. Simply staying in her aunt's house tarnished even the smallest reputation she had. She didn't care. Aunt Bess was fun and exactly what she needed after twelve years wedded to Harold.

She ran her fingers along the titles on the shelves, each one in a different language. Her brows drew tight. What form of reading did her aunt enjoy? She wandered to the table in the middle of the room. Pilled high with books, the round marble surface was surrounded by soft leather chairs.

She flipped open the leather-wrapped drawing pad sitting at the edge. The first drawing was of the back of a man's hand, with a woman's untrimmed fingernail curved about the thumb.

My, her aunt drew well. The entire family had said as much all her life, yet this was the very first drawing Amanda had seen.

She flipped the page and sucked in her breath. Oh, my—a charcoal of a man's firm backside as a woman's hands wrapped about the swells from the front, her nails digging into the firm, squared edges of the lower cheeks.

The only male bottom she had ever witnessed fully unclothed had been Harold's. Harold's bum looked nothing like the one in this drawing. His bottom possessed square edges but no fullness. He also possessed no waist. The man in this drawing looked like a god. Amanda's cheeks grew warm. Well, his bum did. She giggled. What a goose. She shook her head and continued to stare at the image.

Harold had done a decent job of showing what to do in the art of the act, though she had never grabbed his buttocks with quite as much enthusiasm as this woman did. Something she would have to try if she ever took a lover.

A lover . . . hmmm. That thought had never crossed her mind in Kent. She sighed. It was this house! All the nude drawings and sculptures of both men and women flamed her longing for another's touch. She knew her aunt loved to draw and she liked to futter. Up until this moment, she'd had no idea her aunt liked to *draw* futtering. Now she knew.

She flipped to the next drawing. Her eyes widened, and the flesh of her breasts bloomed. She closed her eyes and imagined she was the woman in the drawing, she stood while a man—whose face was hidden behind her—squeezed her breasts, pinching her nipples between his forefinger and middle finger. Her breath hitched, and her sex tensed. The man raised his head as his tongue trailed her neck to her ear.

"*Amanda,*" Devon Ursus whispered against her earlobe.

Typical . . . he would be the one she imagined. *You goose!* She opened her eyes and stared down at the image.

She flipped the page; the drawing on the next one was of her Aunt Bess kissing.

Amanda grinned.

Wicked Aunt Bess kissed a woman, just as Mary and Amanda did all those years ago for Devon. Only, in this drawing, her aunt was Amanda's age. This book had to be twenty years old. Amanda focused on the way the lips touched, slightly parted; she closed her eyes. She spun. She and Mary, spinning in the fields of flowers near her father's estate.

"Spin her faster, Amanda. Indeed, yes . . . I see her ankles. Oh! Her knees! Wicked, wicked girls!"

Her heart pounded, and she struggled to breathe as they laughed and laughed until their stomachs hurt. She put her hands on Mary's slim shoulders to steady herself as the world circled about her. They smiled at each other. Mary's deep green eyes filled with laughter.

"Kiss. I want to see you kiss her, Amanda," Devon's voice choked.

Amanda leaned in, and their breaths mingled. Mary's breath smelled like tea and lemon. The soft, smooth skin of Mary's lips touched, clung, and slid along Amanda's. The kiss, so soft at first, turned wicked as Devon wrapped his long arms about them both, picked them up, and spun them, kissing both their necks.

Mary pulled her lips away; her panting breath warmed her cheeks, and Devon's lips pecked Mary's. Amanda watched, wondering what his lips dragging across hers would do.

He turned to her. His lips met hers and greedily clasped as if sucking on a lemon wedge. Tingles shot through her body, and her toes curled—a wonderful sensation she never would feel again.

Mary giggled, and Devon pulled back. Afraid to close her mouth, Amanda kept her lips slit open, and her chin wobbled. What if the tingling stopped? Her tongue slid out, touched the plump, moist surface, and tasted the vanilla she always smelled on him.

Her gaze settled on his face, and his eyes danced with lust and happiness. Amanda's heart soared on his pleasure.

"My sweet Amanda." Devon's voice filled with love. . . .

Love? Amanda sighed. Her mind crashed back to present day. Devon's eyes had held more than lust that day.

The look of lust in one's eyes . . . Harold had taught her this. Devon . . . His blue eyes had sparkled with warmth, caring, and devotion. To this day, just thinking of that look raised bumps on her arms in longing—longing for a love from a man. Her heart twisted in her chest. Not once in her years of marriage and futter had her husband's gray eyes shown such a look.

Shortly after that day in the field, Devon had started talking to Amanda with his mind, and then her relationship with Devon had screeched to a halt. Amanda's lower lip trembled, remembering the pinch between his eyebrows and the piercing betrayal in his eyes.

No, Amanda. Stop. You will one day make another memory as such.

Amanda shook her head and slapped the book closed. She could not go back to the past. She could not take back the confession that drove Devon away.

She turned and spotted a piece of art paper folded on the

floor by her feet. She leaned down and picked up the smooth white paper. No doubt, the parchment had fallen out when she'd slapped the book closed. She unfolded the book-sized sheet.

Scrolled across the top in black waterpaint was *The Glove*. The image was a vague painting of a man, an orange top hat perched atop his head, standing in front of a deep green door. The colors and shapes all washed together as if the viewer looked through a bottle of oil. Below the painting was scrolled, in quill ink, *Pleasure was had by all us wicked enough to slide into Venus's Glove.*

Wicked Aunt Bess's handwriting? She bit her lip. What was "The Glove"?

Amanda walked down James Street, heading for her first theater performance in years. Her heart hammered in her chest and she grinned as she passed group after group heading to events of the night.

"Good evening, madam."

Amanda stopped; the deep tenor of the man's voice captured her senses from across the street. She turned toward him and watched as a woman dressed in a fine wool cape and red feathered cap exited a home on James Street.

The man, noticing her puzzled gaze, bowed his head. His deep copper-red silk hat glistened in the glow of the streetlights above. "Do come inside." His eyes held playful mischief. "A feat for your eyes and senses."

Her eyes widened, and the painting of the man in the orange top hat flashed before her.

The Glove.

She bit her lip and glanced around her. People scurried about, heading to theater events, not glancing once at this man. She should be headed on her way. *The entire reason you came to*

London, Amanda, was to go to the opera. You should not consider whatever "The Glove" is.

The door to the house he stood before opened once more, and she moved her head to the side to try to glimpse what was inside. A warm glow illuminated as another woman stepped out onto the steps, the faint soft note of a female within moaning, followed by laughter, reached her ears. Amanda's breath caught. The door closed.

Intriguing.

The woman's soft moan and laughter ran through her head once more, and nerves flipped her stomach. They sounded as though they had fun as she and Mary had had fun in the fields with Devon. Her gloved hand smoothed across the bodice of her restrained deep blue gauze.

She was curious.

Only women thus far had emerged from the house. Was she wicked enough? Maybe a new and scandalous experience was just what she needed to forget her staid prior existence. *You just may create a new memory, Amanda. The opera will be there tomorrow.* She glanced about. No one truly knew her to be in the capital anyway, or they had long forgotten . . . Lady Amanda.

No one would notice.

"Do come inside," the doorman mouthed as he motioned to the door.

Amanda stepped off the footpath and into the road.

She would simply ask him what lay inside. If what he said intrigued her, she would enter. If not, she would go on her way to the opera, as was her original intention. She straightened her shoulders.

Glancing to the left and right, she gathered her skirts in her left hand, lifted them, and waited for a break in the carriage traffic.

A hired hack passed, and an opening appeared in the line of

carriages. Inhaling deep, she scurried across the cobbled street. With each step, a stone lifted from her shoulders and excitement pushed her feet to fly. As she reached the other side, her heart pounded in her throat.

The man grinned at her.

Goose . . . what are you doing? She glanced around. No one even noticed her . . . except for the man in the copper top hat.

His smile broadened as she stepped toward him. Her heart beat hard with each breath she exhaled, and sweat pierced her brow. "Sir, what lies inside?"

"Please step inside to see the erotic feat, ma'am."

Erotic?

Her heart sped at the thought. She laughed to herself. Of course, erotic. . . . The painting had mentioned Venus's Glove.

Her sex clenched. Blast Aunt Bess's books, artwork, and sculptures! She had touched herself two nights hence as Devon and Mary had filled her mind. She shook her head. Never once had Devon touched her flesh the way Harold had, yet she imagined Devon in all her wanton dreams.

She shifted her stance and stared at the man once more. His dark brown eyes softened. "Please step inside, ma'am. You will not be disappointed."

Her lower lip trembled. *Do it, Amanda. Do something Harold would have had to have words with you about.* Yes, indeed. She needed to step out of her widow's world. Out of the life she had never wanted with Harold. Start heading in a direction which brought her a bit of pleasure, of excitement. Once upon a time, she had seen and tasted what loving, passion, and pleasure was. She had come to London alone. She could do this. She nodded to the gentleman with the copper hat, and his eyes widened, full of delight.

He walked up the steps, grasped the deep green door's handle, and pushed the door wide. "Please step inside."

She stepped up the stairs, and her knees shook. Never in her childhood would she have believed she would be entering a scandalous hell like this . . . alone. Not that she had thought of entering one with another person either.

She had dreamed of far-off travels and of learning to her heart's content about amazing and exotic things. Never had she thought her life would end up void of excitement, married to a man who had provided her security and a lesson in lust, but nothing else. Nothing.

She crossed the threshold into a softly lit hall. The door quickly shut behind her. Excitement and a bit of fear washed her skin, and she shivered. Soft violin music played from somewhere in the house, and a woman approached from down the long hall.

Simple brown hair was pinned atop her head in a massive coil. Her green eyes twinkled as she beheld Amanda, and she smiled seductively. Warmth spread through Amanda's belly. She was pretty.

"Good evening, ma'am. Come to see the entertainment?"

Amanda fisted her hands. "Yes." The only word she could force past her lips.

"Very well, ma'am. Two shillings, please." She held out her lace-gloved hand for the coins.

Amanda reached into the pocket about her waist and fished out the coins. Her hand shook as she laid the entrance fee into the bare palm of the woman standing before her.

"Thank you kindly, ma'am. Now that the particulars are behind us . . ." the woman's smile broadened, "what exactly would you like to see?"

"Oh, um, I—I'm not sure. An amusing, erotic feat?" Her cheeks warmed. Goodness. She was a woman of thirty. She should be able to say the word *erotic* without blushing.

"Indeed." The woman's eyes grew as big as tea saucers. "There is lots to see. . . . We normally do not receive pretty womenfolk in the door, so you are a treat." Her finger rose, and she bit her untrimmed nail then pointed the tip at Amanda. "I think the group display will ease you into this nicely. Or, wait . . . no. A small private showing before we move you to the other guests." Her nail parted her sensuous lips, and her tongue wrapped about her index finger in a wicked caress.

My goodness! What would her tongue's caress wrapped about Amanda's finger do to her body? Oh! She sucked in a breath as tingles of anticipation peaked her nipples. Never had she thought of kissing a woman besides Mary, yet the thought was there.

The woman's finger left her mouth and headed in the direction of Amanda's face. The wet nail and tip of her finger trailed down the bridge of Amanda's nose, and the nail flicked her nose tip.

Amanda's eyes widened as the moisture prickled, drying in the air.

The woman winked.

Amanda had no clue what either of those two behaviors entailed. The excitement in the woman's voice indicated a display both scandalous and wicked.

Scandalous and wicked.

Indeed, Amanda needed both sensations badly.

The woman wrapped her fingers about Amanda's forearm. "Come with me, dear."

Amanda's feet floated as if on clouds as she followed the woman's swaying hips down the long, dimly lit hall. She was about to see into Aunt Bess's scandalous world. Portraits of man and woman lined the walls. The door opened behind them, and a rush of cool air cooled Amanda's humid skin.

The woman who guided her stopped and gazed back toward the door. "Another guest." Her gazed slid down Amanda's body, and Amanda trembled as if the woman's hands had trailed her skin instead.

"Let me settle this man. I don't want to be rushed with you." The woman's tongue slid along her plush lips.

Amanda shyly smiled. "Of course."

"Pardon me. I won't be but a moment."

The woman turned and started toward the door.

Amanda watched her as she reached the entrance hall.

"Good evening, sir."

"Good evening, madam." The deep tenor of his voice raised every fine hair on Amanda's body in titillation.

Devon.

Amanda's eyes widened. Was it him? She swallowed hard as she studied the broad back of a blue evening coat tapering down to a thin waist and deliciously rounded backside. Oh, my. Better than the one in her aunt's drawing. Even beneath his coattails, the firm muscles showed handsomely.

She bit her lip. He certainly was larger than any man she had seen since Devon, and no one had commanded her attention as he had all those years ago before her marriage. She imagined his lips brushing hers and the sweet smell of vanilla filling her nose as she'd laughed. "Devon . . ." she whispered so soft no one but she could hear.

The man spun around in the hall. His eyes, intense blue, grabbed at her soul.

She sucked in her breath and turned away from him. Devon. Devon Ursus stood in the hall. Chills of longing, anticipation, and fear raced her body. Her nipples pebbled to hard points against the rough fabric of her stays. She inhaled and gasped for air but couldn't move.

She stared at the portrait before her of a man the size of a child who stood beside a full-bearded, skinny woman. Yes, that's it. Amanda focused on the odd painting. She forced her eyes wider and tried to forget the man standing in the entry. Tried to focus on the excitement she had sought only moments before or even on this ridiculous painting. Impossible.

Devon . . . Devon stood in the hall. The man whom all those years ago she had loved with all her heart. She squeezed her eyes shut again. Would he forgive her the folly that pushed him away? Her silly confession came back to her: *"He speaks to me with his mind"*—as Mary's eyes had widened.

"What do you wish to see, sir?" the woman's sultry voice chirped, pulling Amanda's attention back to this day.

"Whatever the woman you were escorting back wished to see."

"A private showing, sir. If you stay here, I will get one of the girls to escort you."

"No, I wish to go with you and the lady."

"I'm sorry, sir, she has requested a *private* showing."

Amanda tensed. She did wish him to join her, but . . .

Amanda, I will be joining you. I knew there was a reason this hell pulled at me when I passed.

Her mind spun. He had spoken to her with his thoughts just as he had all those years ago. Her arms trembled, and she forced her unseeing eyes to never leave the expression of the man in the portrait.

Oh, God. She wanted Devon to touch her. Touch her the way he had so long ago, but more so. The lips of her pussy tingled.

She squeezed her eyes shut. "He—he can join me if he wishes," she said, loud enough for the woman to hear.

"Oh." The woman's tone held question.

Amanda couldn't look at the woman, nor at him. This was a dream. Indeed. One of the hundreds of dreams she had about seeing him again.

No, Amanda, I am here. This is real. And I will not leave you again until you are mine. That was a mistake. A mistake of a foolish young boy. I am no longer foolish.

"What do you wish, sir?" Disappointment filled the woman's voice.

"Well, dear madam, I wish to see the delightful woman down the hall kiss you."

Amanda's breath caught in her throat. He knew! How did he see her wicked thoughts?

"Indeed, the woman is—"

"Indeed." Devon's voice caressed Amanda's nerves, and the flesh between her thighs washed in scorching heat.

"This way, sir. I have lots to show both of you . . . Sights to titillate and shock your erotic senses."

3

Devon's heart lodged firmly in his throat. Amanda was in Venus's Glove. Staggering. Why and how she had arrived in such a place, he simply didn't care.

He laughed to himself. Her being in such a place only proved what he'd remembered about Lady Amanda—she lusted for life and exciting experiences. Her vivid pale hair pulled back from her face was accentuated by the dark blue gauze she wore.

Lady Amanda. His hand brushed against the superfine of his coat. The lock of hair he had carried with him the last twelve years was tucked safely in his breast pocket against his heart. He sighed. No, twelve years was a lie. The first year he couldn't dare to see the keepsake, but he couldn't burn the locks either. Energy and vibrancy had radiated off the tied strands and played their memories in his mind. The way her lips had parted when he'd kissed her the first time. His pure-mate scent, sweet clover honey, had radiated from her being and never left his senses.

His heart pinched. He'd suffered years of acute longing because he had ignorantly turned away from her for telling her best friend about him. *"I spoke to Mary about . . . well, about you and what happened."*

"You mean about me speaking to you with my mind?"

"Yes. The vapors grasped me, and she helped calm me."

Foolishness.

Later he had realized he had never really found out exactly what she had told her friend.

There she was . . . standing down the hall, not daring to glance at him and thinking this was all a dream.

Never would he let her out of his sight, now that he could finally grasp her again. He didn't give a damn what her reason for being in a strange hell like this was.

He prowled toward her, following the extremely handsome guide who had taken his money at the door.

The image of Amanda kissing this woman hardened his cock. Amanda wished it, and he would make her fulfill her desire. This hell was known for sexual variants. A show of sorts. Men with larger-than-large cocks, woman possessing both a cunny and a phallus, and so on—not his typical interest, but Amanda was here for erotic entertainment.

Never had he possessed the urge to enter until this day when he passed the street. The image of Amanda had come to him as he'd passed the door.

What luck! Had destiny brought him to London this very week? He would be thanking Orin for ages for sending him up to safely ensure the port he'd ordered arrived unharmed.

He reached Amanda's side. The woman glanced at him and then stared at Amanda. "Seems we have added to our amusements." Her fingers wrapped about Amanda's arm. "Shall we continue on to the private rooms I wished to show you, ma'am? Or do you now wish to see the group entertainment first?"

Amanda's tongue slid out and wet her lips, leaving a shine Devon wished to taste. She wouldn't look at him. The heat of her embarrassment for being here, and him knowing her thoughts about kissing this woman, kept her at arm's length. Or did she wait for him to decide to tell her what to say? Intriguing....

The group entertainments, Amanda.

Indeed. He wanted to see her reactions with others around to witness her adventurous eagerness.

The muscles in Amanda's neck worked as she swallowed and then inhaled a steady, slow breath. "The group entertainment should do nicely."

The madam of the house licked her lips in a gesture that said to Devon she was ready to taste all Amanda had to offer.

No surprise. Amanda was a rare pale beauty. Hair almost white in hue, fair blue-green eyes, the palest of pale skin, and a mole rested on the corner of her lip. His mouth watered, and the urge to lick the dark dot ran along his skin.

Her father had received a handsome sum for her marriage. His stomach clenched. The announcement had crushed Devon and shocked Amanda as well.

No matter; he was here now and would fulfill every lustful desire filtering through her beautiful full-witted head.

"What is your name?" The madam of the house glanced back at him as she guided them farther into the house.

"Amanda." She licked her lips again and glanced at the woman.

Amanda . . . look at me. I want to see your eyes. Too long has passed.

Amanda's head turned toward him, and her pale blues caught his for an instant. Then she looked back down the hall in front of her.

Duce! He wanted to pick her up and whisk her out into his carriage for a proper inspection of all the charms he had never had the privilege of sighting. *Tsk, tsk, Devon. This could be quite entertaining. . . . Patience, you rogue.*

He smiled and then glanced back at the two women. They

both stared at him as though waiting for an answer. "Pardon, I was wool gathering."

"Oh, indeed, sir." The madam's lips twitched; then she all-out grinned. "Pulling wool off us, I have no doubt."

Devon laughed, as did Amanda. Her sweet laughter warmed him to his toes. Duce. Her happiness lifted his soul and soothed his beast.

"No doubt." Amanda smiled, and smoldering heat sparked her eyes.

Oh, indeed! Staying here in this hell was a grand idea.

"What information were you looking for from me, ladies . . . besides my naughty intent?"

"What do you wish us to call you, sir?"

"Indeed. Hmmm. 'Sir' will do quite nicely."

Amanda stared at him and tilted her head to the side in question. *Not Devon. Why?* Her question was so easy for him to read.

Quite so, Amanda. It is best to simply call me "Sir" here. When I taste you in private . . . you will call me Devon.

Her eyes widened, and the image of his tongue pressed to her sex filled his mind. Duce it. He could see her every sexual impulse. His mouth watered, and he grinned wickedly.

I always knew you were a wanton, Amanda. A woman willing to try things, a woman with an active imagination. I find that quality about you exhilarating.

Amanda's face turned crimson, a striking contrast to her paleness.

He sighed. He had missed her. *Amanda . . .*

"The performance will start at half past, so we will have time to get acquainted." The madam pushed open a door, which led down a small flight of steps to a large room with a stage in the center.

Indeed, I will be requesting you to kiss her, Amanda. Will you do as I ask?

She didn't answer, but in her mind hovered images of her tongue dragging along the madam's plush lips hovered.

Answer enough.

They traversed the steps—the madam in front, followed by Amanda, then Devon. Three chandeliers, with more than thirty candles in each, lit the room. Occupied longues, with small tables set beside them were scattered about the space. On the stage resided an extremely long and narrow bed.

A performance of *the act,* no doubt.

He glanced at Amanda as they situated themselves close to the stage on a deep blue longue.

Devon sat at one end. Amanda sat next to him. He glanced down; a good two hands' breadths lay between them. A frown curved his lips. He needed her closer, to feel the heat of her body against his, to smell the scent of her lust as she peaked in arousal.

The madam stood before them. "Refreshment?"

"Scotch and . . ."

Devon glanced at Amanda. *Claret.*

". . . claret."

"Indeed." The madam turned and sauntered through the settees of men and women chatting quietly and sipping their drinks.

His hand slid across and grasped Amanda's in her lap. His fingers closed around her thumb and trailed the soft flesh of her mound beneath her skirts.

She jumped, and her eyes snapped to his face. "I—I am sorry for how I hurt you, Devon." Her voice was a mere whisper, and remorse and care filled her eyes.

An apology was unexpected and not necessary. "No, Amanda. No apology is required." He stared at her lips, soft and pouting in a true but oh-so-seductive frown. "I reacted poorly to someone I didn't know well finding out I was different." He squeezed her hand and raised the honey-scented flesh to his mouth. Pressing her knuckles to his lips, he kissed her silken flesh and sighed. This was right. His soul had known she was his life mate at the age of twenty and had never let her go.

"I wish you to do wicked, wanton things this night."

Her eyelashes lowered, and she tilted her head down. The delicious blush crept down her neck to the dark lace about the modest neckline of her dress. *There is nonesuch as you, Amanda.*

She didn't tilt her head back up. "Thank you, Devon."

The madam returned with a silver tray in hand, three drinks perched on top.

Amanda, I want you to kiss her before the entertainment begins.

Amanda's head lifted, and she stared him in the eyes. "Pardon?" she whispered.

Quite so. Drink up if you are vexed. She is more than interested in you.

Amanda stared at the madam.

The madam held out a glass of light red liquid to Amanda. "Claret, Amanda."

"Thank you." Amanda wrapped her fingers about the stem of the glass. The madam's long fingers slid across Amanda's hand as she released the stem in her fingers. Amanda's arm visibly trembled.

Don't spill any, my love. It appears you will need it.

She glared at him, and he grinned.

"It appears I missed something." The madam held out his Scotch and smiled.

He grasped the short glass and winked at her and then smiled also. "Indeed, madam. But you will be enlightened in only a moment. Amanda."

Amanda gulped a large portion of her claret. "Indeed, madam."

Devon reached out and curved his fingers about Amanda's opposite side. She inhaled sharply. The erotic energy pouring off her warmed his arms, and his cock thickened. Indeed, he would claim her as his. He pulled and slid her toward him on the settee so the madam could seat herself beside Amanda.

If you are nervous and feel you need instruction, I am here to guide you, Amanda. Though you had no issues the last time I asked.

Years have passed, Devon, but as you know, I had thought about her kiss.

Kiss her; there is nothing to fear, Amanda. It is taboo only to the outside world . . . not here. Not with me.

The madam sat down next to Amanda and raised her glass of wine to her lips. Amanda glanced at Devon once again and then reached out. Extending her finger, she dipped the tip into the madam's glass of wine. She then lifted her finger—a droplet of wine clung to the end—to the madam's lips.

The madam opened her mouth, and Amanda's finger pressed to her lower painted surface. The woman closed her lips about Amanda's finger. "Mmmm."

Devon's lungs locked.

The madam's tongue slid out and curled about Amanda's finger. A shiver racked Amanda, and goose bumps puckered the skin of her chest. Staggering.

The madam's tongue released Amanda's finger.

"More?" Amanda's eyebrows rose.

"Indeed."

Thank the Ursus this settee was slightly curved. Otherwise he couldn't see both of their expressions, and, for him, watching was the entire point.

Amanda's finger slid back into the wine and emerged; the wine clung to the tip and up to her knuckle. She headed in the direction of the madam's lips. The madam opened her mouth in anticipation, and the wine droplet fell, landing on her collarbone, and ran down to pool in the hollow of her neck.

Amanda leaned in; her tongue slid out and licked the droplet of wine from the hollow.

Duce it! She hadn't even hesitated. His heart lodged firmly in his throat.

The madam moaned. Her free hand rose and gently caressed the back of Amanda's neck. Amanda's tongue slid up the madam's collarbone; then she sat back. "Let's try again." Her finger rose and dipped into the wine once more.

Devon could not breathe. Erotic, sensual. A staggering sight. She was the same girl as years ago, but this Amanda was experienced. Just how much so, he had not a clue, but he would find out. He would have the rest of his life to do so.

Her finger rose again to the madam's lips; the droplet of wine clung to the tip as if a dewdrop ready to fall from a spring leaf. The madam opened her mouth, and Amanda's finger glided along the lower plush surface, coating her bottom lip in the wine. Leaning in, Amanda's tongue followed the trail her finger made.

The madam tensed at the sudden caress of Amanda's tongue and then moaned. Their lips melded and then parted slightly. Through the part in their lips, tongues wrapped, stroked, and caressed. Their lips united again, massaging and gliding over and over as they moaned.

Devon swallowed hard and shifted in his seat as his cock expanded with warmth. His gaze darted about the room. Men watched. Women watched. Amanda was an amazing sight. The madam's hand trailed up Amanda's stomach to her breasts as they continued to kiss.

Amanda's chest rose and fell rapidly, and she shifted her position on the seat. Devon leered at them. Was her pussy tingling? Were her nipples hard? Damnit! He needed to know.

He wanted to be kissing her and making her squirm in her seat. His tongue traced his lips. He sure as hell wanted to be touching her breasts and sliding his hand into her cunny to see just how aroused she was.

Jealousy over her lips caressing this woman's, when he had

yet to taste her this night, raised the hair on his neck. His teeth clenched. Would she come and kiss him next if he asked?

"I want to kiss you," burst from his lips.

Amanda trembled, and their kissing slowed. She pulled from the kiss first and turned toward him. Lips, wet from their kiss, and arousal-hazed eyes met his and then dropped to his mouth. His phallus hardened fully, and his animal raged. He repressed an erotic shiver, and his vision hazed.

Hell! His passion for her was strong, but he couldn't allow the animal part of him free. The last thing he needed was to fight his control and change here in a public place. He needed a distraction from her. Duce it! He held back the urge to raise his hand and tug on her hair, exposing her neck for a long, harsh tasting. Maybe . . .

He raised a hand, palm up, toward Amanda. Then, his other toward the madam. Curling his fingers toward him, he indicated his wish. Both of them moved at the same time toward him. Amanda's soft curves draped across his thigh, and her lips smashed with urgent need against his.

The erotic jolt from her harsh, passion-filled caress hazed his vision completely, and his lungs locked. Her lips, so soft, tasted of wine. He feasted; his lips traveled across the plump surface, and then his teeth snagged her lower lip, sucking it into his warmth.

Amanda moaned.

The madam's lips feathered the bare flesh above his cravat just below his ear. His hands rose and possessed Amanda's waist. He wanted to lift her to place her fully on his lap as he kissed her and her alone.

No, Devon. Do not tempt your good luck. She and she alone will fully break your control. You thought Jane challenging your control was amazing, but that was Orsse. A simple kiss and body contact, sexual body contact, with Amanda alone will change you.

Amanda's hands shifted to his lap, and her fingers curled about the top of his prick.

He swallowed a groan, and his chest rumbled.

Devon . . . Devon . . . I have wanted to kiss you and touch you since I learned what this urge and feeling was. I have lusted for you for years. Her lips firmed, and her tongue thrust into his mouth and wrapped about his.

Lust . . . indeed, but there was more to the emotion in his heart and in hers.

Her touch on his pantaloons firmed, and her fingers slid down his length to the ridge of his arrow-shaped head. Her fingers twisted and traced the ridge.

A jolt of erotic tingles shot up his leg. Duce it. He held back the will to surge to his feet and carry her from this room to his carriage. Damn the madam! Not one of her caresses registered against his neck. The madam shifted her hands, and her fingers fumbled to untie his cravat.

Devon . . . you have two beautiful women seducing you, and all you can think of is getting out? Twisted. What is wrong with you? Relax. You have outstanding control over your powers. Live well. Enjoy this.

He pushed the thoughts from his mind as if shutting a door and concentrated on the sensations assaulting him. The soft texture of Amanda's lips gliding along his, the tremors of his muscles as her fingers continued to press and tease his cock through his pantaloons. The whispering breath of the madam as her tongue traced his earlobe and her fingers tugged and un-wound his elaborately tied cravat.

Amanda moaned as the madam's hands brushed the bare skin of her chest above her dress while pulling the length of cotton loose. Amanda was starved for a caress.

He reached up and traced his finger along the neckline of Amanda's bodice. The scorching-hot flesh sped his heart, and he sighed. He loved touching her; her radiance captured his fingertips, and he thirsted for more. He pulled the thin fabric of her neckline slightly from her body and delved beneath.

The smell of honey radiated up and off her. His head spun. He had envisioned touching her in just such a way for years.

Seeing Amanda kiss another woman had filled his thoughts and emotions. Yet, this somehow wasn't quite what he needed. What he wanted. He—

Duce it. He needed to be with her alone, to tell her of all his follies, and for her to speak of hers. He wanted to know everything, every last minute detail that had filled her life since they had parted. Sharing heightened their experience, but adding another person could wait. He tensed and pulled back from Amanda and the madam's caresses.

"Delicious, ladies. But if you continue to attend to me in such a manner, we shall miss the entertainments, and I wish to extend and savor this evening."

What a jest! He wished to end this now and take Amanda to their town residence. Amanda's eyelids hung heavy as she stared at him. Her tongue slid out and traced her puffy lips. He groaned. Damn. He wanted to kiss her again. Her hand squeezed his cock; the heat of the caress pushed stars into his eyes. He clenched his teeth, grabbing for control of his shifting. Tremors slid through his body as his tightly held strings slipped. *Remove your hand, Amanda.*

She showed no sign that she intended to remove her caress.

The madam sauntered around to stand in front of them. "Sir, if you enjoy watching us, and Amanda is interested, we could entertain you in the display?"

Amanda stilled her caress. Thank the Ursus, a distraction. "What is the display this night, madam?"

"The feat for this night is Evan. Evan is filled with lustful talents. But this night he will pleasure six women at once."

"Six?" Amanda's eyes widened and fixed on the madam's face.

Devon chuckled. *Indeed, Amanda. Have you been with more than your husband?* If she hadn't, he would not push her to do this.

She didn't look at him, but the blush intensified on her cheeks. *Indeed, but never to my liking. The men Harold chose always held drunken foul of breath.*

She hadn't minded being with others . . . just that their breath had smelled bad? He held in a smirk he knew would be taken wrong. *Would you like to participate, Amanda?*

I—I wish to continue to touch you.

He gritted his teeth. Indeed, he wanted her touch, and with the entertainment beginning, he could distract himself enough. *Please do, my love. I would never deny you pleasure.*

Her fingers continued to trace the ridge on his pants, and his bum muscles clenched.

"I shall pass on seeing that delight, madam. But if Amanda wishes after the sight begins, may she join?"

The madam glanced at the stage. "Indeed. I need to go prepare. If you so desire, Amanda, you may come and kiss me as Evan makes me spend." The madam's hand rose, and her finger traced Amanda's lips. Amanda opened her mouth and touched her tongue to the madam's caress.

The madam's arm trembled, and then she sighed. She smiled down at them both. "You are both fortunate to have found someone who enjoys exploration." She turned and left them.

4

Amanda trembled in emotional overload. She had kissed a woman. Not simply kissed her but sensually kissed her.

The playful kiss of her youth was a memory she cherished. This full-grown, knowing woman kiss had blazed her mind. She bit her lip, trying to hold in the nervous, excited giggle pushing up her throat. What was even more outstanding was she had kissed a woman at the request of the same man twice over a decade apart. My God! Devon! He had seen into her adventurous soul and fed the fire that Harold had smothered.

Her mind spun with the knowledge that she sat in a club with Devon Ursus. She had wanted this day but had never imagined meeting him in London.

She swallowed hard as chills of ecstasy covered her skin in gooseflesh.

Her hand caressed the long, large prick concealed beneath the pantaloons. Devon's prick.... Only in her dreams had she imagined caressing his phallus, and the shape beneath his pantaloons surpassed her imagination.

"Amanda, lean against me. I want to feel your body against mine."

"Yes, Devon."

She shifted and nestled her body into the curve of his arm. His arm wrapped about her, and he lifted, pulling her bottom on the other side of him, her legs draped across his lap. She trembled, and her eyelids fluttered, pure rapture flooding her senses.

His embrace was better than a French éclair and silk sheets.... Oh! Devon on silk sheets with chocolate and custard drizzled along his prick. Oh . . . oh. Indeed. Her eyes widened as wetness tickled her pussy lips. My goodness. What had gotten into her?

She didn't care; she was enjoying this.

Devon grinned seductively down at her. "Éclair, eh?"

Her cheeks warmed, but she didn't say a word.

A tall, thin, naked man walked into the room and toward the stage, followed by a line of beautiful women, all of varying sizes. The madam Amanda had kissed walked among them. They wore nothing but lacy shifts and stockings.

Devon's hand slid up Amanda's side to her breasts. His other one trailed her flesh at the top of her dress in a heated map leading straight to her pussy. His fingers dipped below the fabric line of her bodice and gently squeezed. Prickles of balmy lust speared through her belly, and her breast bloomed. He pinched her nipple, and the muscles of her pussy clenched. Oh, my! Her breath swirled, caged in her chest, as she forced herself to breathe.

"Indeed, Amanda. I can smell your arousal. The way your body heats and responds to my touch is maddening." His breath warmed her ear.

The wetness of his tongue slid into the cup of her ear, and she trembled, clamping her legs together and shifting them. The slight tension of her legs rubbing together eased her aroused flesh and peaked her desire for his probing touch.

"I will futter you this night, Amanda. Your flesh will be eased into and the ache for me fulfilled."

His voice, deep and playful, filled her mind, and she shook. Indeed, the large prick she had caressed only moments before would press into her cunny and fill her flesh. She shifted her bottom in search for the wide, hard ridge upon which she sat.

"Watch the entertainments, Amanda."

Blast! She slowly turned her focus back to the stage. The man lay on the mat. The madam circled around one of the girls. Hands pinched and rubbed the madam's flesh. Her shift rose, and a flourish of hands lifted it from her body. Fingers delved into the flesh of her legs. Kisses spread along her shoulders, her back, and her breasts. One woman sucked her breast into her mouth, and the madam's head tilted back as she thrust her breast forward.

Oh! How Amanda wanted her breast sucked, to feel the warm wetness of tongue and friction of teeth.

Devon pulled her breast up above her corset. With the nipple barely exposed, the flesh of her breast squished upward in freedom. He raised his thumb to his lips and sucked and then circled her puckered, deep peach-colored flesh.

Oh. Oh, my!

He blew a stream of breath directly onto her nipple. Cool tingles raced across the flesh, crinkling and hardening the nipple fully. She inhaled, shaking, and stared him in the eyes. Deep blue pools of sapphire stared back. The intensity of desire flooding his stare alone brought honey between her thighs.

Watch them, my love. Watch them, and I will pleasure you.

He will pleasure me as I watch? Oh, how delicious. She forced herself to look back to the madam on the platform and not stare at every motion he made.

One of the women now caressed the man's cock, her hand

shimmering in wetness. His cock firmed and grew, standing straighter with each pass of the oil up his prick. The other women all fondled and kissed each other. The madam's eyes strayed to Amanda for an instant and then went back to the sensations around her.

Devon sucked her nipple into his mouth. Prickles slid down her stomach to her womb, and her back arched.

Oh. Oh, God. Her eyelids hung heavy as she watched the unfolding performance on the platform in a haze of arousal brought to life from Devon's skilled hands and mouth.

The man reached his hands up and caressed the breast of the woman who pleasured his cock. Her head fell back, and her fingers squeezed the head of his long, thin prick. Another of the women broke from the group and walked to the man. She stood by his head; his free hand slid up her inner thigh and into her sex. The woman moaned, and the smell of her lustful desire filled the room.

My God. The smell titillated Amanda. She licked her lips. Devon's hand slid down her stomach, and his long, thick fingers pushed her skirts between her thighs. Her legs fell open to allow him access through the layers and layers of cloth. Amanda squirmed against his rubbing in need for Devon's fingers futtering her as the man finger frigged the woman onstage.

The sound of the man's fingers slipping in and out of the drenched woman's flesh added dry grass to the fire building between Amanda's legs. Her hips arched against Devon's caress of her mound as she tried to position herself so his fingers slid lower. He tapped his fingers against the cloth of her skirts, and she moaned.

The madam approached the man. She leaned in, kissed him firmly on the lips, and then straddled his neck. Her pussy opened to his mouth, and she lowered herself, squatting slightly. His tongue slid out, and he licked the red flesh of her sex lips. The madam shifted her hips and closed her eyes. The woman he still finger frigged raised her leg and placed her foot on the mattress by his head. The position opened the eye of her sex to him, allowing him greater access to her pleasure.

Amanda's legs shook, her bottom quivering against Devon's thigh. His mouth sucked her nipple, and his hand rocked on her mound. All her muscles tightened, and her toes curled as she reached for the increasing bliss.

Another woman, with black hair pinned up in curls, went to stand by the man's head. His hand dropped from the woman at his prick and slid into the black-haired woman's sex. The madam wrapped her arm about the black-haired girl, and the new woman leaned in and licked the madam's nipple, sucking the flesh into her mouth. Chills raced Amanda's skin as Devon mimicked the act by sucking her nipple, into his mouth. Devon's tongue swirled her nipple and the muscles of her sex rippled with sensation.

The woman on the other side of the man reached her hand up and pinched the madam's breast as the two final girls—one with red hair and the other a few stone too heavy—positioned themselves straddling each one of his feet. The two girls sank down, sliding his toes into the pink flesh of their sexes.

Amanda's eyes widened. *My goodness, his feet!* What would that feel like? She tried to imagine the sensation of toes wiggling in her cunny and held in a giggle. How odd!

This man pleasured five women, and the sixth continued to stroke his erect cock. The final woman stood, straddled his waist, leaned forward to caress the madam's bottom, and sank down onto his phallus.

He moaned and thrust his hips and other futtering appendages vigorously into the women he pleasured. The woman riding his prick slid her hand along the swell of the madam's bottom and between her legs. The madam moaned and arched her bottom toward the woman behind her. Blast, what the woman did between the madam's legs Amanda could not quite tell. She squinted, hoping to see something. Nope, nothing.

Amanda swallowed hard, and Devon's fingers slid down her leg to her ankle and then up her skirt. She tensed, and her eyes fluttered shut. He was going to relieve her desire here ... in front of all these people. Oh, my, how wicked! But ... *Devon, should you touch me so intimately here?* She shook as his fingers reached the top of her stocking and touched the bare flesh of her thigh. *Did she really care?*

"Indeed. Let this happen, Amanda. If you are nervous, just look around us." She slit her eyes open to meet his. Calm, strength, and desire swirled in their depths.

She nodded her head to him and then glanced around the room. A couple on the longue next to them watched the entertainment unfold. The man's hand exposed the woman's breast as he pinched the nipple. She had his flap folded back and openly stroked his cock. Amazing. Others kissed and groped each other, some even of the same sex. She had never imagined people congregated to watch such a feat.

A moan came from one of the women onstage, and Amanda gazed back at the performance.

The woman on the man's prick rose up and down on him, moaning as she buggered the madam in front of her and kissed her neck. The madam riding the man's wiggling tongue, whimpered and groaned, shaking as both her nipples were pleasured.

Amanda wanted all those caresses. What a wanton she was. She wanted to be possessed in every sensitive orifice of her body. *Indeed, my love, I will give you all you desire and more.* Devon's fingers slid into her labia and across the bud of her sex.

Amanda jerked, and chills raised every fine hair on her body. She spread her legs wantonly apart. *Yes, please, please frig my open cunny with your hands, Devon ... please.* The need to have him give her release possessed her mind, body, and soul.

Devon's fingers traced the opening of her sex, and she bit her lip, her chin wobbling.

"Please," she whimpered, and her hips pushed down.

His fingers eluded her motions, and his lips curved into a smile against her breast.

Please, please, Devon, I—I need you. I wish to feel your fingers in my pussy. I wish to feel your prick slipping in and out of me.

Indeed, my love, but the delight of the full act will have to wait until we leave here. I will frig you in public, but futtering here in this hell, I cannot do. My nature will shift.

His nature. She groaned, remembering his words from all those years ago. *I am not as I seem, Amanda. I am more than human. I am Ursus. And that is more than simply my name. Long ago, my ancestors were cursed by the blood of a bear. We take on qualities of the bear when we mate and become fierce to protect our life mates.*

She had forgotten this large oddity about Devon. Never had she forgotten the mind-speak, but why he possessed the skill she had pushed from her brain. She mentally shrugged. She would never let his oddness unnerve her again. She had learned that lesson all those years ago. The flesh of her inner cunny twitched, and she wiggled her hips in search of release.

Please, Devon, help me reach bliss with your hands.

His finger slid into her open cunny, and lightning flooded her sex; her toes curled tight. She shook about him, her spend shaking her hard as she bit her lip, holding in the scream she so desperately wanted to let free. His finger wiggled against the contractions, and wetness drizzled down her bottom. His lips traveled up her chest to her neck and then to her ear.

My, my, Amanda, one finger and you spend for me. What will my cock sliding in and out of your flesh as I bite your neck do to you? His finger in her cunt continued to slide in and out with ease in her spend. *Watch them, Amanda. I am sure seeing*

them all reach their peaks will bring another wave of bliss to ca-
ress my fingers.

She slit her eyes open and gazed at the stage in hazily aroused
bliss.

The women all trembled, sliding up and down on the ap-
pendage they straddled. They kissed and touched. Pleasuring
and being pleasured. The sight was truly amazing. One man
and six women; who would have thought?

The madam broke first. Her body jerked. "Oh . . . oh . . .
oh!" Legs shaking, she clutched the women on both sides of
her.

The plump woman on his toes spent immediately after; she
rode down hard on his toes. Her scream was absorbed by the
red-haired woman across from her as they kissed. Her spend
dripped down his foot and onto the floor. His foot continued
to wiggle and wriggle.

Amanda's fingers slid beneath her thigh in search of Devon's
phallus. She needed to feel him. She wanted to feel his hot, silky
skin on hers, but the contact of even simply stroking him
through his pantaloons would bring her joy.

She slid along the fabric of his silk pantaloons to the bulging
ridge. The fabric burned beneath her touch, and as her fingers
latched on to the stiffness, his cock jumped in her hand. Indeed,
he did want his cock sliding in and out of her pussy.

"Watch the show, my love. After the entertainment ends, we
will be leaving with haste." His deep, lust-filled voice in her ear
delighted her senses, and she smiled.

The woman who rode the man's cock spent next; her buttocks quivered as passion swept her up and out to sea. The
madam who rode on his tongue stepped forward and off him,
and the woman with her foot on the mat as he'd frigged her
with his hand stepped across his head, opening her cunny up to
his tongue's probe. Her body quivered and jerked at the new
sensation.

Amanda's fingers slid down to the tip of Devon's prick. The fabric covering the plum-shaped head was damp. Heat washed her body. She wanted to sate his desire for her and rekindle his hardness anew.

She kept her head turned toward the entertainments but stroked and lightly pinched the head of his cock as she did so.

He tensed, and his breath deepened. His hand continued to slip in and out of her sex.

Devon, I wish to place my lips here. . . . She gently squeezed the tip between her thumb and fingers and slid down the head to the ridge; then she twisted her hand along the ridge. "Then run my tongue along like this and taste your salty skin."

"Vixen," he hissed through clenched teeth.

"Oh, pardon! I didn't realize you wished for a woman named Vixen to pleasure you in my stead." She licked her lips.

"Duce it, Amanda. I have only ever wanted you."

Her forehead pinched. She wanted to believe his words, but she didn't trust them for a moment. Harold had taught her to futter, but a man only ever wanting one woman? Never. Her gaze focused back on the scene they watched. A perfect example of Harold's teachings.

The red-haired woman riding his toes shattered, pulling the woman across from her from his foot entirely as she kissed and groped. Her body shuddered, and they slid to the floor in a tangle of limbs and urgent kisses.

Harold had insisted that not one man or woman could carnally be satisfied with one futter partner for always. Amanda bit her lip. Funny thing was she had always thought she could be happy with only one, if that man was someone she loved, and he loved her. Her heart constricted.

Foolish, Amanda. You know men can't love. Admire, yes, care for, sure, and lust for, without a doubt. But love?

She sighed and thought of Devon and the swirl of emotions seeing him had evoked in her. She loved him. She always had.

The woman on the man's cock stepped off him. The man's pego stood stiff and glimmering with her oils.

The black-haired woman the man still finger frigged stepped from his fingers and threw her leg across him as if mounting a horse. Her hands slid along his phallus and then positioned the head in her hole. She sank down, sheathing him in her cunt, and shuddered.

My goodness! She wanted to ride down on Devon's thick phallus and shudder at the intense sensation of being filled by him, joined with him in the most intimate of ways.

Soon, Amanda. Soon.

The woman the man frigged with his mouth rode back and forth on his tongue, squatting. Her legs shook, and she moaned.

The black-haired woman on his prick rode up and down on his cock, bringing him closer to orgasm.

His head wiggled, and his tongue speared into the other woman's flesh. His hips lifted off the mattress, and he shuddered, spearing his phallus into the woman who rode him; he groaned. The black-haired woman slid down his phallus and cried out. Her legs jerked as they both spent.

The woman on his mouth whimpered, jerked, and then pinched her nipples and screamed.

Devon's lips pressed to her earlobe and the flesh of her neck beneath. "Ready to depart, my love?"

5

Devon's demons raged, every fiber held in check, in control, but as she had touched his cock and the entertainers had all spent onstage, his eyes had shifted. If he did not have the strength or control he possessed, his dignity would be in a puddle at Amanda's dainty feet. He glanced at her silk slippers as she stepped up into his carriage. Dainty, indeed.

He pulled himself up into the carriage after she settled and unfolded himself into the seat next to her. He sighed. The entire box smelled of Amanda's natural scent of honey. He grinned and ran his hand through his hair. The smell of her pussy honey clung to his fingers, flooding his senses.

He had longed for this day, and she was here. The door to his carriage closed, and the familiar sway jerked into motion, sliding her close to his side.

"Devon." Amanda stared at him in the dim coach light.

"Yes, Amanda?"

Her hand slid to his pantaloons and the buttons at his waist. Passion and devilish desire swirled in the depths of her eyes. "I wish you inside me."

Her fingers deftly undid the buttons and pulled back the flap. The cool night air stung his heated flesh, and her hands slid under the fabric and down his leg in search of freeing his encased prick.

He moaned. He could never deny her futter, not when no one else was in the box.

Her fingers wrapped about his stiff flesh and pulled. His cock pressed against his pantaloons on exit with nerve-shaking friction.

Her hand squeezed the base, and she spit into the palm of her other hand. Holding the saliva above his cock, she drizzled the wetness onto her grip at the base. Her hand slid up his cock on the slickness. He inhaled deep as she glided along the head, sending delightful twinges through his balls. Heat washed his body, and he growled.

She grinned up at him. "Like that, do you, Devon?" Her lust-filled, husky voice set his heart pounding with increased vigor. Truly a vixen.

He reached out and ran the back of his fingers across her cheek. "Indeed, my love."

Her eyes softened, and a crease formed between her brows. His eyes narrowed. What was she feeling? He wished he could read emotions as Mac could at this moment. But everyone was different, and he could simply speak with his mind. Well, and possibly move a feather with his thoughts.

Amanda tilted her head down, and her fingertips caressed the sides of his shaft. Reaching the head of his pego, she flattened her palm and twisted her grip over the tip. Pinpricks of pleasure shot through his veins, and he sucked in through clenched teeth. Duce it. Amazing.

Her hand slid back down, the fingertips touching the sides of his shaft. As she reached the base and her other hand, her lips closed around the crown of his phallus.

His legs jerked as intense tingles pulled his sac up tight to his body. Touching her tongue to the eye at the tip, she pushed saliva from her mouth and down the taut skin. Her lips flared over the taper and followed in her hands' wake, encasing his prick in warm, wet suction.

Reaching her hands, she pulled back up. Her first hand slid behind her mouth back to the tip, pulling his skin deliciously taut. Pinpricks of delight tapped up his belly, and the head of his phallus grew. Her mouth lifted off the tip. Her hand twisted over the top and then descended, lips following back down his throbbing length.

Damn! She was good! Her deceased husband certainly had taught her this skill well. The muscles in his stomach quivered, and each pass of her lips across the tip of his phallus shot twinges of fire to his brain. All of his thoughts exploded in smoke, and he closed his eyes, enjoying the sensations her amazing mouth created.

His breathing deepened, and his prick throbbed. Her lips pulled from his body, as did her hands, and his eyes shot open. "Don't stop." His voice was hoarse to his ears.

She grinned and stood in the carriage, lifting her skirts.

Indeed, even better. Hot, wet cunny.

Facing away from him, she straddled his legs, reached for his cock, parted her wet labia on the tip, and sank down.

Hot, rippled cunny slid along his large prick, encasing his cock in tight, pulsing slickness.

"Oh!" Her hips arched and then resettled his massive cock in her.

"Oh, indeed, Amanda." His hands pulled up her skirts, and his finger reached between her legs, tracing the tight opening of her stretched cunt with his fingertips. She was filled with him.

She wiggled her hips and moaned, rubbing her nubbin against the pad of his palm. He slid his finger up to her large, hard button and circled the turgid flesh.

She gasped, and the carriage rocked, shifting them.

"Brace your hands on the ceiling, Amanda."

She did so, stretching her body upward, her delicious curves accentuated by the pull of the fabric and her confining stays. He slid down slightly, held her waist with his hands, and pulled his hips back. His prick withdrew from her drenched, quivering flesh, creating delectable friction. His stomach muscles clenched.

Rocking the crown of his cock in the tight opening of her cunt, he moaned and then thrust back into her. The waved, spongy walls packaged him in acute lust, the likes of which he had never imagined. His mind spun with the possibilities of all the futters to come with his Amanda, his love.

His finger circled her nubbin again, wanting to bring her the same bliss pulsing through his fibers. Each stroke of his cock gradually increased in speed.

Her body trembled.

His cock throbbed.

He wrapped his arm about her waist as he reached the no-slowing point. "Amanda, I'm going to spend. I want to thrust harder. Are you well with me doing so?"

"Yes, yes, yes," she breathed, all her muscles quivering.

His arm held her firm and anchored her. Her feet parted farther for him, and he thrust powerfully into her, testing her ability to take his forcefulness in a swaying carriage. A shock of the delight speared up his spine. He growled, and his teeth clenched. Her back arched as she moaned.

She could take his hard jabs. His hips thrust up, powerfully and quickly. Each slide of her slick cunt along his prick head sent blissful sensations up his body, and his mind fogged as he chased the peak of pleasure just on the horizon. She moaned and dug her nails into the soft fabric of the ceiling.

Erotic energy flowed through him, and he peaked, falling

into the warming abyss. His balls and cock pulsed in unison, and he burst, spilling forth his seed into his soon-to-be life mate.

Amanda trembled against him. He would always cherish her and this first act. She stilled, and he pulled her back to lay upon his chest. He kissed her ear. "My love, we will futter more this night."

She inhaled a shaking breath and lay her head against the side of his.

"Please don't call me that, Devon."

Devon ran his hands down the front of her dress and slid his fingers along the insides of her thighs, his cock slowly deflating in her womb.

"Call you what, my love?"

"That. 'My love.'" She shook her head.

"Amanda, I don't understand. Why?"

"The endearment, I know, holds no emotion, and I have a hard enough time knowing men don't love. If you call me your love, it only troubles me."

He stilled his caress along her thighs. What was she talking about? She didn't like the endearment because men couldn't love? How silly! She couldn't have meant what he thought.

"I'm sorry, Amanda. I don't wish to trouble you, only to bring you joy. But I don't understand."

"I shouldn't have said anything. I am well, Devon. Call me what you wish." She inhaled a deep breath, and the carriage rocked to a halt in front of the small quarters the family kept in town.

"Where are you staying while in town, Amanda?"

"I am staying at my aunt Bess's. Do you remember her?"

"Who could forget her, Amanda? She was the scandal of her decade. How is she faring?"

"She is in Bath at the moment taking the waters. No doubt tormenting all the old men and their grandsons."

Devon laughed as he stepped out of the carriage and lifted her down. He stared down into her upturned face. "What do you wish me to call you, Amanda?"

She tilted her head to the side. "When we were young, you called me your sweet Amanda. I always liked when you called me such."

He smiled, and his heart lifted. Indeed, she was *his* sweet Amanda, though now she held a very great amount of spice.

"Very well, my sweet Amanda." He leaned in and kissed her forehead. "Come, let's go inside. I am famished. Would you care for a snack?"

Amanda's lips turned up into a devil's grin. "Indeed, starving for more of you."

She was wicked. Much more so than he had imagined she would be. But her comment about not wanting to be called "my love" still puzzled him. There was something afoot with her statement, and he would find out. He had every intention of calling her "my love" once they were joined. He inhaled. The endearment fell naturally from his lips. He watched her swaying hips as she glided up the steps and through the door.

"Good evening, sir."

Devon nodded to the butler, who had been in their families' service since journeying from the homeland, and grunted, "Please have cook send up meat and sweets, Gerald. Oh, and a bottle of wine." Gerald was used to all of them and their ways.

"Indeed, sir." He bowed, and his gray hair glinted in the candlelight.

Devon walked forward, grabbed Amanda's hand, and then placed her palm on his forearm. "Shall we? My l—l . . . sweet Amanda."

She followed his guidance toward the steps and down the long green carpeted hall. Duce it. He wanted to call her "my love." The emotion had been bottled up for a decade, and he wanted to express the emotion now that he could. He frowned.

What had happened in her marriage? He didn't want to press her or ruin this evening by bringing up a topic infused with strife for them. But . . .

"I have no idea how your marriage was, Amanda. I heard of his death. It has been six months now, if I am not mistaken."

"Almost a half year has passed, yes. But I don't wish to talk about Harold, Devon. My life with him was not fun. I simply wish to enjoy this night with you."

"Fair. Though I do wish you to tell me about him and your marriage. I feel it is an important part of knowing you." Very important. But he would simply start Orsse with her tonight. The ceremony would be finished on the morrow; he would do his best to honor her request and wait until the night passed to discuss her comment earlier.

He pushed open the fifth and final door on the left and stepped across the threshold.

6

Amanda's eyes widened at the size of everything in this home. The dwelling's structure was of average size for Mayfair, but the furniture was enormous.

She glanced at Devon, his height and breadth the largest she'd ever seen. She supposed the furniture needed to be large to hold him and his brothers. They were far from petite. She held in a schoolgirl giggle.

"What is so amusing?"

"Oh! I simply had a thought about how dainty you are."

"Indeed, as slight as an Ursus man comes." The corner of his mouth turned up.

"Can you tell me again about what being Ursus is, Devon? I am ashamed to admit I pushed all but the mind-speak from my memories."

"Nothing to be ashamed of, Amanda. Under the circumstances of our parting ways, I can understand. You were betrothed, and I acted like a fool."

"Not a fool, Devon. You were simply hurt that I betrayed a confidence. Rightfully so. I simply was too young to understand how touchy a subject your power truly was. I understand why you left, Devon, and I fully forgive your actions."

"As I forgive you, my love." Devon shook his head. "Pardon."

"All is well, Devon." She never should have said anything to him about *"my love."* Foolish, foolish. "So, the Ursus?"

He strode toward her, backing her up step by step until her back touched the gold wall covering. He sniffed the air, and he shook his head. He opened his eyes, and the eyes of a bear, round and deep blue, stared back at her.

She inhaled a breath and raised a hand toward his face. "May I, Devon?"

"Oh, indeed, you may." He stared at her as though assessing her reaction.

Her fingers glided along the smooth, circular shape of the outside of the eye. His lids closed, and the silky lashes fanned her finger. "Amazing, Devon. How did this happen again?" She couldn't believe she had just seen his eyes change shape. Many humans hid parts of themselves much more heinous than being part bear. She could never hold being part bear against this kind man.

"We were cursed with the blood of a bear in battle. No one quite knows for sure exactly what happened. But the lore says there was a large bright light, and all wearing sarks were forever changed."

"Sarks?"

"Pardon." He raised his hand and pointed to a bearskin on the wall above the mantel.

"A bearskin."

"Indeed, we wore them into battle. I also have these." He raised his hand, and on the backs of his knuckles four slits appeared; the tips of bone poked through.

"Oh! Do those hurt?" The large, bright red slits certainly looked as though they could only be painful.

"No, not at all. The only thing that does hurt is marking at adulthood."

"What is the marking?"

He spun about and shouldered out of his coat and then his waistcoat. He glanced over his shoulder. "Care to help?" He winked.

"Oh! Indeed." Amanda strode forward, the tips of her nipples poking into her corset. She couldn't wait to see him naked, to run her fingers along his heated skin, stopping to touch every indentation, every scar. With claws and three older brothers, there were no doubt scars on his skin.

Her hands slid along his back, and he groaned. She fisted the cotton in her hands and pulled, jerking the hem from his pantaloons. Her hands slid underneath. The skin of his back was butter smooth and hot to the touch.

His well-defined muscles curved and sloped as if sculpted, and a large indentation was formed where his spine was. Images of her naked, seated beside him as he lay on his stomach, came to her. She lifted a grape from a platter, placed the fruit by his neckline, and lightly flicked the fruit with her finger. The round pebble of fruit rolled down the valley of flesh. Her tongue followed the trail, only to lick the grape into her mouth at the swell of his buttocks. She licked her lips.

"Wicked, wicked girl." Devon spun, and the image vanished.

She smiled sunny at him. "Pardon?"

"Eating grapes off my back?"

"You saw that?"

"Oh! Indeed. Wicked." His eyebrows rose. "You were touching me. Though I have always, when in close proximity to you, been able to see your sexual thoughts." He grinned. "Works quite nicely for a chap such as myself."

Amanda's hand flew to her mouth. "You are the wicked one."

"You are only just noticing this? I would have thought you quite aware of this when we met, my love."

My love. He would keep saying the endearment. She would simply ignore it.

A knock came at the door, and a footman entered. Perched on his tray was a bottle of wine with two glasses, a stack of meat sandwiches, a bunch of fruit—including grapes—and a chocolate éclair.

Amanda's mouth watered. The éclair. She stared at the flap to his pantaloons.

"Wicked girl. You may do what you wish with it." The footman uncorked the bottle of wine and poured two fingers' width of the fluid into the glasses. He bobbed his head to Devon and left the room. "As I will do what I wish with the wine."

7

"Who goes first?"

She would ask, wouldn't she? He laughed. "I go first, seeing as you initiated the futter in the carriage." She turned that delightful shade of red he so adored. "Come and finish taking my shirt off."

She sauntered toward him, her deep blue skirts swaying with her hips' sashay. Duce it. She was a seductress. The sweet, innocent girl, full of fun, had turned into a vixen with skill enough to bring a man to his knees for ages. He would bow to her power every day. What had the rogue Harold Dermok taught her? *Back down, Devon. Enjoy her now. The knowledge can come in time.* Indeed. He intended on initiating Orsse with her this night, and she needed to be fully aware of what she was about to do with him.

Her hands grasped the loose tails of his shirt and slowly pulled up. The light brush of her fingers along his stomach and chest made his muscles clench. Goose pins pierced his skin, and he reveled in the delight of her touch.

She pulled the garment up and off his head, his hands still caught in the cuffs of his sleeves.

He lowered his arms in front of him and flexed his chest muscles. "Undo the cuffs, Amanda."

She grinned at him devilishly. "I think not. At least not until I inspect you."

He laughed. "Wicked. Very well, have your fun. Just realize that simple cotton will not hold me."

She smiled. "Indeed."

Her hands reached for the flap to his pantaloons and undid the flap. Pushing them down to his ankles, she gently lifted one foot and slipped the cuff over his toes; then the other. He was left standing naked, except for his stockings and his hands covered in the cotton of his shirt.

The edges of her plush mouth turned up in satisfaction. She circled him and reached out, trailing sensations of fire in an invisible rope about his torso.

His chest tightened. Her fingers stilled on his mark on his back and ran across his upper back from right to left—the length of the largest claw mark.

"This is the mark you spoke of, Devon?"

"Mmm, indeed."

"What was it for? I imagine whoever inflicted the wound must have been terribly angry." Her voice spoke close to his skin, warming the scar she fondled gently.

"Not angry at all, actually. Marking is a ritual for Ursus men when they reach adulthood and are no longer a cub."

"How horrid. What did you have to do?"

He sighed and closed his eyes, remembering. "I didn't want to do the ritual, but it was required. When each of my brothers and I reached adulthood, we were sent to the castle in our homeland for the yearly celebrations specifically to be marked. It was only a year before I had met you, my life mate."

"Pardon?" Amanda's hand stilled on his back.

"The ritual itself really is not strenuous. A few human women are chosen to do their duty to the Ursus in the homelands. They do so knowing they will be well paid for the rest of their lives. Their task. To allow a male Ursus boar to mount her and spend his seed for the first time. It is an honor for the woman."

"I—I'm lost, Devon. Where do the scars come in, and you mentioned life mate?" Amanda's finger continued to trace the raised outlined flesh on his back.

"The scars." A chill raced over his skin as her fingernail dragged up one of the shorter outlines on his back. "In the ritual the chosen woman lies on her back in the center of the chamber. She simply waits. The male Ursus enters after having his cock stroked for hours by various people he never sees—he is tied, face to a wall, and his cock stuck through a hole. He is never brought to spend, only caressed until he starts emitting wetness, then the caress stops and after a bit resumes again."

Her hand dipped into the crevice of his spine and stilled there as though waiting for him to continue.

"We enter the room and futter this woman. Her legs are tied back, and she is secured to the table. She is not a virgin. The pounding of a first futter for a male Ursus is harsh and uncontrolled as he spends. There is another in the room, a male—usually the woman's mate. He unsheathes his claws and marks you as you spend. The pain of the cut does not hurt because your focus is on the spend. After, you can't move for a day without cursing." He grinned. "I did lots and lots of cursing."

She walked around to the front of him, trailing her finger along his arm and down to the shirt about his hands. She looked at him with such compassion for what was a rite of passage in his culture but a total oddity in her world. Her breadth of compassion and acceptance amazed him.

"So you enjoyed pain with your pleasure?"

He chuckled. "No, I definitely would not say I enjoyed it.

Though I do know many who did. Why? Would you offer to spank me, my love, if I did enjoy?"

"I have done so before. Though not to my liking."

"Good. Then we are in agreement. No extreme pain with our pleasure."

"Indeed."

"Undo my cuffs, Amanda."

"No." Her eyes narrowed. "You have not answered one of my questions." Her hand trailed down his stomach and curled one of the hairs near his cock about the digit.

His breath locked in his throat. Duce it. He wanted her to touch his phallus, but he didn't want to ruin a perfectly good shirt when she could undo him. He inhaled a breath and sighed. "Very well, Amanda. What is it?"

"You mentioned 'life mate' and my name. What did you mean?"

"Ah! With pleasure, I will explain, my love." He rolled his shoulders and stared her in the eyes. *You are my life mate, Amanda. I have known it since we met all those years ago. I was foolish when I left you to Harold Dermok because your father had already signed you to another. I was in such a rage at your father, at Dermok, I couldn't think straight. That was why when you told me you talked to Mary about my mind-speak, I angered. Mary, Dermok's sister, would take my family down with such information. Or so I thought. Turned out Mary hated her brother just as I did.* His head spun slightly, as he hadn't taken a breath the entire speech.

"What is a life mate, Devon?" Her eyes held his, filled with fear.

"It simply means we are connected for life. I can love none but you. You fill my heart and always have."

Tears welled in her eyes. "But—but men can't love!" She turned around and bolted for the door.

Damn and damn. "Amanda!"

She turned the lock and yanked. The door pulled half open, and he used all his power to concentrate. *Please . . . please, let me move it.*

Close!

Close and lock!

Close and lock!

He yanked at his hands. Duce it! He bolted at her. The door magically shut and locked. He grinned. *Yes, indeed. Move only a feather no more.*

Devon reached her side and stared down at her as she hid her face against the door, her body shaking. "Amanda, you have alluded to such foolishness twice this night. Where in the world did you get that information?"

She turned toward him. "Foolishness? I have lived it for the past twelve years. Harold told me men were capable of only lust."

Anger radiated off her so hot he was not sure he should touch her, but he needed to all the same. He thrust his hands toward her. "Undo me, Amanda."

She looked down at his hands; her lips quirked up. "You can close a door from across the room, but you can't undo your own cuffs?"

"Please, Amanda."

Her hands shook as she reached out and untied the cuffs of his shirt.

"Thank you." He reached out and scooped her up in his arms. "Harold was a simpleton. Men love just as women do, Amanda. Just as women lust, men lust."

He walked to the bed and sat on it. "I wish to start the ritual to make you mine to bond our connection tight. So tight we will know each others' locations without even having to think about it." His fingers grasped her chin and tilted her head up to look him in the eyes. *Do you want that, Amanda? My love?*

"What does the ritual entail, Devon?"

His brows drew together. He was not expecting a question back.

"Will there be pain? Do you have to cut me?"

"No, no pain, my love." He reached up and pulled a pin from her hair. "We need to futter twice more. First, to open and ready your body, and, second, to claim you as mine."

"I—I want to diddle you again, Devon, so I can futter and decide after if I want to continue. Can we do that?"

Duce it. He wanted to tell her yes, to take the risk, and then she would see the right in them and let him take her both times. But would she? If she didn't, he—and she, too—would go through pain the likes of which he had heard was worse than marking.

"Sort of, my love." He removed another pin, and her hair came tumbling down. "If we futter this time and we don't the third, we both will go through pain. Extreme pain, shedding the connection and fertile seed."

She nodded slowly. "How long before the pain would start?"

"Half a day, maybe a bit more."

She reached out, wrapped her hands about his cock, and stroked him base to tip. "That is something I am willing to chance, Devon. I simply can't decide at this moment, and I need to feel you inside me again. Now."

He held in a grin. She would not be able to deny him a third if she couldn't deny a second.

"Very well. You know the risk."

"Indeed."

"My turn for fun. Stand up and undress for me, Amanda."

8

Amanda stood, her mind spinning. Did he really love her? Could he? She had certainly always thought Devon held a greater amount of emotion for her than any other man, but love?

She busily undid the buttons going down the front of her dress. She wanted to feel his powerful large hands on her bare body.

He stood and went to the tray of food, picked up a larger-than-normal-sized finger sandwich, and popped the entire thing into his mouth. Then another followed the same path. Grabbing a glass of wine, he turned back to her.

She shimmied her shoulders and pushed her bodice down to her waist.

His eyes widened, and she pushed the skirts to the floor and grinned.

He swallowed the gulp of wine hard and coughed.

His gaze swept her from toes to head, then concentrated on her face. "Spin about, my love, and I will undo your stays."

He walked to her and set his glass of wine on the table by

the bed. His hand glided across her shoulder blades and then pulled the laces. Each jerk of the ties loosened the constraint of her torso so he could slide the garment from her body. "Turn."

She did, and he slid the garment across her hips and onto the floor. She shivered, though she was not cold. He bent down and placed a hand beneath her knee and one around her shoulders, then lifted her. He cradled her in his arms then tossed her into the air and toward the bed.

"Weeee."

She landed softly on the bed and giggled. He fanned himself over her. Grasping her hand, he raised fingers toward the headboard. A piece of silk rope was wrapped about her wrist, and he looped the end into a knot. He then did the same with the other arm, securing her hands so she could not touch.

"Well, my love, now I get to taste and tease until my loins are throbbing for your hand's caress." He grinned, and her heart flipped in her chest.

He reached across her and grabbed the wine from the side table. "Watching you lick wine off the madam tonight drove me mad. I wanted the experience of licking wine off you but from a much more intimate place."

He held the glass above her nipples and poured. A drizzling of the sticky liquid splashed her nipples and ran down her pert breasts to pool between them. She trembled in anticipation of his tongue flicking along the tips of her nipples and sucking the buds into his warmth.

"Oh, indeed, wanton. Now I am thinking I shall make you wait for such delight."

"No, Devon. Please. I need your mouth upon my body."

His lips came down on hers hard, and his tongue thrust between her lips. She opened to him, and her heart sighed. He stroked his tongue along hers, never moving his lips from her. She moaned, and her head grew light so she couldn't breathe. Oh, his kiss stole the very breath from her body.

He pulled back from her, and his lips traveled down her neck. His tongue lingered on her collarbone. Her eyes fluttered open and watched the top of his head and the fine blond hairs slide lower to her breasts.

The hot press of his lips caressed the swell, and then he licked. A slow, steady warmth, as if from a fire that had burned for ages, sparked through her veins and straight to her pussy. She squeezed her eyes shut. His tongue swirled in a line straight up to the tip. *Yes, please, please.*

"Mmmm. Sweet wine." His words vibrated the tip of her nipple as his lip latched over the tip and he sucked. His tongue curled about the hard flesh.

Her womb contracted, and her body arched, pressing her breast more fully into his lips' grasp. My, oh, my. Her head spun anew as a feather of wet sensation tickled the flesh of her sex.

He released her nipple and gazed up at her with round eyes. She raised her hand, wanting to run her fingers through his hair to touch him, but the restraint held firm.

Devon grinned at her. "Trying to go somewhere, my love?"

"God, no." She laid her head back and swallowed hard. Never. This was too good. He was too good.

His tongue drew lines on the flesh of her chest and breasts, licking up every spatter of red wine from her alabaster skin.

The need to feel his weight pressed against her set her skin on dewed fire. She wiggled and arched toward him, wanting more than his tongue's caress. "More, Devon. Please, more."

He pulled back and chuckled. "Wanton."

"Yes, please."

He reached for the glass of wine again and moved to kneel between her legs.

Holding the glass above her curly hairs, he tilted the stem. The cool fluid spilled out and into her hairs. She squirmed, and the liquid ran down her pussy lips and into the crack of her bottom.

"Oh!"

"Spread your legs, Amanda. I am going to taste you."

She complied, wanting his thick cock sliding in and out of her, wanting to feel his body press her into the mattress. Her flesh yearned to be filled with him in every way.

"Every way, eh?"

Her lips quirked up. "Stop that."

"No, my love. I will not." His finger ran down the center of her labia, opening the lips. He circled the bud, and she arched her hips toward him.

"Beautiful. You are a sensual goddess, Amanda. A goddess who will soon be all mine."

His mouth came down on her mound as his finger slid into her cunny. She stilled and moaned as erotic heat speared to her toes.

His tongue slid lower, swirling and lapping as if he were a kitten drinking milk in a bowl. The quick flicks and the wiggle of his finger in her womb . . .

Oh, oh, God! He was good. Bliss washed through her pores and tightened her muscles. The flat of his tongue pressed the lips of her pussy wide as his fingers continued to frig her. She pulled on her hands, needing to touch him to feel the soft strands of his hair sliding between her fingers as he tasted her.

She tugged harder, and one of the silk binds slid, loosening. A finger pressed at her bottom. She arched, pulling against the silk binds as her body grew fevered and tight, the bliss building toward a large, delightful spend. Her left bind slid loose, and she grinned. His tongue continued to ripple up her flesh, and she reached across and quickly untied the other wrist. She held no chance against his strength, but the éclair . . . She needed to taste it on his skin.

He chuckled . . . and stopped frigging her. "Go get it, my love."

She sat up and quickly ran across the room and grabbed the éclair.

"Mmmm, you have a beautiful backside."

Amanda spun around and grinned at him. The chocolate from the éclair stuck to her fingers, and she walked toward him.

"Sit on the floor, Devon; lean your back against the side of the bed."

She stood before him and stared down at the delicious cream-filled pastry.

"Do what you wish with it, my love."

"Indeed, Devon, I shall."

She stuck her finger down deep into the cream filling and pulled out a fingerful of custard. Raising her hand to her breasts, she circled her right nipple, smearing the sticky smoothness around. "Mmmm."

"What does it feel like, my love?"

She closed her eyes and continued to circle her nipple. "Smooth. Very smooth." Her hand shifted to her left nipple, and she rubbed the rest of the cream about it.

"Let me taste."

Her eyelids slid open slowly. "You want to taste, do you?"

"Mmmm, indeed."

Amanda looked at the éclair and then at Devon, and her lips quirked up. "Indeed." She stepped closer to him, every nerve in her body on edge. The rug beneath her prickled the sensitive undersides of her feet; the air swirled and hung with the smell of vanilla and honey; her skin was on fire with the need for Devon to touch her and her cunny. . . . She needed him stretching her pussy lips and filling her wide. *Stop that, Amanda. The éclair.*

She lowered the pastry and straddled his legs; the firm, hairy contours rubbed against the insides of her ankles and calves. She trembled, and his hands rose in the air to grasp her thighs. "No. Please sit on your hands, Devon."

He chuckled. "All right, my love."

His hands lowered, and he lifted first one bum cheek, placing his hand beneath the beautiful firm swell, and then did the same with the other.

Amanda swallowed hard and licked her lips. She wanted to lick the skin of his bottom. She placed the éclair between her legs like a prick and stepped forward, lowering her voice into a manlike tone. "Suck my peg. Suck the cream from me." She thrust her hips toward him and the éclair toward his mouth.

Devon's body shook with suppressed laughter. "Yes, sir. Your prick is mighty big and looks oh-so-sweet."

"Stop that. . . ." She laughed.

He leaned forward and placed his lips around the end of the éclair and bit down, biting it in half. The pastry rubbed against her button, and tingles shot straight to her cunny.

"Indeed. I will eat you." He leaned forward and toppled her onto the floor. His hands wrapped about her legs, and his lips wrapped about the éclair, brushing the lips of her sex. He sucked the éclair into his mouth and chewed, burying his lips into her labia. Each motion his lips made, simply by eating the éclair, was like a little kiss to her womb. Heat washed through her limbs, and her muscles tightened. His tongue slid out and licked the last bit of chocolate from her skin.

"Mmmm." The vibration arched her hips up and into him in search of more. More. "Please, Devon, more."

Indeed, my love, I need to be inside you.

His tongue slid up her button, and her hips jerked. Her legs spread wide as his body slowly slid up hers. His tongue licked and swirled, tasting her skin. She moaned, and her head lolled to the side. The tip of his tongue touched her nipple.

"Yummy cream." His breath warmed the skin as his lips latched over the erect peak.

Oh, oh, God! Her pussy contracted, and the lips of her cunny swelled and throbbed with the beat of her heart.

Indeed. I will be filling your hole soon. His mouth moved to the other nipple, and he sucked her flesh into his mouth. The tip of his tongue wound about the tip, and then his teeth bit.

"Ouch!" She thrust her breast up harder into his mouth as heat tightened the muscles of her stomach.

"Pardon. I thought you were an éclair." He moved the rest of the way up her body, and the tip of his cock hovered inches above her cunny. His deep blue eyes met hers, filled with ardor. "I love you, Amanda."

His cock nestled into the eye of her sex, and he thrust into her fully. The muscles of her cunny clenched to his hard, thick length.

"Mmmm, excellent." He pulled out to the tip and hovered there.

Her pussy gasped, sucking at the air, trying to pull his phallus back into her hungry flesh. "Please, Devon, please."

He slid back in. The tip of his cock head nestled to her womb. Her knees slid back, and she wrapped her fingers about her thighs and pulled, holding her cunny open wide for his deep, hard thrusts.

"Take me, Devon. Take me hard. Spend in me." Oh! How she wanted to feel his seed splash her womb. Nothing would compare to that sensation in the world.

Her legs shook, and he pulled out, his body hovering above her. His arms shook, and his hips arched back and forth, sliding his prick in and out of her slick, dripping cunny in rapid successions.

His cock pulsed within her womb as his sac hit her bottom with a slap. "Oh, oh, Amanda." He shook, and gush after warm gush pulsed into her cunny.

His balls pulsed against her bottom, and his hips continued to jerk his peg in and out of her.

My God! She overflowed with his seed. Each rock into her body, wetness squished from where they joined in bliss.

He rubbed his mound against her button, and she arched, rocking in motion with him. Her muscles tightened, and she squeezed her eyes tight, the bliss grasping every nerve, heightening everything he did. His prick stretched her pussy lips as he slid in again and again. With his breath on her neck, his arms and body trembled in a spend that seemed to go on and on forever. She concentrated on the tingling sensation in her womb. *My God! Oh, my God.* The sensation aroused her like no other.

She broke. Her body ignited in trembling convulsions beneath him, each hard contraction of her womb clinging to his hard staff. A prick hit her womb, and her legs shook. "Oh! Oh! Oh, Devon!"

Her lips reached out for him, needing to taste his skin, but the only thing near her was his arm. She hungrily sucked the flesh, and the blissful contraction erupted, slowly fading out as he slowed his movements within her.

She panted as she lay in a haze of euphoria.

His arms relaxed, and his full weight pressed her to the floor. "Amanda, are you well?"

Her eyes fluttered open. Intense bear eyes stared back at her, assessing her expression. "Oh, indeed, Devon. I am quite fine."

Her hands dropped from her thighs, and she reached up and touched his face. "Could we move to the bed, Devon? I would love to lay my head on your chest and listen to you breathe."

He wrapped his arms about her and lifted her, his cock still deep in her womb. Wetness ran down her legs as he laid her on the bed. He rolled so she lay upon him.

"My Amanda. My love."

She settled her head against his shoulder and closed her eyes. A warm, contented haze cocooned her in bliss, and her heart swelled. Indeed. He was hers.

Amanda covered her face with her hands and smiled. Not

only two weeks ago, she had lived in Kent thinking she would never crave futter with a man the way Aunt Bess did.

She shook her head. My goodness! The things she wanted to do to Devon, with Devon, have Devon do to her. Wicked, wicked thoughts, and he knew every one of them.

Her heart swelled again in her chest. It was as if a door to her heart—and thus her sexual hunger—had swung open on the breeze that was Devon Ursus.

She rolled toward him as he slumbered in the bed beside her. She loved him. She had always loved him . . . and he loved her. Tears welled in her eyes, and she smiled. She floated . . . just as if she was in one of those air balloons.

Oh! What an experience futtering in a balloon would be. Her cheeks grew toasty warm. Probably uncomfortable and cramped. But! God! She wanted to try it, gazing out on the world as landscapes passed below her. Her skirts tossed up so her bum was exposed, and Devon's thick, pulsing cock lodged up to her womb as he spouted dirty, nasty tales in her ear. Indeed, a shiver of exhilaration raised all the hairs on her body, and the lips of her pussy trembled. Oh, yes, indeed.

She would remember to tell him her thought when he arose.

No need, my love. The image of your bare ass exposed to the world as I futter you daft in the attic, in a balloon, can be arranged. Devon didn't move.

Amanda smiled. She liked this. She already loved the fact that he knew her sexual desires, yet never judged her. Like kissing a woman. He encouraged her adventurous side.

Oh! And the food! She glanced at the tray and the grapes perched in the silver bowl.

She sat up, scurried to the tray, and grabbed a bunch of the round, purple grapes; then she ran back to the bed. Perching herself upon the mattress, she grasped one grape and plucked the fruit from the stem.

Her tummy growled, and she stared at the crevice on Devon's back. She would end up eating the grape in the end anyway. Indeed. She placed the grape by his neck, and the skin on his shoulders twitched.

She flicked with her finger, and the grape rolled down, stopping at the beautiful swell of his firm, tight bottom. She leaned down and laid her head on his bum.

Grasping the fruit in her teeth, she bit through the skin, squirting the juice all across his bottom.

"Hope you are planning on licking me clean." Devon's deep slumber-filled voice vibrated both their bodies.

"Oh, indeed. Wouldn't want you to be all sticky now, would we?"

"Slick with your oils is incomparable, but sticky is simply not me."

She laughed outright. "Well, I think I shall simply have to leave you sticky then." She sat up, prepared for his revolt.

None came.

"Devon?"

He lay there, not moving. She leaned in and placed her ear upon his back.

Paw-paw-paw-paw.

His heart beat, and he breathed. She leaned back up, and before she was a hand's breadth off his back, his arm wrapped about her shoulders and he rolled her.

She ended up cupped in his embrace, back to his chest, both of them lying on their sides.

"Amanda, will you allow me to be your life mate?" His breath warmed her ear, and he lightly nibbled her lobe.

A shiver of knowing slid through her. The best part of her life was yet to come. Her life, her future, involved Devon.

Her chin wobbled, and tears sprang into her eyes.

"Yes, indeed, Devon. My heart has always belonged to you."

"As you have held mine, Amanda."

His fingers slid down her thigh and lifted her leg over his hip. "Reach between your legs and slide my pego into you."

Her fingers slid down his arm wrapped about her chest and into the curls of her sex. She gripped his length and guided his plum-shaped head to the folds of her completely open sex. Her flesh already was accustomed to him.

The skin of the tip tightened as she placed him into the eye of her Venus. She moaned, and her hand trembled, releasing him to slide in.

This was right. She was his. They had always had fun together. Laughter and love, more than anything, was what she wished for her life.

He pushed forward, the flesh of her pussy stretching about him as he tormented her at a maddeningly slow pace. He licked her neck, and his tongue slid into her ear.

"Tell me again, Amanda."

Her body trembled at the sound of his voice. "You possess me, Devon."

His chest rumbled behind her. "Like a demon, eh?"

Her hands slid up, and she intertwined her fingers with his.

"Again. Try again, Amanda."

"You own me, Devon." Her lips quirked up, and she held in a giggle.

"You are not my dog. Again."

She bit her lip, and he stilled.

"Again."

"Start futtering me, and I will."

He laughed and jerked her body tighter to him. "Wanton."

"Indeed."

"You—" he thrust all the way into her stretched pussy, and her breath caught in her throat; he pulled out to the crown, "—are the perfect—" he thrust back into the giving flesh of her cunt, and her breath jittered once more, "f—fit—" his tongue slid up her shoulder and into the cup of her ear, "—for me, Devon. The sugar in my lemonade." He increased the stroke of his cock, sliding quickly out and slowly back into her greedy pussy. "The chocolate on my éclair." Heat speared up her belly, and she trembled as tears welled in her eyes. "I love you, Devon."

His cock pulsed, and he squeezed her tight, shuddering in bliss about her body. His face nestled into her hair on her neck. "My Amanda. My love. Always."

Turn the page for a preview of
Jodi Lynn Copeland's HANDYMAN!
On sale now!

1

Now, he was the kind of guy she needed to meet.

Parallel parked across the street from the Almost Family youth services building, Lissa Malone stopped examining her reflection in the vanity mirror of her Dodge Charger to watch the guy. He stood in front of the youth building, which was constructed of the same old-fashioned red brick as every other building in downtown Crichton, laughing with a lanky, long-haired blond kid in his early teens. The kid wouldn't be a relative, but a boy from the local community who was going through a rough patch and in need of an adult role model in the form of a foster friend.

Kind, caring, and considerate enough to be that friend, by donating his free time to the betterment of the kid's life, the guy was the antithesis of every man she'd dated.

Make that every *straight* man. And then again, he wasn't the complete opposite.

The way his faded blue Levi's hugged his tight ass and his biceps bulged from beneath the short sleeves of a slate gray T-shirt as he scruffed the kid's hair, the guy had as fine of a body as her recent lovers. What he wasn't likely to have was their badass hang-ups.

He was one of the good ones. A nice guy. The kind of guy Lissa had never gone for and never had any desire to.

There was something about those bad boys that called to her. Not just their bedside manner. Though she wasn't about to knock the red-hot thrill of being welcomed home from work by having her panties torn away and a stiff cock thrust inside her before she had a chance to say hello.

She shuddered with the memory of Haden, the brainless beefcake she ended up with following her latest dip in the bad-boy pool, greeting her precisely that way three weeks ago. What Haden lacked in mentality, he more than made up for in ability. The guy could make her come with the sound of his voice alone.

Show me that sweet pussy, Liss.

Haden's deep baritone slid through her mind, spiking her pulse and settling dampness between her thighs. She caught her reflection in the vanity mirror as she shifted in the driver's seat. Her cheeks had pinkened—an unmanageable tell to her arousal—calling out her too-many freckles.

Yeah, there was definitely something about those bad boys. Something she wouldn't be experiencing ever again.

Lissa wasn't the only woman Haden could bring to climax in seconds. As it turned out, she also wasn't the only woman he'd been bringing to climax the almost two months they dated. Really, it shouldn't have surprised her. With bad boys, something always ended up coming before her. Another woman. A massive ego. Or worst of all, the bad boy himself coming before her, then not bothering to stick around to see if she got off.

She was sick to hell of coming in second.

In the name of coming in first and being the center of a man's attention if only for a little while, she was ready to give nice guys a try. Her housemate and ex-lover, Sam, claimed she wouldn't regret it, since what people were always saying about nice guys was true: they finished last, and it was because they wanted their leading ladies to come in first.

A nice guy like the well-built Good Samaritan across the street, Lissa thought eagerly. Only, a glance back across the street revealed he wasn't there any longer. Neither was the kid.

"Well, shit." *So much for opportunity knocking.*

Not that she had time to do a meet and greet. She had an appointment with the owner of the Sugar Shack candy store for a potential interior redesign job. Besides, Mr. Nice Guy was likely one among a hundred like him who donated his time to Almost Family and similar nonprofit services.

How many of those others had an ass and arms like his?

A dynamite ass and a killer set of arms, and probably a gorgeous wife or girlfriend to go with them.

Her eagerness flame fanned out, Lissa put her nice guy hunt on hold. She returned her attention to the mirror for a quick teeth and facial inspection. Finding everything acceptable and her freckles returned to barely noticeable, she grabbed her black leather briefcase satchel from the passenger's seat and climbed out of the car.

The closest she'd been able to get a parking spot to the candy store was three blocks away. She was a stickler for arriving early, so reaching the place on time wouldn't require sprinting in her skirt and open-toe heels. Hooking the satchel's strap over her arm, she took off down the sidewalk.

One block in, footfalls pounded on the sidewalk behind her. Not an uncommon thing, given the number of people milling about the downtown area on a Friday afternoon. What was uncommon was how noisily they fell, like the person was purposefully trying to be loud.

Were they in step with hers?

Sam's thing was paranoia, not Lissa's. Only, it appeared her housemate was rubbing off on her. Her skin suddenly felt crawly. Her entire body went tense with the sensation of being watched. Followed. Stalked.

Oh jeez! Could she be any more melodramatic?

This wasn't a dark, stormy night scenario. The sun shone down from overhead and, while June in Michigan didn't often equate to blistering temperatures, a warm, gentle breeze toyed with the yellow, green, and white flowered silk overlay of her knee-length skirt. And there was the fact she was surrounded by a few dozen other people.

To prove how ridiculous she was acting, Lissa stopped walking. The footfalls came again, once, and then fell silent.

Her breath dragged in.

What if she *was* being followed? The candy store was still a block and a half away. Sprinting the remainder of the distance might be the safest route. Yeah right it would. She was liable to snag a heel in a sidewalk crack and break her neck. *Then* she would have a reason to be concerned.

Ignoring the hasty beat of her heart, she faced her overactive imagination by spinning around . . . and there he was.

Mr. Nice Guy stood less than twenty feet away. Not following her or even eyeing her up, but standing in front of a coffee shop, peering into its storefront windows.

He moved toward the shop's door, pulling it open with a tinkling of overhead bells and placing his ass in her line of vision. Once more she appreciated the stellar view. This time it was more than appreciation though. This time, just before he turned and disappeared inside, he looked her way.

Lissa's heart skipped a beat with the glimpse of pure masculine perfection.

Stubble the same shade of wheat as his thick, wavy hair dusted an angular jaw line and coasted above a full, stubborn upper lip. Eyebrows a shade darker slashed in wicked arcs over vivid cobalt blue eyes. His cheeks sank in just enough to make him look lean, hungry, and dangerous all at once. Then there was the way he filled out his jeans; his backside had nothing on his front half. Beneath the faded denim, muscles bulged and strained in all the right places. And she did mean *all* the right places.

If not for catching him joking around with the youth services kid, she would have mistaken him for a bad boy in a heartbeat. He wasn't. But clearly her body approved of him.

Heat raced into her face and her nipples stabbed to life, making her wish she hadn't relied on the built-in shelf bra of her yellow short-sleeve top to hold in her cleavage. Her breasts were way too big to be fully constrained by the flimsy little cotton bras sewn into shirts. For whatever reason, she allowed Sam to talk her into giving one a try. Probably because when she slipped out of her bedroom wearing it, he'd taken one look at her chest and offered to give her a pre-appointment mouth job.

Coming from a gay guy, that was a major compliment.

The bells over the coffee shop door sounded as a gray-haired, sixty-something couple exited. Lissa glanced at her watch. Ten minutes till her appointment. A block and a half to go.

She could spend five minutes determining if Mr. Nice Guy was single and searching and then huff it to the Sugar Shack. Or forgo the meet and greet, arrive at her appointment on time, and take Sam up on his mouth job offer when she arrived home.

As much as she loved Sam, there was no future for them beyond friendship. There probably wasn't one with the guy in the coffee shop either.

Lissa walked back to the shop anyway.

To the sound of tinkling bells, she pulled open the wood door with white and red stained-glass coffee mugs designed into its window slats. Entering the shop, she looked up at the bells . . . and nearly slammed into Mr. Nice Guy.

He stood in front of a customer bulletin board, pinning

business cards up with long-fingered hands that bore neither rings nor tan lines. After tacking the last card onto the board, he turned toward her, flashed a smile sexy enough to do a fluttering number on her sex, and moved right on past and out the door.

"Well, shit." *So much for opportunity knocking.* Even worse, she was starting to sound like a broken record.

She should forget about him and get to her appointment. But between his lack of a wedding ring and that sexy smile, her eagerness flame was rekindled.

Lissa grabbed one of the newly posted business cards off the bulletin board. *Thad Davies, Handyman* was written in black, and beneath it, in bold, blue lettering, *Loose Screws Construction.* Was the company name meant to be a double entendre, and exactly how handy of a man was Thad?

Handy enough to leave her his number.

Smiling, she tucked the business card into her satchel. Later, maybe she would give him a call. Or maybe she would pick up a box of Sam's favorite sweets while she was at the Sugar Shack and use them to bribe him into making good on his mouth job offer.